The Sons of Fez

Also by Kay Hardy Campbell

A Caravan of Brides:
A Novel of Saudi Arabia

THE SONS
OF FEZ

*A Moroccan Time
Travel Adventure*

Kay Hardy Campbell

Loon Cove Press
Jefferson, Maine

Quote from "A Community of the Spirit" by Jelaluddin Rumi used with permission by Coleman Barks, translator of *The Essential Rumi,* in which it appears.

Published by
Loon Cove Press
P.O. Box 413, Jefferson, Maine 04348 U.S.A.
looncovepress@gmail.com
www.looncovepress.com

Author website: www.kayhardycampbell.com

Cover Design by Andy Birch

10 9 8 7 6 5 4 3 2 1
FIRST EDITION

ISBN (paperback): 978-0-9990743-2-9
ISBN (e-book): 978-0-9990743-3-6
Library of Congress Control Number: 2021934422

For the students of Arabic and those who teach them

* * *

For Gary

Within the great walls of the Fez medina, every person, every brick, every pack animal and speck of dust is connected. No part is separate from the rest. When you breathe its air, you are taking in the humors of the ages, the essences of eons. In spring, you smell orange blossoms from the nearby hills and fresh rain from over the mountains. When the wind is still, you smell the smoke from the ceramic kilns and the reek of the skins and dye vats from the tanners' quarter. And when you wander through the spice market, mountains of ochre-hued cumin make your heart cry out in longing.

– Diary of John Lombard, 1365

There is a community of the spirit.
Join it, and feel the delight
of walking in the noisy street,
and *being* the noise.

Drink all your passion,
and be a disgrace.

Close both eyes
to see with the other eye.

Open your hands,
if you want to be held.

Sit down in this circle.

–The Essential Rumi,
translated by Coleman Barks

Chapter 1

Summer Rainstorm

Moustapha of the Mountain, that's what they call me. I'm a *djinni* of the male gender, though, given my costume, you might take me for a bony-fingered old beggar woman. My caftan, once an admired pink and white brocade, has gone grey from the dirt in the alley where I spend my days. I cover my hair and neck with gauze, and I shade my head with a scarf of brown cotton. And these worn leather slippers? A kind woman down the street gave them to me. I still can't get used to the way the points in front curl up as if my own toes watch me. My disguise is part of my probation, prescribed by my bosses, the "Powers that Be" who summoned me here. For you see, things are getting out of control here in the medina, in the old city of Fez, and somehow I'm supposed to keep order.

I arrived a week ago, after days of heavy rain filled the roadside gutters, and forced everyone to run for cover. It was a rare summer storm that lingered over the city. In fact, I couldn't recall any like it in my 300 year lifetime. In the deluge, many walls in the old city gave way. Storm sewers backed up, and small streets flooded. Workmen waded in tall rubber boots. Kittens mewed from dry perches. The donkeys and mules pressed on, fighting for each step as they carried their tarp-covered loads up and down the steep cobblestone streets.

They didn't call me in because of the rain. See that stone arch over there? It is no ordinary arch, for it links two times: our present day, and the 14th century by the Christian calendar. They say a stonemason and his friends built it a thousand years ago. They then filled in the arch with stones and walled it in completely. And who were these men? Even if I knew, it would not be for me to say. I'm in enough trouble already without spreading gossip. I have to be on my best behavior, which is why I have this assignment. You see, I'm on probation for laziness, and this job is my punishment.

My task is to guard the arch. Yes, we djinn have jobs. Our society is much like that of the humans, although we are usually invisible to them. This is ironic, since we were here on earth before humans appeared, and now *we* are the ones consigned to the shadows. We can marry and have children, and we have free will, just as humans do. And, like people, we are below the rank of angels, in heaven's view. At this particular time in history, it seems humans also rank above us, though I don't know why. Certainly, they act like lords of the earth.

But back to the arch. In last week's deluge, the stones under the arch began to crumble, and a small hole appeared just under the keystone, which opened the time link. It was just a tiny space, but it was enough for me to be summoned. A sparrow flew from the city to alert me. I had been sleeping, as I do in the calm interludes between jobs, suspended in my hammock of silken threads, which hangs in the cedar forest in the mountains above the town of Ifrane. As always, when I am thus signaled by my bosses, I go where they send me.

Only a few spirits had passed through the opening by the time I arrived. They laughed as they squeezed through the hole, flying to the other side. Yet when I got there, my bosses told me to just sit there, for the time being.

When the rains finally stopped and the sun came out, a work crew arrived from Dar Surour, the *riad,* a sumptuous mansion turned guest house that shares the wall and arch with a neighbor behind it. The work crew was hurrying to repair the damage to prevent pedestrians from being injured if the wall should cave in. I could do nothing as they took sledgehammers and knocked all the stones out from beneath the arch, opening it in its entirety. When they saw the strength of the arch, they stopped work to consult the owner. At that moment, I knew we were in real trouble, as the longer the arch remains open, the more beings can go through and stir up all kinds of mayhem.

Just as I feared, as soon as the arch was fully open, hundreds of spirits, sprites, and ghouls hurried through it like a rushing wind, curious to explore places beyond their usual haunts. They laughed and chattered as they passed me. They walked in the form of humans or appeared as clouds with faces. Some came from the past to the present, while others went from the present to the past.

Compared to us djinn, who admittedly don't have the best reputation, these beings—the ghouls, sprites, and demons— are real troublemakers at best, and at worst pure evil. They cannot be allowed to mix in other times, because they will upset everything on earth.

Of course I tried to stop them, threatening them with djinni insults such as, "Get back, you sons of smoking garbage, daughters of dark swamps and sewage pools!" But they ignored me.

I've had better luck with the animals. For the most part, dogs and cats avoid us. When a few tried to walk under the arch, I shooed them away. Except for Ramses the ginger cat, a magnificent mouser who lives at Dar Surour. The first day the arch was open, he marched under the arch and into the past, his tail held high. I couldn't catch him. Every night since, he has hunted ancient mice and rats to his heart's content. Each morning he returns, first visiting the riad's kitchen for a dish of milk, then retiring to sleep all day. He moves along the roof ledges from one sunny spot to another, ignoring the scolding of small birds. I wonder how long he can keep it up, this diet of ancient mouse and rat. Fortunately, in those long-ago days, the plague was not active in Fez, otherwise we would have an even worse catastrophe on our hands. Things are bad enough as it is.

It was then that I got word that my job had changed. I was not to bother with spirits and animals. No, my job was to keep humans from crossing under the arch. You might wonder why I couldn't just destroy the arch myself, since us djinn can be powerful when necessary. That's the strange thing. I was told that since humans had built it, only humans could destroy it.

One day, the manager of the riad, Khalid by name, returned to the archway with a work crew to clean up the rubble they had created when they knocked out the wall. He stood right under the arch, hands on his hips, one rubber boot in the present, the other in the past. If he'd been paying attention, he would have noticed that the air on one side was cooler and drier. He'd have seen that the very dust at his feet was in two different hues; in the past, soot from wood fires and ceramic kilns darkened the streets. He didn't notice all these things, but he did smell the wood smoke.

"Do you smell fire?" he asked his crew, running a hand through his brown curls. "It's a sweet-smelling fire, like cedar wood." Cedar wood was so rare in modern times that no one would burn it for firewood. Instead, people used electric and gas heaters. But when he stepped back to the modern side of the arch and breathed in, he said, "I guess it's just my imagination."

When he ordered his men to pick up the broken bricks and stones, one of his workers looked at me and said, "Boss, there's a spirit here, a djinni. Please, I take refuge in God from evil. I can't work here."

Though the worker could sense I was a djinni, he didn't realize that I am among the upstanding beings of my kind, one of the God-fearing believers. We have such a bad name in Morocco that most humans fear us. But whatever Khalid thought of the djinn, he sent this man home. The remaining crew would just have to work harder.

After that, Khalid began checking on me every day. At first, he'd look down on me from the roof terrace of the riad. Then he would step into the alley to smoke a cigarette, watching me. One day, he approached and knelt near where I sat on my "easy chair," which was a flattened cardboard box. "Are you in need of some help, Ma'am? I notice you're here every day."

"No, young man," I said in a high voice. "I am content, praise God." I stretched out an arm as if many potential benefactors were about to walk down this generally quiet alley.

"But ma'am, no one passes by to give you dirhams. Is there someone in your family I can bring to help you?"

"No, my son. My family knows I'm here. I rest here, that's all."

"But I worry for your safety. There are bad people in the streets. I think it's best if you go home. Where may I escort you?"

"It's all right. I prefer to rest here."

"Well then, God bless you," he said, standing up. "If you need assistance, I'm here."

Things seemed under control for a few days. The workmen blocked off the alley with their wheelbarrows. Then a deep puddle formed. It had flowed there from somewhere inside the hilly city, and thankfully it prevented humans from passing under the arch. Ramses came and went each day, and the spirits flowed back and forth without impediment. For the spirits, it was a grand entertainment, a curiosity. At some point, someone would have to get them back to where they belonged, but that, they told me, was not my concern.

At first, I wasn't overly worried about the humans, what with the deep puddle and the construction project. Then one morning Khalid gathered his crew and told them to clear out the alley. His boss, the riad's owner, wanted to share the cost of rebuilding the wall with the neighbor, but it would take time to reach an agreement. Once they had cleared the debris away, and the rain puddle dried up, I feared it was only a matter of time before someone walked through the arch into the past, or someone from the past crossed into the present.

One afternoon a few days later, loud laughter echoed from the main street. A group of foreigners was walking by, looking up and pointing at things as if they'd neither been to a city nor seen buildings before. Coats filled their arms, and bulky bags hung off their shoulders.

"Here's Dar Surour!" a man called out in American English. Being a djinni, I can not only understand every language, but I also have a nuanced sensitivity to dialects. This man had an accent similar to a New Yorker's, but when he slipped into Arabic to speak with one of his assistants, he spoke in a Moroccan *Darija* that sounded like he'd come from the countryside, a village perhaps, south of the Atlas Mountains. He walked backward and waved his arms like a traffic cop, beckoning the group to follow. He was a handsome human male, with a prominent forehead and chiseled cheekbones. Yes, a boy from the countryside. You see, I once guarded a cave in that district. Oh, sweet memories of youth.

Soon handcarts full of luggage were brought to the side door, and it became clear that the foreigners were going to stay at Dar Surour, right next to the alley. I knew then that I was in a world of trouble.

Chapter 2

Into the Medina

"Good afternoon, my dears, ladies and gents." The microphone on the bus always made whoever was using it sound as though they were shouting. This time it was the voice of Ibrahim, the Moroccan tour guide in charge, speaking from his seat in the front of the bus. "As we climb up the Middle Atlas Mountains toward the forest and the mountain city of Ifrane, I think it's a good time to talk to you about Fez, our final stop in Morocco and your home for the next three weeks."

Some of the riders sat up, while others stood in the aisles to stretch. Unlike most of the passengers, Barbara had not slept. She had been transfixed by the scenery they were careening past, a dizzying panorama of rock formations and water: cliffs and outcroppings, little stream-beds and a few rushing rivers colored an unlikely pale blue.

Only Mike, who also hadn't been asleep, had approached her on the way to the back of the bus and noticed her staring at the scenery.

"Incredible, isn't it?" he said.

"Sure is," she said.

"I think I know why they call the country Morocco." She looked at him, waiting for the rest. "It's really 'More Rock, Oh.'"

They shared a laugh, and he continued down the aisle, stretching his legs but holding onto the luggage rack as the bus swayed.

The busload of students was taking part in a summer intensive Arabic study program. They studied on the road, first in Casablanca then moving on to Marrakech, with tours and treks on weekends. It was late July, and they had three weeks left before they would fly back to their home countries.

Even Barbara, who had savored every second of the trip, was starting to dream of going back home to Maine. She missed her parents, her dog, and the comforts of the familiar, especially the luxury of having her own bedroom. But she wasn't ready to get on the plane just yet.

Hers was one of many programs offering Arabic study in Morocco. After the 2001 terrorist attacks in the US, Arabic became one of the most popular languages among college students, and, in Morocco, teaching Arabic had become a thriving business. She'd heard that in that summer, 2018, more than 5,000 foreign students were in the country studying Arabic. More than half were Americans. She had seen many groups from other programs when her group visited famous tourist sites.

Her particular Arabic program had attracted students from colleges across the US and Canada, as well as a few from Japan, France, Germany, and England. They were united by their ambition to master the challenges of learning Arabic. Most were undergraduates, but a few graduate students had joined, too. No matter how much they had studied Classical Arabic, that summer they all had to learn a second Arabic language, *darija,* the Moroccan dialect. No one had it easy, and each student was faced with particular challenges. Nearly everyone had arrived at the program having read different textbooks, so they knew different vocabulary. The Japanese students had pronunciation difficulties. These struggles, along with their shared adventures, bonded the group as a whole. That didn't mean that the constant companionship didn't occasionally grate on their nerves, though. Things that summer went as might have been expected. There were some romances, spats, and break-ups among friends. Some people got sick, while others seemed to have guts of steel.

Now they were reaching the final stage of their journey, in Fez. What a funny name for a city, Barbara thought. It sounded like fuzz, or fizz, with only one z.

Dr. Charles Khamis, whom the students called Dr. Charles in keeping with Arabic custom, stood at the front of the bus, mic in one hand, gripping the back of a seat with the other as the bus rocked this way and that. "Fez is also known as Morocco's Imperial City. This is where sultans once reigned. The city also gave its name to what we in the west call the fez, or the men's red pill-box hat. Of course by now you know that the proper name for that hat in Arabic is *tarbush*. Still, I do believe Fez is the only city that gave its name to a hat."

They had just come off a four-day camping trip in the Sahara, during which they'd sweltered by day and shivered by night, but had also kicked back and spent hours each night around the campfire, playing drums and dancing to desert music. They spoke in Arabic without prompting, and they called each other by the Arabic names that had been assigned to them in class. Barbara had become Basma. She liked having two syllables instead of three, and she felt that Basma, which means smile, suited her.

The trip was a much-needed break from their language studies. Their teachers had also taken a break from the group and would meet them in Fez. Though they were returning to city life, many students still wore colorful scarves wrapped turban-like around their heads as they had in the desert. They'd been warned to be careful about the cultural implications of donning traditional garb, but their desert hosts had insisted on teaching the young men how to wrap a desert turban, gifting them each a scarf as they arrived in the desert encampment. Barbara draped a dark plum scarf that she'd bought in a desert town around her neck every day. Purple was her favorite color, and she'd been buying bargain-priced tunics, caftans, and scarves all summer, draping herself in everything from light violet to the almost-black hue of her scarf. Most of the time she had one or two shades on at once.

While Dr. Charles droned on about the history of Fez, Barbara put in her earbuds and tuned him out, playing Moroccan pop tunes on her phone. She noticed that more trees had begun to appear, and soon they reached the mountain forests and the resort and university town of Ifrane, where they stopped for hot chocolate. How amazing, she thought, to wake up in the desert and to arrive in a mountain forest the same day.

After the break, the bus continued north. But since they had crossed the mountains, they were now headed downhill. After the stop in Ifrane, everyone was wide awake, and conversation buzzed. Someone started singing a desert song they'd learned, and others joined in. Mike pulled out his drum and soon everyone was clapping and singing along. Barbara danced in her seat, waving her arms and tilting her shoulders up and down to the beat.

It was late afternoon when they reached the outskirts of Fez. At first, it seemed just like every large city they'd visited.

The traffic picked up. Vespas and motorcycles buzzed by, some with three people perched on them, weaving past stopped cars. Rush hour was in full swing.

The bus slowed, and it had trouble making its way through streets that seemed to grow smaller with each turn. The bus pulled over and lurched to a stop next to an old archway the width of a single lane road.

Ibrahim jumped up and said, "Okay folks, we're here. Our home for the next three weeks, Dar Surour, is down this little street. It's only a five-minute walk. Let's gather outside, and you can follow me on foot. My team will bring the luggage later. This is the edge of the medina, Fez al-Bali, the Old City, and no motorized vehicles are allowed inside. So it's on foot from here."

At that point, Barbara wished she'd paid attention to the lecture. A city district with no motor traffic? Even Marrakech didn't have that.

She stood and stretched. The bus was big enough that each student had half a row to themselves if they wanted privacy. There had been an installment of a long-running card game in the back, but those had broken up, owing to the weaving motion of the bus as it turned along the switchbacks. It had been a long day on the bus, almost seven hours.

"I've heard this place serves a mean Gin Fez," Mike quipped as he stood and pulled his backpack down from the luggage rack. Groans only encouraged him, but they couldn't help it.

After climbing off the bus, Barbara arched her back and swung her backpack up on one shoulder. It must have weighed twenty pounds by then, and the zippers were giving way. She had duct taped a couple of rips to keep them from opening further. Her worn out flip-flops were still hanging on, though the cushions were getting thinner by the day. Soon she'd be basically going barefoot, but she was determined to make it all the way back home in them.

Laughter bubbled up, as it always did, between the two Texans, Jenn and Carla. They were already attracting admiring looks from nearby men. They could have been twins with their slim figures and waist-length blonde hair, and they attracted stares and comments wherever they went. Barbara was usually too far away when they were laughing like that to know what was so funny. Even when she sat with them at a meal, it was as if they had a secret line of communication, and they would start laughing uncontrollably. Something would just set them off. "Going Texan," the others called it. Still, at times it really was infectious, and soon all 40 of them would be laughing. Often, they didn't know why, but that in itself was funny, so they kept laughing.

"Okay everyone, stay close," Ibrahim said. "That means you, Munir—er, Mike. No wandering off." Mike nodded and rolled his eyes, acknowledging his tendency to disappear into the markets. Mike's Arabic name, Munir, meant brilliant, which even he recognized as ironic.

Within a minute of passing under the arch into the medina, the sounds of honking and roaring engines receded. The streets were packed with pedestrians, and they had to give way when a donkey laden with lumber was led past.

They walked along a small street lined with little shops, many of which were closing up for the day. But above them, the upper stories of ancient whitewashed stucco buildings glowed in the late-afternoon sun. The scents of home-cooked dinners, with cumin, paprika, and Moroccan spice mixes, filled the air.

People in the streets were going home from work or school, and they didn't pay much attention to the students. It's not that the other cities weren't filled with industrious people, but it was different without cars careening and motor scooters trying to weave among the walkers. Everyone was simply going about their own business, at a walking pace.

Barbara stayed toward the back of the pack with Maureen, her roommate and also the faculty escort. Maureen had been a last-minute substitute for the famous ethnomusicologist who had been expected to accompany the group, but he broke a leg just a week before the trip. Maureen had been recruited to fill in, but as a specialist in French medieval textiles, she was out of her area of expertise, and most of the time she seemed miserable.

Though her fluent French served her well throughout the country, Maureen had no interest in Arabic. She kept her distance from most of the students, yet she and Barbara often sat at meals together, and they passed the time with small talk and comfortable silences. Once, while sharing a cup of tea away from the group, Maureen had confided that she didn't understand why anyone would want to study Arabic. Barbara was familiar with the sentiment, since she often heard it from her friends and family.

Barbara watched the heads of her fellow students bob above the crowd. Way out front, Ibrahim stopped and turned toward them, raising his hands. He gestured toward a stately three-story riad, an ancient mansion recently restored for touristic purposes. "This is our home in Fez, Dar Surour. Please take a seat in the courtyard and wait for your room assignments."

Two by two, Barbara watched the heads of the students bend down as they ducked beneath a massive beam to enter the riad, then disappeared. They could have been entering another dimension as far as she could tell. She and Maureen were the last to step through, finding themselves in a small whitewashed stucco foyer with a brilliant red tribal carpet and a painting that featured women's hands decorated with geometric patterns of russet-colored henna.

They were led to a small courtyard open to the sky, with a tinkling fountain at its center, tiled walkways and pillowed alcoves all around. All summer, they had been staying in budget tourist hotels or even college dormitories. This was different—a real historic riad. The group made themselves at home, sitting in the little booths, or cross-legged along the walls, enjoying the cool green of the towering banana trees and other exotic flora that surrounded the fountain. Already, young men in long white *djellaba's* and red vests were pouring out small glasses of sweet mint tea with characteristic flourish, raising their pouring arms high to produce foam in each glass. Barbara had come to love this welcome ritual and relished her first sip of the minty sweetness.

As was the usual routine, Ibrahim explained when and where dinner would be. Until then, the students were to watch for the porters to bring their luggage to the courtyard and then the students would carry it to their rooms. They were meant to stay on the grounds of the riad until a neighborhood orientation after supper.

With room assignments in hand, the students scattered in search of their rooms, heading down hallways and up stone stairways that wound their way up three stories. Dar Surour had three separate courtyards, one of which featured a small swimming pool. The riad had once been home to a wealthy merchant, and it had been converted to a hotel by the local architect who now owned it.

Each courtyard was surrounded by three stories of balconies, and behind them, the guest rooms. Barbara and Maureen laughed with delight when they stepped inside their room. It was on the second floor, overlooking one of the largest courtyards. Each of the two beds was beautifully made up, with luxurious white cotton sheets, light wool blankets, and rose petals sprinkled on the pillowcases. The window to the courtyard had wooden shutters that they could open all the way or leave partially closed for privacy. While they had to climb a narrow staircase to get to their bathroom, it was a fanciful bath, fitted in the latest European style.

Maureen said she wanted to take a nap, but being twenty years her junior and ever-curious, Barbara had no such need. She felt the pull to explore the rest of the riad and slipped out to have a look. Half the students were doing the same. Splash! They were already using the swimming pool, and laughter echoed through the place. She looked down into the courtyard and spotted several students curled up in little nooks, doing homework for the next day's classes.

"Wow, what a view!" she heard from above, and she looked up to see some of the students pointing out over the courtyard. They were on the roof. She found the stairway that led to it and skipped up two steps at a time, as she always did, and came to a heavy wooden door that led to the roof. It had been propped open, letting the breeze fill the stairway. Out on the roof, she was delighted to find several patios surrounding each open courtyard. Luxurious cushioned lounge chairs were arranged to catch the best views. The heat was still intense, but the sun was sinking toward the horizon, and the breeze kept the air moving. She found them huddled in the shade next to a roof-top utility room, gazing out over the city.

All around them, from the elevations to the slopes, the magnificence of Fez spread out like a maze of golden-pearl building blocks. Being on top of one of the taller riads, they could see well beyond the neighboring houses into the distance. There was something about the medina. It was so harmonious somehow, but she couldn't say why.

"Notice, no skyscrapers," someone said. "No modern buildings."

"And no sounds of cars," someone else added. "The whole thing is a UNESCO World Heritage site. Can you believe even though it's less than a square mile, more than 150,000 people live here?"

That was when it hit her. The quiet of this great city. Even though it was filled with people, the sounds of motors and horns were gone. They were far enough inside the old city that they couldn't hear the cars just outside its walls. Not even the whining buzz of a Vespa passed by.

When the others moved to the third courtyard to watch the swimmers cavorting in the pool, Barbara remained, letting the wind catch her loose cotton tunic and baggy cotton slacks. She looked over the wall to the neighborhood below, enjoying the sights and sounds.

In the alley below, she noticed an old woman sitting alone on a big piece of cardboard. She wore a greyish faded pink caftan and had her arm outstretched, propped on one knee, waiting for a little change. They'd seen women like her in other cities that summer. She felt sorry for them, and most of the students would share a coin or two when they passed them in the streets. But this woman was in a deserted alley, where no one walked.

The old woman had positioned herself next to an ancient stone arch that bridged the alley. She looked up and glared at Barbara, who backed away, feeling uncomfortable.

She heard a commotion in the alley and looked down again. A crew of men was pulling several metal handcarts piled high with luggage into the alley where the old lady sat. They started unloading the bags, carrying them through a side door. The old lady stood up and waved her arms and shouted at them, but they just ignored her. She then stood under the stone archway and stretched her arms out to its sides, as if blocking them. The men kept on working. One of the riad staff members emerged from the side door and spoke a few words to her and managed to calm her down, so that she sat back down on her sheet of cardboard.

After supper that night, the group gathered on the rooftop. While they drank mint tea and ate orange slices sprinkled with cinnamon, Ibrahim and Dr. Charles introduced everyone to Khalid, the riad manager. Khalid told them a bit about the neighborhood and passed out simple maps of the medina to show the location of the riad and key landmarks in case they got lost. The next day, they would go on a walking tour after morning classes.

Abdul-Lateef, the owner of the riad, also made an appearance. An elegantly dressed architect in his 40s, he gave Dr. Charles and the students a warm welcome. He explained that this was the first time Dr. Charles' program had stayed there. The arrangements seemed ideal to Barbara. The classrooms were just next door, in a building that had once been a carpentry workshop, and it was also owned by Abdul-Lateef. So, for the first time that summer, the students didn't have to ride the bus or even walk very far to get to class. Barbara was beginning to think this would be the best city yet.

Dr. Charles took a deep breath and said, "One last announcement. As you know, when you signed up for this trip, you agreed to surrender all your electronic devices during our stay in Fez."

A collective groan rose from the crowd. Like everyone else, Barbara had forgotten about that clause in the program agreement that they'd all signed.

"We will store your devices in the hotel safe. The day after your last exam, you'll get them back."

Those who had not been paying attention were now focused. Maureen smiled with enthusiasm at this news, since she had been critical of how the students spent a lot of time posting on social media and chatting with friends back home.

Dr. Charles continued, "Remember, Fez is a unique and historic place. We believe that while you are here, nothing should come between you and your surroundings. In the medina, you can actually converse in classical Arabic with the shopkeepers. And in class, we don't want you recording. Learn directly from your ears and your handwriting, the way humans have learned languages for thousands of years. This way, you'll be better prepared for the final exam, which is in three weeks."

Dr. Charles waited for verbal protests, but got only groans, sighs, and shaking heads.

"This is the only intact medieval Arab city in the world. We want you to experience your days here directly without digital interference. Professor Maureen and I will be collecting all the devices you listed when we arrived in the country."

Maureen brought out several large canvas bags filled with padded envelopes and pulled out a clipboard. Dr. Charles gave everyone ten minutes to get their devices.

Though the students had known this was coming, it seemed to Barbara that everyone had put it out of their minds. And while at first Barbara had been upset about turning in her phone and tablet, she realized that she had stopped taking pictures and checking messages and social media since their second day in the desert. She realized that it wasn't so bad to be disconnected from the outside world.

Once all the devices were turned in and registered, Khalid and his staff carried the bags down to the hotel safe.

As soon as they disappeared down the staircase, two loud drumbeats rang out from another roof entrance. A line of ten drummers paraded out onto the rooftop patio. Dressed in white djellaba's, with red tasseled tarbushes on their heads, they held frame drums in front of them at shoulder height as they pounded out a catchy, complicated rhythm.

Barbara jumped up and swayed in place, dropping her shoulders to catch the rhythm of the syncopated beats. Others joined and clapped with enthusiasm. The drummers smiled and laughed, enjoying the effect their surprise entrance had on the students.

Some of the students ran to their rooms to get their own drums and join in. They'd been collecting Moroccan drums throughout the trip. By the time they reached Fez, they had double-headed bongos, darbukahs, and many sizes of frame drums, and they loved to jam at every opportunity. They joined in with the drummers and kept in time with the tricky syncopated rhythm as best they could.

Anytime the drums came out, or they watched a folkloric group, the students were encouraged to dance. It was something Barbara had come to love about that summer. She'd joined the belly dancing club during the spring semester at school, so she knew a few moves, though the Moroccan rhythms were different from the Egyptian beats she'd learned. They danced almost every night, no matter where they were. She tried to imitate the Moroccan dance steps, but knew she wasn't getting it. Still, the music always made her dance, and she wouldn't sit down until it stopped. Her enthusiasm got the others dancing, too. She had taught the Texan girls a few moves, which earned them even more attention.

Barbara always danced for herself. She was not aware of anyone else in the room at times like this, only her and the music. Her mind wandered as she danced, as she let the sounds lead her thoughts this way and that. Dancing gave her pure joy and stress relief. It had been belly dancing that piqued her interest in studying Arabic in the first place. And she wasn't going to give up studying the language, despite the difficulty, because the dance had become the center of her life. Even in her first belly dance class, she'd found that, when she was dancing, joy bloomed in her heart and she couldn't stop smiling. The dance felt right. When the Moroccan rhythm changed, sweeping her thoughts away, she pranced across the terrace toward the drummers.

Barbara was so distracted by the daily excitement of being in Morocco that she'd had a hard time focusing on her studies. In fact, she was one of the worst students in the program. She had to fight her way through every class: to catch each concept of grammar, each family of vocabulary.

At least she wasn't the worst. Mike, who was always wandering off, held that honor. He was the youngest in the program, a rising sophomore from the University of Minnesota. He struggled with the simplest sentences and exercises. Every day, they would go around the room, taking turns reading exercises out loud. He never got it right. Some said he would probably fail and not get a certificate of completion at the end of the course. Talk about embarrassing. One thing about Mike, though—he could drum much better than any of the others, and that night he was grooving right along with the Moroccan group.

The drummers ended the jam with a flourish, and the students sent up a cheer. Barbara stood still, her right hand over her mouth, and let out a long loud *zaghroota*, a trilling cry of joy. Barbara had an unusually loud and piercing zaghroota that always got its own cheers. Throughout the summer, she'd had many opportunities to show off. After she'd finished by fading her trill to silence, she took a bow to the cheers of students and musicians. She was so grateful to have learned that from some older Egyptian women at a restaurant near Boston.

When the riad staff brought out another round of tea, a new calm seemed to settle over the group. For Barbara, the night and the sky and the music banished thoughts of texts and posts, though she was sure a few fingers twitched at not being able to take a selfie or post a video clip of the impromptu party.

Barbara wandered back to her previous lookout and peered into the alley below. Even in the dark, she could see the woman was still sitting there, her arm outstretched. The beggar looked up at Barbara, and her eyes reflected green light like a cat's eyes. Barbara backed away in shock. It was as if she'd seen a . . . djinn. If it was anything, she thought, it would be a djinn, those spirits that share the world with humans. They were said to be thick and close in Morocco. They'd been hearing stories about djinn throughout the trip. They were advised to be careful when opening closets and stepping into houses and rooms. At such times, they needed to utter God's name for protection.

Barbara called Maureen over, and they peered into the alley. Again, the green eyes glowed in their direction. Maureen let out a scream and Ibrahim dashed over.

"Look, down in the alley," Barbara said. "That old woman has green eyes, and they glow."

For just a moment, a look of fear appeared on Ibrahim's face, and he muttered, "In the name of God". Barbara could see that he was willing himself to calm down. By then the group knew that he was incredibly superstitious. He had told them a lot of Moroccan lore about the supernatural. He pulled his shoulders back, stepped to the edge of the wall, and leaned over. He jerked his head back, then looked at the two women in alarm. Without saying a word, he dashed down the stairs.

Ibrahim's quick departure caught the attention of more of the students, and soon a group was looking over the wall. A minute later, Ibrahim and Khalid appeared in the alley and approached the woman. Ibrahim was shouting at her, while Khalid gripped Ibrahim's shoulders and pushed him back. The woman stood in the middle of the alley and started talking back, waving her arms dramatically. They were speaking in lightning-fast dialect, so no one on the roof could make out any words.

After a few exchanges, she seemed to calm them down, and it looked as if they had come to an understanding. They gave her some coins and left her alone. Khalid put his arm around Ibrahim's shoulder, who shook his head as they headed back to the riad's front door. The old woman sat back down, then directed her gaze up at the students, who leaned back so they couldn't be seen.

"Wow, I wonder what her story is," Barbara said.

"I've never seen Ibrahim so freaked out," Mike added.

Laying in bed that night, Barbara was grateful that her room opened only onto an interior courtyard, not the alley. Yet she pitied the old woman and wondered if she still sat there, all alone, and if she had a home at all.

Chapter 3

Moustapha's Alley

The morning after the students arrived, everything seemed calm again. I had just been lulled into a lovely nap when the riad door squeaked open and woke me. Khalid brought the Moroccan guide and some of the students into the alley. By that time, I had concluded that they were mostly Americans, based on their speech and their studied disregard for fashion, as compared to other foreigners. There were a few from Asia, but the majority seemed to be American or European.

Khalid spoke to the others, ignoring me. "What with all the rain, we've had some construction issues. This wall gave way just the other day, revealing this old arch. See how the stones are set in it? It has to be centuries old. And the green keystone—it's so carefully placed. The arch is solid, won't budge," he said, pushing his whole weight against one of the lower stones. "I grew up here and never knew this arch was hidden in the wall."

"What did they use for mortar?" the young Moroccan asked, his smile a dazzling white.

"Well, Ibrahim, I don't know, there's so little of it left. And even so, it seems it's so well built that gravity is holding it together."

Ibrahim. The city name didn't match his country accent at all.

As they turned toward the street, some of the Americans stopped to look at me as I sat, motionless.

Ibrahim said, "Like in many of our old cities, in the medina many of the beggars you see are widows, and they don't have any means of support. Some people say that giving them a coin only encourages them. Others say it's bad luck to pass by an old woman like this without helping her a little bit. It's up to you." I could tell that Ibrahim suspected I was more than what I appeared to be. He stood back and wouldn't look at me directly.

Two students stepped forward and handed me coins. Then a third young man crouched beside me and looked deep into my eyes.

"Here, ma'am," he said, smiling as he pressed a dirham into my hand. "God bless."

"Come along, Mike," Ibrahim said, "They're serving lunch." The group moved down the alley toward the front of the riad.

I got a good look at this human named Mike, since he stayed at my eye level for a moment. He seemed different from the others; more Mediterranean. Perhaps he had Italian ancestry, and who knows, back some centuries, perhaps an Arab forefather. His skin was the olive tone of many Moroccans. He had a round chin, and his dark eyes peered out from beneath a prominent brow that reminded me of a desert cliff. As he paused for a moment, I sensed something about him, or rather about his spirit. It was an openness, a vulnerability. If I'd been an evil sort, I'd have taken advantage of him, no doubt. But I am not evil, and, as he stood up, I closed my finger around the coin and nodded my thanks, making my chin quiver for added effect.

Khalid and Ibrahim lingered after the others had gone inside. Khalid spoke in English, assuming I wouldn't understand. "We don't usually have beggars around here. This one came after the rains, and she hasn't moved since."

So the Fez days of the Arabic school began. And what a school it was! Birdsong accompanied their conjugations. During class breaks, they sipped sweet mint tea and strong coffee in a courtyard with a tinkling fountain.

Each afternoon, they went shopping or touring. In the evenings they studied or enjoyed traditional performances. One night, a group of women healers came to the riad to sing blessings in a ceremony. The women paused at the opening to the alley and looked at me, muttering, before they went inside.

After a few days, I concluded that the locals wouldn't be coming down the alley, as they have set walking routes through the old city. Even the people in the past didn't seem to pay any attention to the newly opened arch.

As the students got used to their surroundings, they also didn't show any interest in coming down the alley. The lure of the great market streets was too strong and they were drawn there, away from me, every time. Maybe I was scaring them, just a bit. I began to think that my job might pass peacefully, that the arch would soon be filled in again, and I could return to the quiet of the mountains.

And so the days passed peacefully, that is until the night of the *gnawa* ceremony. I might have known that the gnawa would come along, upsetting the balance and churning things up. But what were the chances they would be asked to perform at Dar Surour? No matter, so it was. Being a djinni, I was drawn to the smell of the incense they lit, which was my favorite: rich aloeswood. That was how I knew they were having the ceremony. The incense.

I flew over the riad's rooftop and hovered there in the dark, looking down into the open courtyard where the musicians had gathered. The students were lounging on big pillows and bolsters, unaware of the powerful ceremony they were about to witness. A cloud of incense billowed up. I flew right into it and bathed in its delicious aroma. Other spirits hovered nearby, waiting and watching. That was when the trouble started.

Chapter 4

The Gnawa

Ibrahim never understood why foreigners were so fascinated with gnawa musicians. They knew only the basic facts about Islam, so how could they hope to comprehend the subtleties of the gnawa ceremony? And what did foreigners know about old traditions, anyway? They couldn't possibly understand something as ancient and mysterious as the gnawa, yet here they were, eager for the performance.

"Please, folks, just a few words," Ibrahim said, quieting the group at dinner. "Tonight we'll have the chance to see an all-night gnawa ceremony, a *lila*. We've seen gnawa musicians all summer performing in public for tourists, but this will be different. We will experience an authentic lila.

"According to legend, rulers many centuries ago brought soldier slaves to Morocco from sub-Saharan Africa, who became known as gnawa. They became Muslims and gradually, they won their freedom. They are not just musicians, they are a Sufi brotherhood that attends to the community's needs for spiritual healing. Over the years they tried to preserve something of their old spiritual ways, which live on in these rites. It takes years for the musicians to learn gnawa music, and to perform the ceremony. Sometimes a ceremony can go on for days, but they have agreed to do an evening session for us. Their main instrument is the *guenbri,* a kind of bass guitar. Here in Fez, they call it the *hajhuj.* Many street musicians we've seen play those loud double-headed finger cymbals, the *qaraqib*, and they're also a key element to this music and the ceremonies.

"Tonight, the *mu`allim*, the musicians' leader, will call up specific spirits one by one, using incense, colors, melodies, and rhythms. If a certain rhythm speaks to you, feel free to get up and dance. Maybe you have a connection to that spirit. Otherwise, just enjoy the evening, and if the music lulls you to sleep for a while, that's fine too. There will definitely be time for dancing." Ibrahim winked at Barbara who reacted with a smile.

"We'll gather in the main courtyard around ten. Ladies, this is a nice occasion to wear your beautiful caftans," he said, smiling as he remembered the commissions he'd earned from the caftan merchants earlier that day. His phone rang just as he finished. He pulled it out and glanced at it. It was his wife, Laila. After sending the call to voice mail, Ibrahim excused himself and went to the roof. He listened to her message, the same message she'd left every day for the last week. He hadn't called her back, since he was still seething mad from their last conversation.

"Sweetheart," she'd said. "I hope you haven't been buying too much on this trip. Remember what we talked about, what happened the last time you shipped a container? You'll just get ripped off again, and we can't afford it, not this year with the baby coming." He knew she was right. When the last container had arrived, half the items were broken, and most of the rest were substandard, substituted for the top-quality goods he'd ordered. He'd lost several thousand dollars on the last shipment, and they couldn't afford another like it. Still, he hated to hear these criticisms in her *diplomatic* tone of voice. Didn't she know he was doing his best? Besides, she knew that this tour wasn't just to earn money, but was also a chance to buy things from across Morocco.

He didn't know how to tell her that he'd already placed enough orders to fill a container. While he felt guilty that she was back in Pittsburgh with their two young sons, he was also glad to be away from her. On the tour, there was no question that *he* was in charge. When guilt made him call her back, she didn't pick up. She was probably at work. He hung up before the beep. At least she'd see that he tried to call. He went to his room, and changed into a royal blue *gandoura*. He wound a black turban around his head like a Tuareg and left his modern persona behind. He emerged in the courtyard wrapped in the clothing of his ancestors, the men of the deep Sahara.

The flickering light from candle lanterns sent shadows dancing across the courtyard's whitewashed walls and arches. The students had gathered there, eyeing the gnawa musicians with respectful curiosity. The gnawa sat on the carpet in a semi-circle, cross-legged. They wore their distinctive costumes: skull caps decorated with cowrie shells and long tassels, and vests of bright red, green, and blue. A glowing brazier sat in front of them, sending clouds of incense into the night sky.

Many of the students had followed Ibrahim's suggestion and dressed in their Moroccan clothes. The women showed off new tunic sets and caftans, fringed scarves at their waists or wrapped around their heads like fanciful turbans. Faded traces of their recent henna night lingered on their hands. Silver earrings jangled, kohled eyes flashed, and bangles jostled and clinked with merriment.

The leader of the group, the mu`allim, smiled at the audience. Behind him, a man with a long face and dark mustache who was lighter-skinned than the others, began a subtle improvisation on the hajhuj, coaxing soft, deep-toned bass lines from its gut strings as it explored the notes of a five-toned scale.

While the hajhuj player continued his solo, the mu`allim wandered through the group, greeting each person them with a nod and a smile. When he smiled, his face folded up in long wrinkles, framing his five gleaming front teeth, three of which were gold.

The mu`allim knelt down and began to sing, and the hajhuj followed his notes. After a few minutes, the musicians marked out a slow waltz-like rhythm on the qaraqib with their unique metallic clank. Together, the mellow bass line of the hajhuj and cymbals began to work their hypnotic magic.

Typically, Ibrahim would have hired a particular brotherhood that performed rituals in Moroccan homes, but they weren't available. He'd invited this group on their recommendation. They seemed competent, and the mu`allim had a gentle manner. He hoped the students would appreciate the ceremony. Some of his tourist groups had been rude and made fun of the ritual. Others dismissed it after a few minutes and left. This kind of thing wasn't for everyone.

Ibrahim watched the students' faces as their senses were assaulted by the ancient melodies, the rich incense, the bright costumes, and the clank of the qaraqib. This was an interesting group of students. Each was on a unique personal quest to learn Arabic. One wanted to read Khalil Gibran in Arabic. Another wanted to study the poetry of Andalusian Spain. Several were graduate students in political science and history whose serious research required them to learn to read Arabic.

Whatever their motivations, Ibrahim sympathized with them, because, for nearly all foreigners, learning Arabic was like climbing Mount Everest. Few ever achieved the ability to read, write, and speak with ease, because to do so required that they learn the standardized language of scholarship and the media, as well as at least one spoken dialect. They had many dialects to choose from, and it was inevitable that foreigners mixed them up when they spoke. Ibrahim admired their persistence and dedication. Well, perhaps the Texas gazelles were concentrating more on what they called "foreign affairs" than on their Arabic studies. Though Ibrahim couldn't stop them from going out at night to prowl the discos, he sent one of his crew along to make sure they didn't go to the wrong sort of club. Tonight, though, they sat cross-legged in front, spellbound. Jenn and Carla could have been sisters; they both had long blonde hair, tight jeans, and Moroccan tunics that were just a little too small and outlined their dangerous curves. Ibrahim wondered how long they could take the intensity of the gnawa music.

Even though Dr. Charles and Professor Maureen were around to help keep an eye on things, Ibrahim had hired extra guards for the front door, just in case. He checked on the two young men outside; they were leaning against the wall near the door, smoking cigarettes.

Foreigners were usually safe in Fez, but over the years, Ibrahim heard stories about gangs preying on tourists, and he wasn't taking any chances. This was his first time taking a group to this riad, and while the manager Khalid seemed like a nice enough fellow, Ibrahim had hired his own helpers for the Fez visit.

Ibrahim turned the corner and peered down the alley. He was not surprised to see the old woman still sitting there. Ibrahim was suspicious of her. Maybe she was some kind of lookout for a gang. Khalid had assured him that she was just

an old woman from the neighborhood, that it seemed her
family kept an eye out for her.

Chapter 5

Female Spirits

The mu`allim took gentle steps in time to the slow music. He stepped on the carpet as if it were a soft cloud. His short frame tilted as he marked each rhythm's heartbeat, his robe rippling slightly. He had been looking down, but raised his head and searched the crowd, looking for someone or something.

The old man approached Barbara. Ibrahim wasn't surprised that he sought her out, for the gnawa had a way of knowing things. When he reached out for her hands, she let him pull her up. Standing next to him, her round face beaming, she held his hand, and imitated his slow careful steps in time to the rhythm. Her generous figure barely moved with the beat, and her long chestnut-brown braid swayed on its own behind her. Others joined them in the line, the mu`allim's smile and dancing eyes welcoming their enthusiasm. This group really did seem to get it, Ibrahim thought. Was that possible?

Everyone stared at the mu`allim's feet as he did his simple step dance on the carpet. He turned slowly, walking forward and back. After many mesmerizing minutes of this, he sat down and the musicians took a break. The students drank more mint tea and nibbled on sweets, their ears still ringing from the clackety-clack of the qaraqib.

The gnawa started up again and lit another kind of incense. The qaraqib picked up speed, and the others clapped faster and faster, thundering like horses galloping across the desert. The mu`allim pulled bright purple scarves from a basket. Purple was the color of Lalla Malika, the spirit of dance. The old man tied a scarf around his head and handed scarves to the audience.

Barbara tied one around her hips and began to make slow, wide hip circles, around and around, bouncing subtly in time with the music, like a dancer in a Cairo nightclub. It was good to have someone who loved to dance in the group. She had a lot of soul. She started turning slowly in place, in contrast to the fast rhythm. She slid her head from side to side with her eyes closed, her arms at her sides, elbows bent and palms out. She looked like a goddess as the cloud of incense enveloped her. The mu`allim stood nearby, skipping in time to the fast rhythm, almost jumping up and down in place.

The next song was for Lalla Mira, the spirit of fun and frivolity. Ibrahim noted that they were calling up spirits out of the usual order. Usually, they did the female spirits at the end of the evening. He wondered if they were going to cut the performance short, and that made him suspicious—perhaps they would demand full payment for half a ceremony.

Khalid didn't seem to mind. He ran to the front and grabbed a scarf in yellow, Lalla Mira's color, from the basket. He tied it around his head and began to dance. Barbara continued her inward turning, while Khalid began to weave his head back and forth as he put his arms out and spun, stepping to the lively rhythm. Ibrahim figured Khalid was just hamming it up for the visitors. How could a city boy from Fez be so into a gnawa ritual?

At the back of the room, others held hands, dancing in a long writhing snake of a line that wove and looped in on itself. Even Dr. Charles joined in. The musicians' faces lit up in response.

Professor Maureen seemed uncomfortable, as usual. Ibrahim sighed as he watched her sitting alone, casting a disapproving gaze toward Barbara, her lips pursed, her chin angled upward. As usual, her graying brown hair was pulled back in a tight braid. She looked grim and austere, like a prison guard.

Even though she was on staff, Maureen was definitely "the one" on this trip. From the moment she was added to the team, she'd sent him daily e-mails. She needed to know the details of the food they would be eating, to make sure it was up to her exacting preferences. What type of pillows and linens would they have? What were the cleanliness standards of the hotels? Were there bedbugs? Would the tap water make her eczema flare up? Would they accommodate her very particular diet?

Once they'd arrived in Morocco, and she found that he'd met all her requests, she began obsessing about "the poor animals", although she never remarked on the human poverty they encountered. She ranted about the skinniness of street cats and fed them table scraps at roadside stops. She threw a fit the first time she saw a fully laden donkey being led through a country market. After the first few days, everyone ignored her, but this only made her more indignant.

Maureen could hold forth on the origins of linen, weaving techniques, and the natural dyes still used in Morocco. But after a while, even when she was sharing her unique expertise, everyone but Barbara tuned her out.

Ibrahim had found her highly irritating until he realized that she'd never had a family of her own to distract her from herself. He thought of how his boys never allowed him or his wife to become too self-absorbed. Once you were a parent, you were no longer the center of the universe. Now he just felt sorry for Maureen, and he was grateful for her roommate's patience.

Scanning the group, Ibrahim noticed that Mike hadn't moved from his seat. He was leaning against a pillar, his feet tucked beneath him. Of all the people not to take part, this made no sense. Mike played bass guitar, and he loved traditional Moroccan music. Ever since he'd arrived in the country, he kept saying how much he looked forward to the gnawa ceremony. He had been obsessed about buying a guenbri since day one, and he'd disappeared in every city and town they'd visited, in search of the musical instrument makers.

Mike was not only the worst student in the group, but he also seemed to be in another world. He, too, had gotten on Ibrahim's nerves. He was late for every appointment, including bus departure times—forcing everyone to wait. Mike frequently wandered off, and Ibrahim would have to look for him. He found Mike in all kinds of strange situations, sitting among street sellers, watching artisans work, and playing soccer with young boys in vacant lots. But this night was something Mike had looked forward to for the whole trip, and he was just sitting there with his eyes closed.

Ibrahim knelt next to him and asked, "Mike, Munir, are you okay?" When Ibrahim nudged him, Mike rolled off the pillow onto the floor, his left hand curled under his chin. He was asleep. No. He was unconscious.

Khalid came over to see if Mike was okay, and then spoke to the mu`allim, who joined them at Mike's side. The musicians played on as the mu`allim spoke to Mike in a strange dialect that Ibrahim didn't understand. Mike's eyes fluttered open. He looked up at the old man, and his face curled into a wide but strangely sinister grin. Then he rolled over and went to back to sleep.

"Someone is with him tonight," the mu`allim said. "He'll wake up when we play the right rhythm. Until then, just let him sleep. God willing, he'll be fine."

During the next break, some of the students gathered around him. He was still sound asleep, stretched out on his side on the carpet. Professor Maureen propped a pillow under his head.

The musicians lit a new kind of incense, an ancient and rich scent that smelled like a combination of amber and licorice, and more smoke billowed up from the censers. Again, the lighter-skinned tall man with the long, Arab-looking face began to play a soft melody on the hajhuj. The others sang and clapped, and the qaraqib joined in.

Ibrahim joined the rhythmic clapping. After a while, he grabbed the hand of the old man and danced. Before long, a new group was up dancing. Even Maureen joined in, trying with great concentration to move gracefully.

Barbara danced by herself in the corner, waving her arms like a writhing snake. The men watched her, their eyes smoldering. *Barbara sure does know how to move*, and Ibrahim's thoughts wandered. He remembered he was a married man, and she was just a college girl. Yes, he admitted to himself, wild ideas pass through the mind of a tour guide, and strange things happened on tours.

People on tours seemed so normal at first, on the surface. But after a week on the road, he would often conclude that the entire tour group should start on medication, or be in therapy. Sometimes the group dynamics grew quite intense, but fortunately most tours didn't last long enough for things to erupt into anything serious. Student groups were different, since they had a definite focus and task, and they weren't just passively taking in new sights and sounds while also growing irritated at their fellow travelers' quirks.

Chapter 6

Shafiqa

It was after two a.m. when Ibrahim checked his watch. He'd warned everyone that the gnawa lila would go on until near dawn. Always, at about this time in the ceremony, he wanted to stretch out with a pillow on the rug and sleep. But he was afraid to doze off even for a few minutes. After all, he was in charge, and the last thing he wanted was some kind of trouble. If he got reported as an irresponsible guide, he could lose his license. So he gulped down another glass of tea and resolved to stay awake until it was over.

Just when it seemed the ceremony would never end, the qaraqib broke into a pounding rhythm as fast as the wind, as frantic as a storm. Mike sat up as if someone had yanked him with a rope, his eyes wide open. He rushed over to the old man leading the ceremony and began jumping in time to the music, laughing, waving his arms and rolling his head in circles. He stretched his arms up to the heavens and laughed aloud as he turned in place. He spun and cavorted in an eerie ecstasy.

The mu`allim grinned as he danced along with Mike. The other gnawa made remarks to each other as they played on, their eyes riveted on every move Mike made.

Shocked out of his late-night haze, Ibrahim stood up to watch. He had never seen a Westerner trance out like this before. The mu`allim wrapped Mike's head in a long black scarf, like a turban, while Mike kept dancing. He said something to the old mu`allim, who laughed.

The mu`allim pushed Mike to the center of the room, and Mike started to sing along to the tune, using the syllable, *la la la*. The gnawa group seemed re-energized. They clapped and rang the qaraqib so loudly that Ibrahim had to cover his ears. Mike flailed his arms around, shouting, *Allah Allah*.

Khalid pulled on Ibrahim's sleeve and nodded. Dr. Charles joined them as they tried to grab Mike's arms from behind, but he pulled free. The gnawa shook their heads at them, but Ibrahim felt the situation was out of control and they had to do something. The audience watched with the usual dazed look that they got when their minds had been overwhelmed by hours of dancing, incense, and ringing qaraqib. Meanwhile, Barbara kept dancing by herself in the corner.

"Leave him alone," the mu`allim shouted over the music. "You have to let this happen. If you try to stop it, it will be bad for all of us. Don't interfere."

Mike kept shouting as he rolled his head around. He ran up to the few people who were awake and shouted gibberish at them. He was trancing, all right, but Ibrahim was shocked, because he'd never seen a foreigner do this before. Ibrahim wondered whether Mike hadn't been mentally unstable to begin with.

After several minutes of this, the old man nodded at one of the men playing the qaraqib; he immediately left the room, then emerged from the back room dressed in street clothes and darted toward the door. Khalid questioned him as he slipped out.

"He's gone for help. He's getting someone from a healing group who can help." Khalid said to Ibrahim, yelling over the music. "The mu`allim thinks that he's possessed by Aisha Kandisha."

Ibrahim's eyes widened. There were groups that specialized in spirit possession, especially with Aisha Kandisha, the djinnia people always invoked when there was trouble. For sure she was bad luck, a bad spirit all around, and very powerful. You never wanted to mess with her. If you got sick, or tripped on a carpet, or if you fought with your wife, then you blamed it on Aisha Kandisha.

As Mike danced on, everyone was drawn into the mysterious drama. Dr. Charles reassured Maureen that things like this often happened and that no one was in danger. One of the musicians told Ibrahim, "We'll make sure he's okay. It's just that Aisha can be difficult sometimes."

The mu`allim addressed Mike, and he answered as he danced on. Sometimes he laughed and made a strange clicking sound, *zhzhzhzhzhz,* then nodded his head in answer. Other times, he just shook his head. Soon three of the gnawa stood near him. Khalid joined them and they formed a circle—shielding him from the eyes of the others, who had now been drawn into the spectacle.

A few minutes later, the man who'd left the riad returned with a slender dark-skinned woman. She strode into the room, carrying herself like a young queen, despite having been woken in the middle of the night. She wore a striking caftan of aqua and a matching headscarf worn turban-style, wound atop her head. First, she spoke to the mu`allim, then bowed her head and closed her eyes, her lips moving. She moved forward, always in time to the music, as if she were sneaking up on Mike. She stood behind him, moving with the others, who made furtive eye contact with her, as if they didn't want

Mike to see. She took their hands and joined the circle around him.

She called out to him. He stopped dancing and stared at her wide-eyed, his limbs frozen. She shouted at him again, and he began to let out cries that sounded like an animal howling. Then he roared like a crazed lion. The men backed away, but the woman stepped forward with her arms out and took both his hands.

"In the name of the Almighty!" she shouted. "Who are you, spirit? Answer me!" She let go of his hands with a great sweep of her arms, as if she were scaring off birds.

Mike's eyes widened, but then he just laughed at her.

She shook her head, stomped a foot, and called to the spirit again, but once more Mike laughed and shook his head. After instructing the men from the group to clap and keep playing the qaraqib as loud as they could, she had others join her in a circle around Mike. She led them to a small salon just off the courtyard. Once the door closed behind them, the students could hear the woman yelling, and Mike shouting back. Meanwhile, the remaining musicians tried to cover it up by playing and clapping louder.

After a few minutes, the rest of the musicians stood up, still playing, and walked to the back room, making it look like part of the ritual. They were playing a song for Aisha Kandisha, usually done at the very end of the ceremony, and they were playing it twice as fast as usual. The mu`allim was the last to go, trying to veil the seriousness of the situation by smiling and nodding at the audience.

"What's going on?" Maureen said to Ibrahim. The gazelles joined her at his side.

"I'm not sure," Ibrahim said, "but that lady's some kind of…."

"Exorcist?" Maureen said.

"Yes, I think so. Best to stay here," Ibrahim said, urging them to sit down. He promised himself that this was the last time he would hire a gnawa group, no matter how much people begged for it. From now on, he'd just take them to a restaurant to see the floorshow version done for tourists.

Someone started banging on the other side of the salon door, as if they were trying to get out into the courtyard. Then all the other doors and window shutters around the courtyard flew open and slammed shut, again and again. The night staff came out to the courtyard, their eyes wide with fear.

A hot smoky wind that smelled of burning hair swirled around them like a dust devil. It seared their faces, blew up the long panels of their tunics and caftans, and unwound Ibrahim's turban. It finally blasted out the top of the courtyard and into the night. The shutters stopped banging and the air cleared. Then there was silence—blessed silence.

Everyone in the courtyard was frozen in place, looking around. Even Ibrahim, who had been to hundreds of these evenings, was shaken. He tried to compose himself, scanning the room to count those who remained. No one was missing. "It's always like this with the gnawa," he said. "You never know what's going to happen. We have to be careful." Ibrahim reassured the group that Mike was all right, that the gnawa would make sure of it.

One of the girls from Texas said, "That sure was worth the price of admission," and laughter broke the tension.

The mu`allim and the woman in aqua emerged from the back room, their arms around Mike's shoulders. He was a bit unsteady on his feet.

Mike sat down next to Barbara and took a cup of tea. He rubbed his eyes and stretched. "What did I miss? Must have fallen asleep." Barbara put her hand on his knee and raised her eyebrows at Ibrahim.

The rest of the gnawa returned to the courtyard and had tea with the woman in blue who spoke quietly with the mu`allim.

By this time, nearly all the students had staggered back to their rooms and only a handful remained.

The musicians lit more incense, then the mu`allim knelt and chanted rapidly. The hajhuj player started to pluck out another melody, this one relaxed and filled with peace. The other musicians put the qaraqib away, knelt in a half circle with their eyes closed, and offered a prayer to the Almighty for protection and safety. After they had finished, they bade everyone goodnight and retired to the back room salon for a traditional post-lila couscous. Ibrahim, Khalid, and the woman in blue joined them.

"So what happened with our young man?" Khalid asked.

"Shafiqa is an expert in these things," the mu`allim said, deferring to the woman.

"Like you, at first I thought it was Aisha Kandisha," Shafiqa said. "But no, my friends, this is an old spirit, an ancient one. Evil and very powerful. You heard its voice, did you not? This spirit is a sign of something my Aunt Shumaisa told me. She's our leader, but she insisted on sending me in her place tonight. She said something about a door being open. I advise you to keep this boy away from more ceremonies. I think he's vulnerable. And if bad spirits are near, they might try to find him."

After Shafiqa and the gnawa had left, Ibrahim and Khalid sprinkled salt at the threshold of the riad's front door, and outside every door in the building. Ibrahim would instruct the staff to salt the doorways and thresholds every day. His grandmother always said that was the best way to keep the djinn away, and he didn't want to take any chances.

Chapter 7

Muezzin's Call

Mike woke to the sound of muezzins calling the faithful to dawn prayers. He listened through the small arched window next to his bed. His room was on the third floor, overlooking the same courtyard as Barbara's, and he could see the sky through his window. Water gurgled in the courtyard fountain, and his roommate occasionally let out a snore from the other bed. The melodies of the muezzins meandered high and low through the ritual call. Why were some of them so out of tune? he wondered. He had learned that educated muezzins would sing in a certain *maqam,* musical mode.

His sharp ears picked up an old man's voice, very faint among the other younger voices. His voice had a raspy quality that tore at Mike's heart. It had so much soul, and he was perfectly on key. The more he listened, the more this voice intrigued him.

Anxious to pinpoint the source of the old man's voice, Mike got up, wrapped himself in a blanket, and slipped on his white leather slippers. He had to hurry or the calls would be over, so he scrambled up the tiled stairway to the roof. There, he stood on the highest patio and stretched his neck over the wall and listened. A flock of doves circled overhead. The moon still hung in the western sky. He cupped his hands behind his ears and turned his head to scan the buildings all around, trying to pick out the voices more clearly.

A young man was calling from the main mosque at the Qarawiyyin, the central mosque of the old city, its green-tiled roof poking up like a faceted emerald a few blocks down the hill. Over by the tomb of the saint, another young voice called out. His voice was a strong tenor, and he hit the high notes just right. At last, he heard the old man's voice again during a random moment of silence, when the other muezzins were taking a breath. It was coming from high on the hill. *He's somewhere up there,* Mike thought. *I've got to find him.*

The calls died away, but Mike stayed on the roof, listening to the sounds that floated up from nearby courtyards and alleys. A rooster crowed. Doors slammed. Mothers called to children, whose sandals slapped against tiled patios. A cat meowed. A donkey brayed. Wide awake, Mike went back to his room and checked the clock. It was only 6:45, and breakfast didn't start until eight. He knew he should go over his Arabic lesson, but instead he succumbed to an impulse to go for a walk.

Soon Mike was out on the street, dressed in a gandoura he'd bought when the group was camping in the desert. They'd been cautioned not to wear this kind of native garb because it was cultural appropriation, but Mike was in such a hurry he forgot. Being up so early was an adventure for him. Back home in Minneapolis, he was a night owl. His studies and music gigs usually kept him up late at night, so he rarely rose before noon.

At that early hour, the pack animals—horses, mules, and donkeys—walked with calm surety along streets that would soon be congested with people. Above him, a sparrow chirped from a nest tucked behind a utility box. A teenaged girl in a modest brown caftan glided past him, balancing a wide cloth-covered board on her head with her right hand. Mesmerized by the sway of her long black braids, Mike followed her until she ducked into a small bakery. He lingered long enough to see the baker nod as she left the board and returned down the road toward home, taking no notice of him.

He began to walk uphill along the main road, Rue Tala'a Kabira. Though the shops hadn't opened yet, artisans and tradesmen streamed into side streets and alleys to the workshops where they would toil all day. As the road grew steeper, Mike paused to catch his breath near a seller of Amazigh carpets, where a black and white cat crouched and blinked at him, unafraid, its elbows sticking out like a praying mantis.

Mike's eyes filled with tears. Not again, he thought, wiping his eyes with the heel of his palm. Ever since they'd come to Fez, he would tear up at the oddest times. He'd feel overcome with an emotion he couldn't name, like a deep yearning. As he stood there, taking in the scene, he recalled what Dr. Charles had told them about the city's history.

Fez had been a famous center of learning in medieval times. At its center were the Qarawiyyin Mosque and the university that was attached to it. In fact, a woman founded the mosque, back in the ninth century. She had donated her inheritance to build it; it was named for her ancestral hometown, Kairawan in Tunisia.

Dr. Charles had said, "Fez linked the knowledge of the old world and Europe. Many great minds of the medieval world, such as Ibn Khaldun, and the great Jewish philosopher Ibn Maimun, or Maimonedes, studied and lived here. Mathematics and science were taught and debated. In this way, many believe that Fez helped sow the seeds that grew into the Renaissance."

Resting there and leaning against the wall, Mike believed in his deepest being that it was true.

An old man strolling down the hill caught his eye, interrupting his reverie. He had the air of a gentleman, and his white turban seemed to connect to his trim snowy beard. A tan cloak edged in gold rested on his shoulders. He carried a wooden walking stick in his right hand, nodding and smiling as he greeted men coming the other way, looking briefly in each man's eyes as he did so. Could he be the muezzin? That would be too lucky, Mike decided, though his eyes were riveted on the venerable figure. The moment he drew near, a man leading a donkey laden with leather skins appeared, and the old man stepped to the other side. After the donkey had passed, the old man continued down the hill, greeting everyone until he reached a bend in the road and was gone.

At the top of the hill, Mike noticed a sign in English advertising the Café Clock. He'd heard it was an interesting place, so, following the enticing scent of freshly ground coffee beans, he turned down a narrow alleyway. He came upon a dimly lit courtyard filled with small round tables. Three backpacking tourists, two men and a woman, were drinking *nusnus*—the Moroccan version of café au lait—half espresso, half milk. They spoke German and were typing messages on their phones.

The waiter, a young Moroccan with long Rasta locks, spoke to Mike in Darija, Morocco's distinctive dialect. Mike knew enough to order coffee and a croissant to tide him over until breakfast, and he wondered if the waiter thought he was Moroccan. He was exhilarated to be out in the city, far from the riad and his fellow students. Mike liked to have time to himself so that he could experience things in his own way.

The people in the group were nice enough, but he needed to breathe, to have some private time and personal experiences that no one else could analyze, dissect, and discuss on the tour bus, or over dinner. Sometimes he wondered if the people he was with were even traveling in the same country. He had to point things out to them. His roommate walked with him through the maze of streets in Marrakesh and didn't even notice the men pouring into the mosques in the middle of the medina, their shoes lined up carefully in rows outside the entrance. He was sure he was the only one whose eyes had lingered with fascination as their bus passed a group of village women, their colorful dresses hiked up around their knees as they did their wash by hand in an oasis stream.

Then again, he had always felt like an outsider, someone in the margins of every group, every class. Yet for some reason, learning about Arab culture and language was like coming home.

Though his sister had given him a leather-bound journal for the trip, he hadn't written much so far, just a few scattered words to remind him of the rhythm of the desert musicians' clapping, or the smell of the spice souq in Marrakesh.

And then they'd come to Fez. The moment they stepped into the medina, he felt as if he were being pulled even further away from his fellow travelers. At least that's what he told himself. History seemed so close, as if he could reach out and taste it. It was in the very air and he wanted to breathe it deeply, alone.

As he waited for the coffee, he realized he should have brought his Arabic exercises with him. *Why did I think I could actually learn Arabic?* he asked himself for the thousandth time. He remembered his mother's reaction to this trip. She said she admired his persistence in studying Arabic, but she didn't understand why he would study something so hard, and most of all, why he wanted to spend three months in Morocco doing it.

"For sure it's difficult, and not only the script. The structure of Arabic grammar is completely different from European languages. Then they have these strange sounds that we don't have at all."

"But seems you're hell bent on learning it. And it's all because of the music?"

"I know it sounds crazy, but yeah, it's the music. The first time I heard it was in Nadia's Deli. I was the only customer, and the woman behind the counter turned up the music playing and sang along. Turns out the singer was this famous Egyptian diva, Um Kulthum. Her voice and the orchestra, they just grabbed me and the next thing you know I'm taking Arabic. But don't get me wrong, Arabic's a really beautiful language. I love every moment of torture studying it."

He had waited for his mother to say something, but she just smiled, so he filled the silence. "This program's a great chance for me. It will be like immersing myself in the language and culture. Maybe I can skip a year of study at school and save some tuition."

"Well then," she said, her hand on his arm. "You've always chosen a difficult path, ever since you were a young boy. Maybe that's your father in you, God rest his soul. I wish you'd study something more practical, but you're as stubborn as he was, and I can tell you're set on this. If you win the scholarship, you've got my blessing."

When he got to Morocco, Mike was horrified to find he was completely unprepared for the program. He'd never imagined that, of all the students, he'd be the worst. He was at least a year behind anyone else. Every lesson was a struggle. When he spoke in class, making mistake after mistake, the other students were very kind, but he could sense their impatience. Though the teachers took great pains to help him, it was humiliating. He hated to think about the final grade he'd get, doubting he'd even receive the certificate of completion. He knew he could forget about skipping the next year of Arabic at university. And it was doubly embarrassing because many of the students in this program weren't even Arabic majors. Although his studies were torture, outside of class, Mike was having the time of his life. He had fallen in love with Morocco.

It was only as he sipped his coffee, sweet and strong, and gobbled up a freshly baked croissant, that vague memories of the gnawa ceremony surfaced in his consciousness. The meandering melodies of the hajhuj, the loud qaraqib, the clapping, and the incense came back to him. He remembered falling asleep, and then leaving the ceremony feeling refreshed.

But how could he have slept through the gnawa lila? He was a connoisseur of their music and had listened to hours of gnawa recordings back home. It didn't make any sense. Why hadn't they woken him up? Had he fallen into a trance? He hoped someone in the group had got it on video then remembered no one was filming. He sipped the last of his coffee and checked the wall clock. He had to hurry and prepare for classes.

Mike decided to take a different route back to the riad. He noticed that he was attracting attention in his *gandoura,* and he wanted to avoid that. No one was impolite, but when he walked by some young bead merchants, one of them nodded toward him and elbowed the others. Mike nodded to them in greeting, and one of them said something that he couldn't quite catch. He wondered if the man had been speaking to him. Was he so obviously an American? And were they offended that he was in dressed like a traveler from the Sahara?

As he pondered these things, Mike lost track of his surroundings. He became part of the crowds on the streets, people on their way to work and school, and he forgot his worry about being noticed. He careened with them like blood cells along the artery of the living, beating heart of the city. He dodged animals and carts, young boys and girls, old men and old women. They bumped shoulders with others, but there was no aggression. He felt a different kind of energy, vital and real. He focused on the flow of people around him, how each person had many close calls with others, with the curb, with stray cats darting across the road, with load-carrying donkeys and carts, but carried on effortlessly. There was something so human about this chaos, and even though he was a stranger, he fell into it and loved it.

If he hadn't been so transported, he probably would have made it back to his room. But he was deep in thought as he approached the riad that he walked right past its front door and turned, absent-mindedly, into the alley. He didn't notice the old beggar woman grabbing at his gandoura as he passed her, and he sauntered right under the arch. He continued down the alley, his long robe swinging behind, his arms held straight in his side pockets. He didn't hear the old woman call out to him, urgently trying to get his attention. He turned the corner at the end of the alley and kept walking.

Chapter 8

A Gentleman of Fez

Mike noticed that smoke curled skyward from the roof of every home. He concluded that he'd entered a conservative enclave, since everyone around him was dressed in traditional clothing. Gone were the jeans and black leather jackets.

He was overcome by the pungent odor of horse and donkey manure. It was some time before he reached what he thought was *Tala'a Kabira,* the main road, and he concluded that he'd walked in a big circle. It was getting more crowded, so he leaned against a wall out of the foot traffic to get his bearings. Where had all these flies come from, he wondered, shooing them away from his eyes and mouth.

"Make way, make way!" a man yelled, leading a line of men up the hill. Each man was bent over, carrying two-foot stacks of bright yellow and lapis-blue animal skins on their backs. *That's a new one*, Mike thought. He'd never seen people being used as pack animals before.

Mike kept walking. "Delectable saffron, best quality, your wife will be the envy of the quarter!" a vendor called, holding out a handful of delicate red saffron tendrils. Mike hadn't noticed how fragrant this part of the souq was before. He could pick out the cinnamon, the curry, the turmeric, the pepper and the cumin. He paused to breathe it in and caught a strong whiff of fresh mint as an old woman passed him, carrying a large bundle of mint on her head. It was so fragrant, he inhaled deeply as she passed. She noticed him and stopped. She held out her hand to him, saying, "That'll be two riyals just for smelling!" Everyone around them laughed.

A handsome young merchant, his black beard cut close and tipped in a pointed curl, sang in a lusty tenor as Mike approached. As he sang, he waved a horsetail switch over small bottles of jasmine perfume. Passersby of all ages stopped to listen. Mike counted the rhythm of the song. It was in 14/8, but he didn't recognize the musical mode—it was an unfamiliar combination of east and west.

> *Her eyebrows arch like palm branches,*
> *May I always sleep in their shade.*
> *May her slender trunk always sway next to me,*
> *As she dances in fair weather breezes.*

The crowd let up a great cheer. "Brilliant!" one of them shouted. As they dispersed, the singer smiled as he made a few quick sales.

As Mike walked up the hill, the merchant's song still playing in his head, two boys ran past him in the opposite direction. "Hurry up; they saw us!" one shouted. The other said, "Quick, down here! We'll go to my Uncle's." They disappeared down an alley. It was only then that Mike realized that he had understood every word. The poetry, the remarks of the onlookers, the cries of the street vendors, the boys' chatter. He understood everything. He, the worst student in his class, could follow every conversation. What was happening? Was he dreaming?

To test whether he could speak, too, he approached a merchant selling birds from cages nailed to a wall. "Sir," Mike said, "What kind of birds are these?"

The merchant leaned back in his wooden chair, twirling his prayer beads in one hand, then using it to grasp his ample belly. "Why these are canaries, of course, from the Canary Islands."

Mike marveled that he could even tell that the man had an accent. He was lisping all his 's' sounds in Arabic.

The merchant said, "And these, these are finches from the mountains of Yemen."

"How much are the finches? I think I'd like a pair."

"Five riyals," he answered quickly.

Riyals? Mike thought. Morocco uses dirhams. He reached into his pocket and felt the wad of dirham notes and coins and pulled them out.

"How much is a riyal, Sir? I only have dirhams."

"Well, yes, but a dirham is 100 riyals. I won't be able to make the change." When Mike handed him a dog-eared five dirham note, the man held it in his hand and rubbed his fingers on the paper, saying, "I've never seen such a thing. And if you think I'm going to accept this as currency, you're mistaken. I'm from al-Andalus, but I've been in Fez for ten years and I know for a fact this is not a dirham. I'll have the market inspector over here in a minute if you don't pay."

He's a Spaniard, Mike thought. He'd had some basic Spanish in high school, so he tried it out on the man. "Do you understand Spanish?"

The man looked at him, one eyebrow raised. "Very strange accent," he said, in a kind of sing-song voice. "But I do understand. What is your accent?"

"Castilian, I guess," Mike said.

The man stepped back, looked him over from head to slipper, and murmured, "Of course, from Lisbon, I suppose," he said. "You definitely *look* Portuguese." Then the merchant tried out another language that sounded like Spanish, but not quite.

"Sorry, I don't understand," Mike said, shrugging.

"In any case, we can communicate in the language of the Arabs, so I ask you, do you have any intention at all of buying any of my birds, or are you just wasting my time? If so, please move along. I have to feed my family, and I can't spend all day talking to strange people who don't even know their own language."

"I'm sorry Sir," Mike ventured, "It's just that I don't understand what's happening. I can understand you, but everything is all wrong." Then Mike thought for a moment. "Do you know the Café Clock?" he asked.

"No, never heard of it."

"Do you know Dar Surour?"

"No, young man, never heard of that either. Now move along and find someone else to pester with your questions."

Mike walked up the hill, trying to console himself with the idea that sometimes the locals didn't know all the new renovated riads in town. Why would this character, obviously from Spain, know it?

He stopped when he came to the place where he'd seen the little cat crouching by the side of the road near the Berber carpet store. He was sure it was the same place—there was the same archway, the same curb. But everything else had changed. Instead of a small carpet store, it was a ceramic shop. Plates were hung up, covering its walls, and they were all painted with delicate blue geometric designs radiating out from the center. A young woman sat inside in a shaft of sunlight, painting a large plate that she held in her lap, deep in concentration. Holding a long wooden brush in her right hand and balancing the plate on her lap with her left, she made decisive brush strokes before she went over the plate again slowly, adding more color. Only after she had lifted the brush from the plate did she sigh and look around.

Mike was transfixed watching her work. A few days before, the students had spent hours at the state-run ceramics factory on the outskirts of the city. There, he had watched a roomful of young people, men and women, painting just like this. Only something was different, he thought. They'd been wearing jeans, while she was in a simple caftan of grey cotton, a navy-blue scarf tied over her head.

She looked up at him and broke the spell.

"Yes Sir, can I help you with something?"

"Good morning, Miss," he said, and his voice broke in the middle of the word Miss. Had she noticed him staring? "No thank you, I was just admiring your work."

"I take refuge in God," she said, nodding, then smiling at him.

Even though her friendly gaze bore on him, he needed to move along. He nodded and said, "Good day, Miss."

"In peace," she answered, and he responded in kind as he walked on.

Though Mike was quite sure he was on the Rue Tala'a Kabira, nothing seemed the same. He had to reorient himself and find a familiar landmark. The Madrasa at the top of the hill, he thought. Of course. Everyone knew where that was. The next shop he came to was a tailor. Four young men sat next to each other in the sun, hand sewing braided buttons on elegant linen coats.

"Excuse me, Sir," Mike said, addressing the oldest one.

All four of them stopped their work and looked up. "Yes, my dear Sir," said the oldest after a split-second appraisal of Mike's costume and size. Mike noticed that the others were also assessing his clothing. Of course they would, he thought, they're tailors.

"I'm sorry to disturb you, brothers, but I'm quite lost. Can you kindly direct me to the Madrasa Bou Inania?" Mike was amazed at the flowery speech flowing from his own mouth.

"You are quite close," the oldest fellow said. "You need only continue up the hill, and you'll see it, in its blue resplendence, on your left."

"Thank you," Mike said, and he began to walk away.

"Pardon me," the oldest tailor said. "May I ask where you purchased your gandoura? The fabric, it is most unusual." He laid down his work and approached Mike, his eyes focused on the material. "Is it silk?"

"No, not silk at all." Mike laughed. "Polyester or maybe rayon."

"Bol-ee-es-ter? Ray-on?" the tailor said, still staring at the fabric, his head tilted. "May I?" Mike nodded, and the tailor reached out to feel the fabric. It did shimmer in the sunlight a little. But surely they'd seen this fabric before. Who were these guys, tailors who didn't know polyester?

The tailor took the fabric in his fingers and pulled it up close to his eyes.

"How much would you sell this for, young man?"

"Sell the gandoura off my back? Why, I, how about…"

"Would you take 50 riyals?"

"Why I was thinking more like 75," Mike said. He was enjoying this, the oddity of selling the clothes off his back, and what's more, the reversal of bargaining. He'd grown so tired of bargaining for things in Morocco that he'd just stopped doing it. But this was different. He had all the power. "But I will also need something to wear—so 50, and you also provide me with a complete ensemble."

"Well, I…" the tailor said. When one of his brothers whispered in his ear, he said, "We will pay you 45 and dress you so finely that you will be the most resplendent young master of Fez."

"Done. You've got yourselves a deal," Mike said, wondering if that expression came out sounding correct, or somehow too American. He smiled as the oldest tailor assented with a nod. His friends would never believe that somebody bought a cheap gandoura right off his back.

They led him to the back of the shop and told him to undress. When he handed them his gandoura, they marveled at his underwear and t-shirt. *How strange*, he thought. *What's going on?*

"Pardon, Sir," one of them said. "We are providing you with a full ensemble, and so would you mind also giving us those underclothes? They are unlike anything we've seen."

This is too much, Mike thought, even as he stepped out of his briefs. He was glad he was wearing a relatively new t-shirt without any holes. The men didn't stare at his nakedness; they'd seen plenty of men before, he assumed. They handed him a sarong to tie around his waist. But they did stare at his tattoo, a multi-colored compass rose.

"It's a compass rose, like you see on a map," he said as he held out his arm for them. They all touched the skin of his tattoo.

"These colors are so bright, not henna or indigo." one of them asked, touching his skin.

"It is ink, but I don't know what kind they used," Mike said.

"Salman, get a medium set of *sirwal* for our gentleman. Er…may we know your name, Sir?"

"I'm Mike—er, Munir." He had the sense to use his Arabic name from class.

"Right away, then, Mr. Munir."

The tailors worked quickly, using string instead of measuring tape.

"Try this on," one of them said, handing him a handsome ivory cotton gandoura with glistening pearl piping and embroidered buttons. He slipped it over his head and they stood back to admire him. "Yes, this quite suits you, good Sir."

"Do you have a mirror?" he asked.

The tailors laughed, and one said, "Alas, Sir, we cannot afford one, but they say the Sultan has one!"

What a bizarre encounter, Mike thought, thanking them profusely as he left the shop. They directed him toward the Madrasa, where, they told him, there was a daily lecture before the noonday prayer. If he went straight there, he would arrive just in time to hear it. He walked along the cobblestone street, up the hill toward the Madrasa, almost strutting in his new outfit. He marveled at the matching ivory *babush* slippers they gave him, and he reached up to feel the finely embroidered turban that they'd wound carefully around his head, leaving one fringed end to trail down his back. Passersby nodded in greeting, and their admiring glances took in his finery.

As he passed another man selling birds, he jingled the riyals in his pocket. The bird-seller called out to him, "O elegant Sir, do you not need the music of the heavens in your courtyard? Does not your young mistress long for the birdsong of her childhood? My birds are from the farthest reaches of the earth, and they bring good luck!"

He merely nodded and continued up the hill. He would have loved another cup of coffee, and he was getting hungry. He wondered if he'd already missed class—he'd forgotten to put on his watch.

He spied the blue tiled minaret of the Madrasa up ahead, and he joined the throng of men streaming in through its massive cedarwood doors. He left his slippers just inside like everyone else and climbed the steps to the main courtyard he'd toured just a few days before. But today it was filled to capacity with all manner of men dressed in colorful clothing that would have thrilled Maureen, though he noticed there were only men there. All were dressed like him, in turbans and fabrics that seemed almost Shakespearian in their layered elegance. He swore at himself for not having his camera.

Mike marveled at how he could understand the Arabic being spoken around him. The accents—well, he couldn't place them, but he could hear the nuances as the men spoke to each other as they found places to sit, cross-legged, on red tribal carpets that covered the open courtyard. He'd heard somewhere that if you study a language long and hard enough, you can break through to fluency in strange ways, suddenly realizing that you understand everything. Yet this seemed far beyond that kind of breakthrough. He'd been studying Arabic for only a year, and every lesson had been a colossal struggle. Maybe his stubborn persistence had finally paid off. It was just so unexpected.

"Here, Sir, there is a place where you can see and hear quite well." Someone was touching his arm. Mike turned and took in the figure of a skinny boy, smiling up at him. Twelve at the most, the boy was dressed in a grey gandoura, with a simple white turban. Mike nodded and let the boy lead him to a shady spot in the loggia of the courtyard. He bowed to Mike after seating him next to older men who were dressed as he was, more prosperous looking than the rest. Then the boy disappeared in the crowd. What a trip, Mike thought to himself. Whatever's going on, it really is a trip, far more amazing than any Arabic class!

An older gentleman wearing a chestnut-colored cloak over his spotless white robes entered the courtyard and sat facing the crowd, which grew silent the moment they saw him.

"Peace be upon you, as well as the mercy and blessings of God," he said.

"And upon you be peace," the group responded, as one.

"Today's lecture concerns the importance of the sciences. Of what importance is earthly knowledge, if we follow the true religion? Is our faith not enough? We hear whisperings that we have no need of these sciences. That the heathens of old—the Romans and Greeks—left us these sciences to beguile and distract us from the true religion.

"When we search the Qur'an and hadith for guideposts to help us answer this question, we find a clear indication. Not only are we advised to seek knowledge, we are asked to better our community and to support our families. It is science that lets us do that. We need it to fulfill our roles, to move forward and to continue to build this great city for the glory of God.

"Today, 775 years after the founding of the One True Religion, our city continues to attract men from the Frankish countries, from al-Andalus, even from the Romish cities. Some come here to trade, others to study the books of the great thinkers. In so doing, many of them have found the True Faith. So I submit to you that the sciences lead men to the truth and to faith. And in this way, one cannot dismiss these sciences as evil. All of God's creation has the potential to lead us astray.

But with a strong faith and trust in God, we can fulfill our duty as true believers."

It took Mike a minute or two before the lecturer's mention of the year 775, in the Muslim, or *hijri* calendar, sunk in. He turned this number over in his mind. From courses on Islam at college, he knew that the Islamic calendar begins in 622 CE, so he added 622 to 775 and got 1397 CE. That was the first moment he began to wonder if he had somehow traveled to the past.

The lecture continued for what seemed like an hour. The sun climbed higher, and Mike was grateful to be seated in the shade. His mind raced, remembering everything that had happened that morning. He stayed still, looking around at the scene in wonder. What was going on? If he was dreaming, he'd wake up soon and all would be well. But somehow he knew this was no dream, and after admitting that to himself, the enormity of his predicament filled him with fear—because if he had slipped into another time, and he didn't know how he'd gotten there, then how could he ever find his way back to his own time? He'd often gotten lost in Morocco, but those episodes were nothing compared to this.

At the close of the lecture, it was time for the noon prayer. Though he was not a Muslim, he felt he should join the men in the ritual, trying to be inconspicuous. He followed them to do the ritual ablutions, taking care not to expose the tattoo on his arm too much. He just wanted to blend in.

The men prayed facing the beautiful tiled *mihrab* that marked the direction of Mecca. The tiles looked much brighter than they had a few days ago, when he'd come here on the tour. And the repair work they'd been doing at the entrance was all finished. As he followed along with the prayer ritual, he realized that there was no longer an admission booth near the front door.

At the end of prayers, the men made their way to the exits. He stumbled down the front steps of the Madrasa and began to walk. He didn't know where he was going, but he needed to walk to figure how to get back to the present.

Chapter 9

775 A.H.

Mike had dreamed of time travel ever since he was a boy. He'd lain in front of the television late at night, watching dozens of shows and movies about it. But how could he tell if it had really happened? Yes, it *was* a summer day, just as it had been yesterday. It was supposed to be the first of August. So, if he had traveled to the past, was he in a past that was somehow in sync with the calendar of the present? Could it happen like that?

Trying to fight back a growing panic, he wondered if something had happened to him at the gnawa ceremony. But in time travel stories, there was usually some kind of gateway—a porous wall or a round space, or a machine through which the time-traveler had to pass. So maybe he'd stepped through a portal. If so, he had to retrace his steps. Yet that seemed impossible since he'd been lost most of the morning. No matter what was going on, he had to calm down and get his bearings.

As he walked unnoticed in the crowd, his mouth grew parched and his stomach ached with hunger. He needed to eat, but there didn't seem to be any cafes on the main road. He reached the tailor's shop to ask for a recommendation, but it was closed for the midday siesta.

As he stood outside the shop, wondering what to do, a riderless donkey approached amid the throng. No one paid it any attention, even though it was laden with golden jewelry, a gold diadem on its head. Necklaces, earrings, and bracelets were sewn onto its saddle as if it were some kind of pagan idol. It wore bracelets on its delicate hairy legs. They jingled with every step as it got closer, until it was just feet away. It even had a gilded bridle, decorated with tiny glittering teardrops of gold leaf. Mike blinked a couple of times to be sure he wasn't imagining it, but it was still there. Only an arm's length away, Mike reached out to touch the donkey's saddle. But when his hand got within an inch of it, the donkey jerked its head, reared up on its hind legs and brayed. It looked down at him with fear in its eyes and then galloped away, weaving among the people before disappearing around the bend. Yet no one else in the crowd seemed to notice. It was as if the donkey was invisible to everyone but him.

I really need to eat, he thought. Just then his nose and stomach got a whiff of spiced lamb being grilled, peppery and inviting. The smell slowed his steps, and he stood at the corner of a side street inhaling the fragrance, holding his stomach.

A young man about his age with brown curly hair and a long European-looking face approached him from the alleyway and beckoned him to follow. "O sir! Are you hungry? Taste our delicious food! Strangers and travelers are welcome!"

"Yes, in fact, I'm quite famished. And is that lamb you are serving today?"

"Indeed, indeed, and at a mere two riyals, it's a gourmet bargain."

Two riyals, Mike thought. He wondered how much that was in dirhams, and then in dollars. And was he being offered a fair price? Was he supposed to bargain?

The young man led him to a room lined with cushions woven in the tribal style they'd seen in the desert. He joined a half dozen men. They looked like Europeans, with long faces like that of the café owner. In their long robes, they seemed to be actors in a Shakespearean play: they were swathed in dark green fabric, wore pointed leather boots, and had loose beret-like hats set on their heads.

He sat down in the corner nearest the door. The others nodded in acknowledgement.

One of them said, "You were at the Madrasa today, were you not?"

"Yes, I was. Very interesting. My first time," Mike said. How amazing that he could understand the man, even though his words had a strange accent! "Where are you from?"

"Rome," he said, shifting in his place, no doubt uncomfortable sitting on the low cushions rather than on a chair. Mike noticed that there was no cutlery anywhere, just a bright red and yellow weaving laid out like a tablecloth in the center of the room. So these were Europeans, strangers like him, visiting Fez. "And you?" the Italian said.

"I'm also a stranger. From Pisa," he said, naming the city of his ancestors.

"My name is Marcello, and this is Dominic."

"I am Michael."

"Then you are Christian?" Marcello said, his surprise unconcealed by both this voice and arched eyebrows.

"Yes, I am Catholic," he said. In all his years of attending church and Sunday school, he had never imagined he would be in such a situation.

"But you're dressed as a Muslim," Marcello said.

"Yes, I am fortunate. A tailor made me this ensemble for an excellent price."

"It is a fine garment, to be sure," Dominic said, "But do you not worry that you'll be mistaken for a Muslim?"

"And what harm would that be? Are we not all brothers?"

"Well, I should think you would want to be distinct from…" Just then a boy entered, carrying a wooden tray piled with grilled lamb, eggplant, onions, and peppers. Another brought in a covered ceramic dish filled with steaming couscous and round flat bread, reminiscent of modern-day pita, but darker brown.

The proprietor had hung cotton partitions over the doorway, but it kept out only some of the flies. Mike waved a hand over his plate to keep it clear enough to eat.

"What are you doing?" Dominic asked.

"It's the flies, I can't keep them out of my mouth," Mike said. He watched the men chew, in spite of blackened and missing teeth, ignoring the flies on their faces and hands.

He had so many questions for these men who were visiting Fez as strangers from another land. But the unusual spices in the meat and the grittiness of the bread distracted him, and he soon tucked into the meal with the vigor of the others.

A while later, the boys poured fresh water over the men's hands, which they held over a bowl, and they wiped their hands on a clean cotton cloth.

"And who is the proprietor of this place?" Mike asked, as the diners sat back, some picking their teeth with gusto.

"He's one of us, from Florence. He came here to buy spices for his father's business, but he fell in love with a Muslim girl and married her. And converted too. If you ask me," he added under his breath, "no woman is worth that much—giving up your faith, leaving your family."

The servants brought a brass tray with small ceramic cups filled with a hot mint beverage, but it wasn't exactly tea. The two Italians said they were staying at a hostel attached to the restaurant.

After paying for his meal, and saying goodbye to his new friends, Mike continued his walk down the hill. The streets were quiet, so the way seemed clearer. He planned go down to the end of the street, turn right, and walk along the outer walls of the Qarawiyyin mosque. After that, he'd take the third right into the little neighborhood where, hopefully, Dar Surour would still be standing.

As he walked, however, his stomach started grumbling, and within minutes he was suffering from severe stomach cramps. *Even I, with my iron stomach, have limits*, he thought. *Who knows what exotic microbes lurked in that food. I should have known better.*

He stepped off the main street into a little alleyway and vomited his lunch, but the stomach cramps continued. Finding relief in a dirty alley where others had clearly been doing the same, Mike stumbled back to the main street, only to find himself feeling very light-headed. Dehydration, he knew, can come on very fast. But any water he'd drink would be dirty, too. So he stood at the side of the street, holding onto a wall with one hand, leaning back, waiting for the next wave of nausea to come. He began to sweat, and his stomach was churning again, so he started to walk back down the alley, but light-headedness overtook him, and everything went black.

Mike opened his eyes and found he was alone. He was in a small room, lying on a thin mattress stuffed with straw that crunched when he moved. A window with carved wooden shutters was open to the afternoon sun. A wooden bowl filled with water lay next to him on the floor. He was dying of thirst, but he was afraid to drink. What he wouldn't give for a bottle of Pepsi or Coke! He moaned and began to shiver, fearing another round of nausea would overtake him. And what if he needed to relieve himself, where would he go?

The door opened, and the familiar face of the boy who had welcomed him at the Madrasa floated toward him. He was carrying a pot of a hot liquid, and it smelled of mint.

"Ah, I see you are awake. You are back at the Madrasa now, and you can stay here until you are well." The boy sat down near Mike's feet, on the edge of the mattress. "What is your name, good Sir?" he asked. "If you don't mind me asking."

"Munir."

"I am Hameed," the boy said. "I found you, Sir, lying in the street. I woke you enough to walk you back here." Mike nodded and thanked him.

"Drink this, and then you must rest."

After a few gulps of the sweet mint drink, Mike turned over and fell back to sleep. Hameed watched him for a long time, and then he went back to sweeping the hallway just outside, until he heard his name called from downstairs. Then he abandoned his broom and scampered off.

Chapter 10

Tannery Poofs

What was it about Fez? Ibrahim was clenching his fists as he stood, pressed into a crowd of pedestrians, stuck behind a slow mule cart overloaded with ten-foot lengths of PVC pipe. The packed frenzy of the old city was getting to him. Especially after their recent visit to his home village, which was full of friendly faces. Ibrahim couldn't wait to get out of Fez, but, on this trip, he had to spend nearly a month here. The daily rhythm of a bus tour was so much easier than elbowing around in old Fez.

People from Fez, Fezzis, were so proud of their ancestry. They thought they were better than anyone else in Morocco. They traced their bloodlines to Arabs from the East and Andalusians from Spain. Ibrahim was proud of his own ancestors, the ancient indigenous people, the Amazigh, the people called Berbers by the Romans. Yet every time he had to deal with a Fezzi merchant or craftsman, Ibrahim felt they looked down on him because he wasn't from Fez.

His feelings went deeper than that, though he'd never admit any of this to the people on his tours. He always felt he was being cheated in Fez, that his tourist clients were about to be pickpocketed or overcharged.

That morning, while the Americans were in class, Ibrahim had called on a leather dealer. If they had come to terms, he'd planned to place a generous order for handbags. He'd sat with the merchant on a balcony overlooking Chouara, the ancient leather tannery, an acres-wide space filled with hundreds of round vats of dyes, chemicals, and rinse water.

The barefoot workers performed the same tasks that had been done by generations of men before them. Some stood in the vats stirring dyes and solvents with sticks. Others pulled wet skins out of the vats and slapped them into piles. Still others carried the skins from one basin to another, their spindly legs dyed red, blue, saffron, and purple. Hides of saffron yellow and lapis blue were laid out on every available flat surface and hung off roofs to dry in the sun.

A dozen European tourists wandered among the vats, aiming their cameras in all directions. When the odor of ammonia solvent drifted in his direction, Ibrahim breathed through his mouth and took a sip of tea. He wondered whether the tannery workers ever got used to that smell—the reek of ammonia from pigeon droppings, a centuries-old recipe.

The leather merchant's leather poofs had just been featured in a European home décor magazine, so his goods were in high demand. Ibrahim focused all his persuasive power on leaving the store with a verbal contract. But his polite cajoling produced no deal. Once the merchant learned that Ibrahim would be in town for a few more weeks, the man apparently decided to string him along in hopes of a higher price later on.

Fuming, Ibrahim elbowed his way back to the riad through the medina's crowded streets. Every time Ibrahim dealt with this man, he felt dirty afterward. And he hated to admit that Laila was right, he was always getting ripped off in Fez. She'd called him during the meeting, and he'd sent her call to voice mail.

It frustrated him that the best handcrafts in Morocco were made right in the medina's tiny shops and workshops, so he was forced to deal with the locals. He felt they were arrogant, looking down on him because he was an outsider. And why should these uneducated and unsophisticated people look down on him? Most of them had never left Morocco, and some, he had heard, had never ventured outside Fez.

Admittedly, the commercial system allowed Ibrahim generous commissions when he brought his tourists to the shops. Everywhere else in Morocco, Ibrahim was content with his contacts, but he bristled at every turn when negotiating with a Fezzi merchant or craftsman.

As soon as the crowd grew thinner, Ibrahim turned off the main road and made his way to an area where leather craftsmen worked. He would show this merchant a thing or two about doing business.

"Good morning," Ibrahim said, stepping into a workshop where a dozen men sat at sewing machines, piecing together sections of leather poofs. "Where's your boss?" he asked the youngest, who was sitting near the front.

"That would be me," a voice boomed behind him. Ibrahim turned and took in the form of a burly man in a dye-stained djellaba. His basketball-sized pot belly preceded him as he approached. He had the typical rounded head of a man from Fez, his ears sticking out beneath his skull cap. Unsmiling, the man reached out and shook Ibrahim's hand, a wary look in his eye.

"Can we speak privately?" Ibrahim asked, noticing that all the men had stopped working to look him over.

"Whatever you want to say, say it here."

"I've a proposition that I think you'd..."

"Then it can be proposed here and now."

"My name's Ibrahim, and I import to the US. I'd like to buy leather poofs from you." He handed the man one of his Arabic business cards.

"Sorry, we're fully booked for poofs for the next year. Can't take on any new customers now."

Ibrahim didn't believe him.

"Fully booked for the next year? Well, how about women's handbags?"

The man shook his head. "Sorry, we're backlogged."

Ibrahim turned to the front of the shop and noticed that there were plenty of poofs and handbags of all designs on display. "But you've got plenty of merchandise in the shop. How can you be—"

"Look, I said we were fully booked. We can't take on any more export clients. Now, if there's nothing else, I've a busy shop to run. Go in peace." With that, the man turned and walked away.

Ibrahim walked out of the store, shaking his head. *What's with this town*, he wondered. He wandered back to the main road and let the crowd draw him along the outer walls of the Qarawiyyin Mosque, the center of the medina, the hub of the bicycle wheel from which the city's most ancient roads spread out. When his mobile rang, he stepped into an alley to answer.

"Mike's missing." It was Dr. Charles. "He hasn't turned up at class this morning, and he wasn't even in his room when his roommate woke up."

"Be there in five minutes," Ibrahim said.

Normally, Mike's disappearance was just a nuisance. He often wandered off on adventures and got lost, turning up hours later bursting with excitement over the musical instruments he'd found, the artists he'd met, or the café where he'd won at backgammon. Still, after falling into that trance at the gnawa ceremony, he might not be in his right mind. That woman, Shafiqa, had said he was vulnerable. Ibrahim had a different opinion. Mike was just plain thick-headed. Unfortunately, Mike was his responsibility, and, in Fez, he could get into serious trouble.

By the time Ibrahim opened the heavy wooden door of the riad and stepped into the reception office, he had decided his course of action. After a quick lunch, he gathered out in the alley with Khalid and three of his staff.

"Mike disappeared sometime early this morning," Ibrahim said. "Now, we know he likes to wander, but I don't think he'd leave the medina, so let's concentrate on the old city."

The old woman in the pink caftan was still sitting near the arch. She stared at them as if she were listening. Ibrahim wondered why the old crone was so interested in their conversation.

Ibrahim passed around two photographs of Mike. One had been taken while they were in the Sahara. In it, Mike was smiling, wearing the lapis blue Tuareg turban that Ibrahim had wrapped around his head. The other photo showed Mike at dinner with the group, bareheaded and in western clothes.

"He wears a small gold hoop earring in his left ear. Not on the lobe, but higher up along the outer rim. And his roommate thinks he left wearing a blue gandoura he bought in the desert. If that's true, I'm sure he would've been noticed."

Ibrahim sent Khalid to search the district above the brass souq. Two others also went outside the medina, just in case, to visit the discos and talk to the managers and bouncers before the clubs opened in the evening. The last man went to shops that sold musical instruments and leather goods, places Mike would likely go.

Ibrahim went off on his own, walking down quiet streets and visiting out-of-the-way squares, asking shopkeepers if they'd seen someone fitting Mike's description, with no success. Ibrahim concluded that Mike had probably wandered into the labyrinth of streets near the riad and the Qarawiyyin, where the alluring shops and galleries would distract him. This often happened in Fez and Marrakesh. Foreign tourists were so bedazzled by the shops and markets that they strayed off their path, finding themselves in one of the medina's large antique emporiums, notorious places where foreign travelers were invited to sit and have tea, usually emerging hours later, hundreds of dollars poorer. He checked every antique store he knew, but no one had seen Mike.

Returning to the riad, Ibrahim learned that the only lead they'd found was at Café Clock. The young waiter remembered Mike, since he had been wearing traditional Moroccan clothing. This surprised Ibrahim, for the merchants along the main thoroughfares sized up every potential customer that walked by their shops, judging whether they appeared to have money. They noticed everything about tourists—who they shopped with, what they wore, what language they spoke, and what they bought. None of them had noticed Mike. Ibrahim concluded that either he had gone somewhere else, or else he must have passed by early in the morning, before they had opened.

While the others discussed it over tea, Ibrahim excused himself. He went out to the front of the riad to think and leaned against the wall at the opening to the alley, watching people pass by. Unless Mike had gotten into serious trouble, Ibrahim was sure he'd eventually return to the riad. Besides, Mike had the phone number of the riad written on a business card—all the students did. If he were carrying the card he'd been given, he'd be able to call for help at any hotel or riad in the medina. But if some harm had come to him, God knows where he'd be.

"Young man!" a voice called to him from down the alley. It was the old beggar, her arm outstretched as always. "Come here a moment, I have news."

Now what, Ibrahim thought. Normally, he felt sorry for women like her. He still didn't trust this particular character, but, in the end, his lifelong training to respect his elders won out, and he approached her. Besides, he was desperate for any leads.

Ibrahim squatted next to her. "Do you know who we're looking for?"

"Is it the American, looks Italian, with the gold earring?" she said, a cackle in her voice.

"Yes, that one, his name's Mike. Have you seen him?"

She nodded.

Ibrahim turned to face her, his hopes overcoming his suspicion. "And what did you see?"

"This morning, early, he walked down the alleyway, under the arch, and I haven't seen him since. He was wearing a blue gandoura."

"Thank you, I'll check it out. And if you see him, please let me or anyone at the riad know."

As he tried to stand up, she grabbed his arm. Ibrahim was surprised at her strong grip.

"Wait, young man. There's something you need to know. This arch, if you go under it, you'll walk into the past. Mike has gone there, and he's there now. Until he returns through this arch, he remains there. He could be in serious trouble.

You must find him and bring him back, exactly this way, through this arch. And you must be careful—for your own safety."

"Yes Ma'am," Ibrahim said, trying to be polite, deciding that she was demented and harmless after all. "I see. This is a doorway, an archway to the past?"

"Yes. And a very serious one, I might add. For when the now and the then meet, it's like striking flint against stone. A big, big problem."

Ibrahim nodded. She reminded him of a feeble-minded neighbor in his village who everyone had humored with kindness and pity. "Well, I'll go through. But if it's the past, how do I get back?"

As he stood up, the old woman raised her voice. "Like I was saying, to return to this time, you must pass back through the same archway. It's your only way back."

"Yes, thank you Ma'am," he said, smiling. Then he strode under the arch and down the alley.

"Don't get lost!" she called after him in a voice so loud that it sounded like it belonged to a street hawker, not an elderly woman.

"Oh my, oh my," Moustapha said. "Another one's gone through and now it's going to get complicated, I can just feel it. Why is it always me who gets this kind of job?" Just then, a ghoul flew down from the sky and landed near where Moustapha was sitting, on the modern side of the arch.

"So, lovely lady, what have we here, an open gate?" it said, clicking its fangs and slobbering with every word. "Don't mind if I do," it said, stepping forward.

"Argh, get back!" Moustapha stood up and tried to push the ghoul back with his walking cane. But the ghoul just laughed and jumped over his head, flying through to the past.

Chapter 11

A Guide's Nightmare

"Prisoners! Make way! Make way!" Ibrahim stepped aside as a chain gang climbed the steep road behind him, guards parting the crowd. The prisoners—a dozen of them, bareheaded and dressed in rags—struggled up the road with great difficulty. Ibrahim turned away from the sight of the bruises and sores on the men's bodies. Only one of them held his head up and stared straight ahead. The others kept their eyes cast down in obvious shame. In all his life, Ibrahim had never seen such a thing.

"Burn in hell, sons of dogs!" a shopkeeper said, spitting on the ground as they passed.

"Thieves, God will mete justice to you, even if the Sultan sets you free!" an onlooker called out, shaking his fist.

The Sultan? Fez hasn't had one of those, well, for centuries, Ibrahim thought. He stood to the side, letting the crowd pass, listening to the clink of the chains as the prisoners moved out of sight around a bend in the street that he had walked hundreds of times. Everything around him was somehow different. The people wore traditional clothes and the air smelled of wood smoke. Nothing unusual in that. A donkey ambled past, laden with bundles of cedarwood. The side streets were filled with the familiar sounds of hammering on wood, brass, and iron. Standing on his toes, Ibrahim peered over the wall against which he'd been leaning. On the other side, tendrils of a thick jasmine vine, woven like a woman's braid, poured over a green tiled rooftop. Inside the walled-in yard, two giant date palms rustled in the breeze. He had never noticed the place before.

As Ibrahim continued up the street, which he had walked hundreds of times, he began to wonder if, indeed, he might have crossed over into the past. He could have noted the lack of power and phone lines, or the absence of music blasting from radios, but instead his mind was fixed on the layout of the medina. One of his merchant contacts had a store up ahead, but when he got there, he found a ceramics shop instead, selling hand-painted plates and bowls. He was sure it was the same address; he'd been there so many times. The shop faced a small road that led outside the walls of the old city, and there was a green-tiled roof on the house next door. He was standing in the same place, but everything had changed—except for the green roof. He took the alley out to the edge of the medina and, instead of the dusty open parking lot, there were vegetable gardens and small pastures, but no cars in sight.

What if it is *true?* Ibrahim thought. He approached the proprietor of the ceramics shop. "O Sir, can you tell me what day it is?" he asked.

"Certainly. It's Tuesday, the 21st of Safar," the man said, his shaved head gleaming in the sunlight.

"And the year?" Ibrahim asked, without thinking how strange it would be for someone to ask that.

"Well, of course everyone knows it's the hijri year 775."

Ibrahim stood still, blinking, estimating what that would be by the Gregorian calendar. He guessed between 1350 and 1400. *God help us, this has got to be a nightmare*, he thought. *The tour guide's ultimate nightmare.*

"Are you all right, my son?" the man asked. "Say, I can't help but notice how short your jacket is, and, pardon me for commenting," he said, pointing at the jacket's shiny silver zipper, "What in heaven is that, I have never seen..."

"A zipper," Ibrahim said absent-mindedly as his mind tried to absorb what was happening.

"A what?"

Ibrahim improvised an answer. "Something my grandmother invented, to ward off the cold winter winds up in the mountains." He always thought well on his feet; it came in handy in his line of work.

"Can you show me how it works?"

Ibrahim obliged, and the man said, "By my life, I've never seen anything like it! Badriyyah, come here and look at this."

Ibrahim realized he was going to cause a scene, and he made his excuses. But then he stayed, waiting for the young woman to approach. She held a delicate paintbrush in her left hand and wore a loose scarf of navy-blue cotton draped over her head and shoulders. The end of her brown braid fell below it, to her waist.

"Look, my dear. Have you ever seen anything like this?"

"No, I haven't," she said. "Do you mind if I have a closer look?"

As she stood close to Ibrahim, staring at his hand that held the zipper half open, the old man said, "My daughter Badriyyah is a ceramics artist, but she's an excellent seamstress, too."

Badriyyah reached out and examined the zipper. "Your grandmother made this?"

"Yes, she's very clever. The best seamstress in our village."

Extricating himself as quickly as possible, he bade the old man and his daughter farewell and pushed on up the steep street, imagining what might be possible if he really had slipped into the 14th century. He began to dream of filling a shipping container with authentic medieval antiques. He'd make a killing on them, and he'd be set for life. Well, maybe not for life, but at least they could buy a house sooner rather than later.

As he walked, Ibrahim listened to conversations around him. The people sounded as though they had small pebbles in their mouths, and they rounded their vowels. Some spoke classical Arabic, while others used what sounded like an archaic version of the modern Fezzi dialect. He also noticed that his clothing had begun to attract unwanted attention, mostly lingering stares and furrowed brows. He stopped at the first tailor he found. The men inside gasped when he stepped into their shop—he supposed it was due to his jacket. They were all wearing ivory turbans and costumes made of matching linen, their hands busy sewing. One man was finishing off the piped buttons on a lightweight grey woolen cloak. That would do just fine, Ibrahim thought.

"Sir," he said. "How much for this cloak?" He used his formal Arabic.

"It is 30 riyals."

Riyals? Ibrahim did the math in his head. Morocco had abandoned the riyal system years ago, but some older merchants in the cities still calculated prices that way. But 30 riyals would mean just three dirhams, about 35 cents.

"Well Sir, I have no riyals at the moment, for I have been traveling in the north, beyond al-Andalus. I have some coins of silver and brass. Perhaps these would suit you? You could have them melted, perhaps, or sell them to a metalsmith."

Ibrahim handed the tailor a few five-dirham coins. They were rimmed in silver with a brass center, and the dates on the coins, both Western and Islamic, were faded, so Ibrahim hoped the men would have a hard time reading them. The profile of the King was clear, but the words underneath, The Kingdom of Morocco and King Hassan II, were well worn and barely legible.

"This is a fascinating coin indeed," the head tailor said, turning it over and over. "It is both gold and silver, as you say. Is this some kind of Frankish coin?" The tailor picked it up and bit it with his teeth, then examined the writing closely. "But there are both Arabic and Frankish letters on it. Where did you get this?"

Before Ibrahim could answer, the man changed the subject. "Pardon, Sir, but what is that metal decoration there on your jacket?"

"It's called a...a...zipper. My grandmother invented it. It's made of iron."

"I see. Well, if you would like to try on this cloak, you must take that off, no?"

Ibrahim began to wonder if it was such a good idea to be telling people about the zipper. If they didn't have them in this time, then wouldn't he be changing history? How would they make them? Did they even have the skill with metal to do it?

"No, thank you. I intend to wear the cloak over my other clothes, like this." Ibrahim took the cloak and tried it on. It covered his jacket and jeans completely. "This will do perfectly, thank you."

Ibrahim noticed a blue, modern-style gandoura hanging on the wall. It was just like the one Mike had been wearing.

"Excuse me, if you don't mind me asking, but where did you get that gandoura?"

The tailor was still examining the coins, inches from his left eye. "Earlier today, a young man came in wearing it. It's of such an unusual fabric that we exchanged it for a new suit of clothes. In fact, he had the same strange accent as you."

"I think I know him, yes. When he left the shop, where did he go?"

"Up the hill. He said he was going to the Madrasa."

The purchase concluded with modern coins, Ibrahim strode up the hill, draped in his new grey cloak. The Madrasa—of course. It would have been there in the late 1300's. In fact, it had just been finished at that time. When Ibrahim reached the Madrasa's front door, he could scarcely believe how new it looked. Its carved wooden doors glowed. The brass lanterns and brilliant mosaics gleamed. Young men streamed in and out of the entrance, carrying leather-bound volumes. And there were Europeans there, speaking in classical Arabic.

Three classes were being held in the courtyard at once. Teachers and students sat in groups on colorful woven carpets. Ibrahim scanned each group, looking for Mike. One lecture was about astronomy. He couldn't understand all of it, as it was rather technical, but he recognized the names of the planets, *Zuhra,* and *Mushtari,* Venus and Jupiter.

"Pssst." Ibrahim looked up toward the sound, and there, in a small arched window on the second floor, was a be-turbaned Mike wearing an impish grin.

Ibrahim slipped up the stairs and found Mike in one of the students' rooms, resting on a simple mattress, dressed in a sumptuous linen costume fit for a pasha. Ibrahim had taken many tour groups to this very room, explaining that students would board there. Now he could scarcely believe that he was seeing it fully furnished, with Mike there, seemingly at home.

"Boy, am I glad to see you. How did you find me?" Mike asked as they clapped each other on the back. "We're in another time, man, can you believe this? Or maybe I'm just dreaming."

"Either we're both dreaming, or we're mixed up in a major mess. You all right?"

"I had some bad food earlier, but I'm okay now. Just a bit shaky."

"So this is the 14th century."

"Yeah, I know. Someone told me the date. Unbelievable, huh!" Dizziness overtook Mike for a moment, and he grabbed Ibrahim's arm. "What I wouldn't give for a café nuss-nuss right now."

They waited until the lecture was finished, and the students began milling about. Mike left a coin for Hameed, and the two men slipped out the front door and onto the street. Arm in arm, they started down the hill.

"Ding!" a metallic ringing startled them both. Everyone in the street looked up, and the two men followed their gaze.

"It's the water clock. I can't believe I'm seeing this," Ibrahim said. "Remember how I pointed out that clock when we toured here the other day? Remember how it looked in our time?"

Mike nodded. Little remained in the present day, just a few pieces of wood left from the once-famous medieval water clock, set into the wall of a building near the Madrasa around 1350. And they were seeing it, newly built and functioning perfectly. The sound they'd heard was a metal ball falling into a bowl, and it sounded like the chime of a grandfather clock.

They took their time walking down the hill, taking in the sights, talking about how incredible it was to walk through the old city of the past. It was so little-changed in some ways, and much more vibrant in others.

"The weirdest thing, Ibrahim, is that I understand Arabic perfectly now," Mike said. "From classical lectures at the mosque to people talking on the street."

"Really?" Ibrahim said. Then he blurted out a tongue-twister in dialect, *"Mesh khbesh khabsha f khashba."*

"Hah! That's great," Mike said. "The cat scratched a scratch in the wood."

"Wow," Ibrahim said, testing him on three more in rapid succession. Mike got them all right.

Ibrahim wondered if Mike really understood the enormity of what was happening, or whether he thought this was just another adventure of being lost, then found, in Fez.

Neither of them noticed that Hameed had followed them down the hill. He kept a discrete distance between them, and he watched as they turned into the alley.

"Unbelievable luck," the old lady said, shaking her head, as Ibrahim and Mike stepped back through the arch. Ibrahim nodded at her and rolled his eyes.

"Mike, you should go inside and change into some regular clothes."

"I caused this mess, so if you don't mind, I'd like to stay and get some answers, too."

Surprised that, for once, Mike was taking some responsibility for getting lost, Ibrahim beckoned him to sit down beside the old lady.

"So tell me," Ibrahim said. "What's going on here, and who are you, anyway? I seriously doubt that..."

The old lady interrupted him. "Actually, my name is Moustapha, if you must know, but Ma'am will do just fine for now."

Mike laughed. "But Moustapha is a man's name, and you're dressed like..."

"Yes, it is. And yes, I am. I'm a djinni, for heaven's sake. I happen to be a male djinni, and I'm dressed like a female human. It's just the way it has to be right now, for me to blend in. I'm in charge of this arch, you see. I must guard it while it's open, to keep humans—and also animals, if possible— from crossing through." Just then, Ramses the cat jumped down from the riad wall and sauntered through the archway into the past, tail held high, ignoring the humans.

"As far as Ramses goes," Moustapha said, "he can come and go as he likes. And on top of that, the spirits—the ghouls and djinn—are flowing back and forth, and there's nothing I can do about it. Evil is spilling from one time to the other, and each time has more than enough of that already. I'm telling you, until they rebuild the wall and seal up that arch, or knock the arch down, the balance of things is in danger."

"I take refuge in God from Satan," Ibrahim said, standing up and backing away. All his life, he had been told that the djinn were dangerous and evil. Why should he trust this one?

Moustapha sighed. "I know what you're thinking, Ibrahim. Yes, despite what you have heard, there are djinn who are obedient to the Almighty. There are those who cause trouble, yes. But I myself am a faithful believer in God. And when my higher-ups, who are also of the good legions of the djinn, ask me to do something, I do it. You have nothing to fear from me. In God's name, it's the truth. Now, come and sit with me and be sensible."

Ibrahim sat back down. After what he'd just experienced in the Fez of the past, he wanted desperately to believe that Moustapha was what he said he was.

Moustapha continued: "I've been hesitant to mention—well, I suppose I must tell you everything. Among these spirits is the one that took hold of you, Mike, er, Munir, during the gnawa ceremony. It is an ancient malevolent being, and wherever it alights, it causes mayhem on a scale that affects all mankind. It brings famines, wars, plagues, and catastrophes wherever it goes. And it found delight in the gnawa evening, as well as in this present time. The Fez of 1374 already had its plague and its wars. No doubt your modern world is far more alluring. The name of this spirit is Haqud."

At the mention of that name, a slight tremor shook the ground, as if a building was being demolished somewhere in the neighborhood.

"The spirit certainly is well-named," Ibrahim said. "It means Hating One, Mike."

"I know. Remember, I understand everything now."

"But what if this spirit is here in the present?" Ibrahim asked. "Then what can we do?"

"My duty is to make sure that humans stay in their right times and to help to fill in or destroy the arch as soon as possible. The rest is up to others more powerful than me. You could say I'm here for damage control. Isn't that the phrase you use?"

"But wait," Mike said. "You're a djinni. Can't you do it yourself?"

"No. I cannot destroy a time link. It's not allowed. I need to have the help of humans. Humans built it, and humans must destroy it. This is my assignment—as, you see, they're testing me because of something I did, or rather didn't do, in the past. I slept through something bad that I could have fixed easily, and so I must do this job with less than a djinni's usual powers."

"So *you* need *our* help?" Ibrahim asked. Moustapha nodded.

Shafiqa had hardly slept at all after the gnawa ceremony. She'd turned over in her bed, agitated by what had happened, haunted by the strange voice of the young man when he was possessed. Dawn soon came, and she was up, making tea and breakfast for her elderly aunt.

Her aunt was a healer, the head of a women's *hadra* group of singers and spiritual healers that helped with spirit possessions, when needed. Shafiqa told her aunt about the incident, and the old woman prayed with her about it. She told Shafiqa to keep an eye on the riad where it had happened. So, just after lunch the next day, Shafiqa walked by Dar Surour. She passed by the alley as Moustapha, Ibrahim, and Mike were talking there, and she slowed down to take a look. What astounded her was that the two men were dressed in what she could only describe as costumes from historical TV dramas, of the sort broadcast at Ramadan. They were even wearing turbans. She shook her head and looked again, not believing what she'd taken in at first glance. Seeing it was real, she walked on, vowing to return every day.

Chapter 12

An Ancient Weave

Maureen was reading in an alcove near the riad entrance when Mike swept in, heading to his room. She looked up and, in that instant, she dropped her book and reached out for his flowing cloak as he passed her. "Oh my God, this fabric, it's...." She fell silent as her eager hands explored the weave. He kept walking, hoping she would let go, knowing she wouldn't. "Where did you get this? It's unbelievable!"

Her pulling stopped him, and he was trapped. "I was lost and stumbled onto a place. Got a pretty good deal on it, too."

Never letting go of the cloth, Maureen trailed him up the stairs, along one of the colonnades and into his room. Normally, she would never have followed a student into his private room, but she could think only of the fabric.

"This piping is exquisite," she said. "Even the handmade buttons, such quality. This is all skilled handwork. Even the fabric is hand-woven. Any chance you could take me there? Having a sample like this would really help my research. If only I could talk to the tailor and the weaver!"

"Sorry, I'll never find it again. I wasn't feeling great and was lost. Maybe Ibrahim can take you somewhere that does the same work. Now, do you mind? I'd like to shower before dinner." He took off the cloak and tossed it on his bed. She didn't notice he was only in his drawstring pants—her eyes were bedazzled by the fabric.

Maureen grabbed the cloak and took it out into the courtyard to examine it more closely in the sunlight. Mike let her go—at least she stopped pestering him. All he wanted was to get into a hot shower and have a cup of coffee.

Barbara, fresh from a swim and wrapped in a towel, found Maureen hunched over the garment in the courtyard below their room. She was caressing it with both hands as she held it up to the light. She had never expected to see fabric like this in modern times.

"Look at this fabric. Mike just came in wearing it. It feels like a silk-cotton blend, something that Fez was famous for hundreds of years ago. And the weaving pattern is just like one I've seen in old diagrams. You see, these patterns appeared in France around 1400, and no one knows where they came from." The possibilities of articles or even books she could write filled in her head.

Barbara ran her hands along the fabric, but stood back, afraid her wet hair would drip on it. She imagined how it would feel to wear a caftan made of that fabric in a muted violet.

"Let's find out where he got it," Barbara said. Maureen nodded, and they smiled at each other. What could be more fun than an expedition to the souq in search of exotic fabric?

At dinner, Maureen watched Mike from the other end of the long low table where everyone was eating, leaning back against the bolsters as they did every night. Mike seemed different, and not just because he'd been lost all day. Maureen wondered whether he'd gotten into some serious trouble. Ibrahim sat with Mike, and he spoke to him quietly as the conversation around the table got boisterous and loud. Each evening, the group downed two bottles of wine before dinner, but, as usual, they quieted down when the main course arrived. Everyone tucked into the chicken tagine with olives and turmeric.

"Now this is a recipe I would love to try," Barbara said in the sudden silence, her sentiment echoed around the table. Even Maureen seemed taken with it.

"I have the recipe. I'll e-mail it when we get back home," Ibrahim said. Then, taking advantage of the silence, he added, "By the way, the management of the riad has asked us to stay out of the side alley. There's some construction about to start there, and they don't want any of us getting in the way."

Maureen and Barbara took their mint tea to the roof patio after dinner. They stood at the wall of the roof and watched the silhouettes of birds flying overhead, slicing the turquoise and orange sky. Below them in the alley, they watched Ibrahim having tea with that person they'd seen the first night, who they learned was just an old woman begging in the street. He was sitting next to her, his back against the wall.

The women heard shouting from the road out front. They strained to see, and saw the riad manager Khalid come sprinting up the street. He turned down the alley at full speed, running right past Ibrahim and going through the arch. The old lady seemed very upset about it, which seemed odd. Why would she care who ran by?

Ibrahim stood up and shouted in English, "Hey, hold onto your horses!" But Khalid had already disappeared around the corner at the end of the alley.

About 20 seconds later, half a dozen policemen ran up the street to the riad, seemingly in pursuit. They stopped at the opening of the alley and looked down it, pausing to catch their breath. Ibrahim stood up and said something to them, shrugging his shoulders and pointing down the street out front, away from the alley and the riad. The police walked on in the direction he'd pointed. After a few moments, Ibrahim ran through the archway and down the alley, apparently chasing Khalid.

"Figure that one out," Barbara said. They looked at each other with raised eyebrows. They agreed to keep what they'd seen to themselves. They both had come to like Khalid, and hoped he wasn't in too much trouble.

Chapter 13

Home No More

Khalid nearly tripped as he rounded the corner. Recovering, he sprinted as fast as he could up the hill, weaving through small streets, assuming the police were right behind him in pursuit. He stopped to catch his breath, his heart pounding. When he didn't see the police catching up, he sensed he was safe, that they had given up the chase. But why would they? After chasing him for about half an hour, they'd been gaining on him, and now they were gone. It made no sense.

His meeting with Suhaila had gone terribly wrong. They'd grown up together as neighbors, and their families had always been close. In the last year, they'd fallen in love and Khalid was planning to propose marriage. But everything fell apart when her second cousin returned from abroad and sought her hand. With his engineering degree and a stable job at his family's well-known firm, he offered prospects for a life that Khalid could never match, and her family agreed to the engagement. She felt forced to comply, since she could never admit that she and Khalid had been seeing each other. In the eyes of her parents, dating was wrong, so she and Khalid had pursued their romance in secret.

Khalid had only a commercial certificate. With his job as riad manager and assistant to the owner of the riad on building restoration projects, he could hardly compare to a professional engineer. Still, Suhaila had agreed to meet him one last time at a quiet café. The fiancé must have followed her, to make sure she was scandal-free. He found them at the cafe, just an hour before. He started shouting at Khalid, and then pulled him out to the street. Suhaila couldn't separate them, and a crowd gathered. The fiancé taunted Khalid, saying he was an uneducated fool to think that Suhaila would love him. That's when Khalid snapped and went at him with a pocket knife. Afraid a knife fight would hurt his business, the restaurant owner called the police. When they arrived, the men had been separated by the crowd, but Khalid bolted and the police followed in pursuit.

No longer being chased, Khalid paused to catch his breath and take his bearings. He was surprised to find he was lost. None of the shops had the ubiquitous metal grills pulled down in front. Instead, they had sturdy wooden doors with old-fashioned iron locks. He listened. There were the usual barking dogs. He heard some muffled voices. A donkey brayed, and then nothing. And it was far darker than usual. No lights anywhere.

His family had lived in the same sprawling house for generations, and he knew the old city and considered it all his neighborhood. Then a familiar fear rose in him. Ever since he'd been a boy, he'd had a nightmare of getting lost in his own city. In fact, Khalid often dreamed about the medina, about adventures he'd had in it, finding strange places that never existed, only to wake up and be relieved that it had only been a dream.

He calmed down as his eyes got used to the night sky, for there was a half moon overhead, and he took in more of his surroundings. Where were the signs over the shops? There were no electric wires overhead, and no street signs nailed on the corner walls. He started walking down the hill, toward the Qarawiyyin, knowing he could find his way home from there. But when he approached the shrine of Moulay Idriss, he stopped short in shock. He was standing right where it should be, but it wasn't there. Instead of a shrine, there was nothing but a bare wall. He felt sick to his stomach.

He was happy to find the Qarawiyyin Mosque was where it should be, and he followed its wall down the hill about a quarter mile. But as he came around a corner of the mosque, everything looked different. Where was the Museum of Berber Antiques, the bakery, and the tiny café where his uncle spent hours every day? Nothing was familiar.

He continued on until finally he began to recognize a few things. When he turned onto the open square, he sighed with relief at the sight of the arched double doorway of his family's home. He pulled out his key and sought out the keyhole. There was usually a light on above the neighbor's door, but now it was dark. He couldn't find the lock, where was the doorbell?

He rapped his knuckle on the door as loud as he could and called out, "Saleh! Saleh, it's me, Khalid. Open up!"

He waited for a response then banged on the door again. This time he heard a voice inside, "Who's there at this ungodly hour? What's your business?"

"Let me in! It's Khalid!"

Khalid heard the sound of a primitive latch turning, not the modern one that they'd installed a few years ago. A bolt scraped across the inside of the door and the door cracked open. Light streamed from a candle and an old man spoke, "And what do you want, young man?"

Khalid said, "Who are you? This is my home!" and tried to push the door open, but the old man must have had someone with him, and he resisted Khalid's efforts.

"No, this is not your home." the old man said, his boney features etched in the candlelight. "You are mistaken, young man. This is the home of Faruq al-Kandili, second minister to the Sultan. Now, good night, and go in peace." The door shut, and Khalid heard the latch slide shut.

"Some kind of lost spirit or drunkard," the old man said in a muffled voice behind the door.

"God protect us from the evil ones," a younger voice answered.

Second minister to the Sultan? Khalid thought of banging on the door again and trying to force his way in, but decided against it. He was tired and maybe he wasn't thinking straight. He made his way to a low archway above the side alley and pulled himself up into a small hidden alcove just above it. As a young boy he'd retreat there to hide or just to enjoy a little peace. At least that hadn't changed, he thought. He sat there, alone, trying to make sense of the situation. But logic and reason were no help to him that night, as he waited for the dawn.

Chapter 14

One Meter

As Ibrahim combed the streets looking for Khalid, he couldn't fathom why the police would have been chasing him. "Khalid!" he called out half-heartedly in a hoarse whisper, fearing that he would wake someone. He tucked into the shadows as a night watchman passed by, his lantern light dancing along the whitewashed walls with the swinging rhythm of his gait. At sunrise, Ibrahim gave up and returned to the riad, finding Moustapha at his post.

"Any news?"

"The police just stopped at the riad, and I assume they were asking about him," Moustapha said. "But that's not all. About a hundred ghouls and djinn slipped through, going in both directions. It's a disaster. There's got to be something to lure the spirits back to their own time. But that isn't your concern, or even mine. We just have to keep control of the humans. And we've got to get Khalid back and destroy the arch as soon as possible or things will get even more out of hand."

The two of them sat as the sun rose higher in the sky. They sipped tea in silence for a while, both deep in thought.

"Tell me, Moustapha. The people who return, how much will they remember of their time in the past?"

"That's a blessing for most humans. Much of what happens there will fade from the top of their mind, except for those who are sensitive, like your friend Munir. But the longer they stay in the past, the more they will remember of the time they spend there. In the end, even if they only cross for a few minutes and forget what happened in that other time, kernels of knowledge from the experience will always stay with them. Yet the source of their knowledge will be a mystery. They will find they know things and will not understand how they learned them." He crunched on a butter cookie, scattering crumbs all over his dusty caftan. "How has it affected you, young man?"

"I really can't tell, nothing seems different."

"Spend enough time there, and it will come to you, sooner or later."

The next morning, Ibrahim met Abdul-Lateef, the riad's owner, at the door to the latter's apartment, just as he was going out. This was the first time they had worked together. Even though they were from different circles, one professional and Arab, one commercial and Amazigh, both considered themselves excellent judges of character, and they had come to trust each other. Besides, Abdul-Lateef had reasoned, if Dr. Charles had hired Ibrahim for such a long tour, he must be reliable. And Ibrahim had trusted the school organizers to know a good landlord. Abdul-Lateef welcomed Ibrahim, inviting him to sit on the white leather sofa in his salon.

"Sorry to disturb you. I'll be brief," Ibrahim said, as the two of them sat down at the same time. Ibrahim enjoyed sinking into the cushions, the leather smell enveloping him.

"Yes, my friend," Abdul-Lateef said, centering the sharp crease in his slacks with a thumb and forefinger.

"Any news of Khalid? I was just out looking for him," Ibrahim said. "I understand the police have been round asking about him."

"I'm afraid that Khalid's a bit headstrong when it comes to girls. He's in love with a young lady from his neighborhood, but unfortunately her family pressed her to accept a better proposal. He got in a fight with the fiancé. Apparently, Khalid went after him with a knife at a café. Cut him, but nothing serious."

"And no one has seen him since?"

"No," Abdul-Lateef said, shaking his head. Then he looked up from inspecting his nails and gazed at Ibrahim. "Do you know something? If you do, we must inform the authorities."

"I only know that the police were here, and that our own search turned up nothing."

"I have no further information, either. But if you learn anything, let me know immediately. His family is worried that he'll do something rash and come to harm."

"Of course, of course," Ibrahim said. They exchanged small talk for a while. Then, as Ibrahim was leaving, he said, "I was also wondering, what's the holdup with rebuilding that wall in the alley?"

"It's the neighbor just behind. He claims the wall should be moved one meter toward my property. We've got a perfect case to defend the current wall location, but we have to leave everything just as it is until it's sorted out in court, which could take months."

Ibrahim left, more worried about the arch than ever. He also knew that the police might start scrutinizing him and his group. Any suspicion at all on the part of the authorities would make his life miserable until he got everyone safely on the plane home. And they had weeks to go before they left Fez.

When Ibrahim got back to the riad, he went to the roof and called home. He knew he'd overreacted to Laila's reminder that they'd lost money on the last shipment. The phone rang at their rented house. It was dinnertime, and Laila should have been home, but no one picked up. He left a message, apologizing for being out of touch. He didn't mention the arch, though. He wouldn't know how to explain it without sounding crazy.

Chapter 15

Rooftop Refuge

The hinges of the great door squeaked as they swung open, waking Khalid with a start. The sun was bright; morning was well underway.

"Ali! Ali! Come for breakfast, you'll be late to school!" The woman's voice was high and shrill, sure to carry.

Khalid had spent the night curled up on the hidden alcove, outside his home. He craved a cigarette. His neck, arms, and legs ached, and though he wanted to stretch, he had to stay still.

Below him, a young woman, probably a housemaid, swept the threshold with an old-fashioned broom made of palm leaves. When Khalid was young, they'd hired a country girl to clean who used a broom just like that. He closed his eyes, comforted for a moment by the familiar sound and rhythm of her sweeping. He snuck a glance at her, careful not to be seen. She wore a tan caftan and had covered her hair with a long white muslin scarf, wrapped around her head several times, with the ends hanging down her back like long hair. He could tell she was young, because her fingers looked full and soft. "Where is that boy?" she said, looking down the street.

The sound of sandals slapping on stone approached from the side street. Khalid held his breath as a young boy ran inside. The door closed. Khalid was so confused. That could have been him running down the alley. How many times had he woken early in the morning to go next door, making sure the pigeons his grandfather kept on the roof had returned to roost? Then he'd run home, eat breakfast, grab his schoolbag, and walk to school arm in arm with his friends.

The door opened again, and a man emerged. An ivory-colored turban topped his head, and he carried an ebony walking stick. His cloak was made of black and white brocade. He must have sensed something, for he turned and looked up to where Khalid was hiding. Khalid pulled back before he could be seen.

A young man joined him, saying, "Well then, Sir, let's go. It certainly is a fine day for a walk."

"Indeed, indeed it is. Praise God," the old man said.

The two men walked up the street, the wiry figure of the elderly one dwarfed by the tall frame of his companion, equally resplendent in dark blue brocade. He was two heads taller than his elder and walked with an easy elegance. Khalid had never seen such people, apart from actors in the television soap operas aired on Ramadan nights. Most were set in Baghdad, during the golden age of Islam, with a few in the heyday of al-Andalus. But this was Fez, and it wasn't TV. He was obviously still dreaming.

Khalid stretched, then climbed up onto the roof just as he always did. He needed to eat. He realized that he'd never dreamed about being hungry before. As he looked around, he was astounded to see that even at his own home, there were no electric lines or satellite dishes in sight. He opened his mobile, but got no signal. He crouched near the front wall of the roof and watched the passersby in the small square out front. Everyone wore old-fashioned clothing, and the women were wrapped in white *haiks* like his grandmother used to wear. He considered his own clothes. A pair of tight jeans, now dirtied from sleeping on the ledge all night, a black t-shirt, and a jean jacket. He'd have to find something more suitable to wear until he woke up from his dream, even though, in most of his dreams, no one noticed what he was wearing.

Still, he sensed this was different and walked to another section of the rooftop, where the ladies usually hung laundry to dry. He was lucky, for before him hung a selection of spotless white linen tunics. He swam through the hanging garments until he found a matching turban, tunic, and drawstring pants. Surrounded by the hanging laundry, he changed into the outfit and wrapped the turban around his head as best he could, imitating the style the men of the house had worn. He folded up his own clothes and hid them, along with his watch and phone, in a spot where he used to hide things as a boy, a cubbyhole set between the outer walls of his house and the house next door. He kept his black leather shoes on, for the alternative of going barefoot was never a good idea in the medina.

While he was tempted to search the house for food, since the men had gone, he'd be in serious trouble if he were discovered, so instead he climbed back down to the alcove and slowly dropped to the ground. He walked toward the Qarawiyyin mosque, looking for something to eat.

Khalid was relieved to find the mosque's entrance, but he was vaguely unsettled when he realized the building's emerald-tiled roof was shining and bright, as though it were new. Across the small, triangle-shaped square, the doors to the Madrasa al-Saffarine were wide open, a crowd gathering inside. To his surprise, they weren't all Moroccans. There were Europeans, also wearing old-fashioned clothing. Some had blonde beards as long as the dark ones of the Arabs around them.

Despite his hunger, Khalid was drawn in. He had walked by that madrasa all his life, seeing scholars come and go from its door, thin from poor men's diets of rice and bread. This was different, somehow exciting. It reminded him of the time he'd gone with Suhaila to a well-attended anthropology lecture at the university she attended.

Doing his best to blend in, Khalid walked inside. His beardlessness had started to make him uncomfortable, because it seemed everyone around him had at least a close-cropped goatee. He reached up and felt his face, noticing that stubble had begun to grow, so perhaps he was all right.

He followed the others inside and removed his shoes and socks, hiding them as best he could and emerging barefoot. The courtyard was packed with men of all ages and races, sitting cross-legged on maroon woven carpets. They were all speaking at once. He sat down near the back at the end of a row, sinking slowly to his knees, mimicking the way the others sat cross-legged.

Next to him, an old man with a snow-white pointed beard sat still, listening. Staring straight ahead, he said, "I can't see anything, young man, but I know you're there."

"Yes, I am, Sir, indeed. Good morning to you."

"And to you," the old man said, reaching out to shake Khalid's hand, and after they had greeted each other, he touched his hand to his heart. Khalid did the same.

"Young man, is Ibn al-Khatib here yet? My son and I have been waiting for nearly an hour. He went to get some nourishment, but he's been gone a while."

"I'm sorry I don't know him. What's he like?"

"I can tell you only of his voice. When he speaks the whole world goes silent, listening to his calm and quiet wisdom. He's an advisor to the Sultan, a scientific thinker, and a gifted poet."

Never having been a serious student of history, Khalid couldn't remember the name from his school days.

"But tell me, young man, how do you not know of him? Are you not from Fez? You speak just like someone from this very quarter, by my life."

"Yes Sir, I am from here, but I've been, er, traveling on a long journey and only just returned."

"Well then, you'll be interested to hear Ibn al-Khatib speak, for he is a brilliant lamp of wisdom."

The old man's son returned and unfolded a piece of cloth to reveal a round of flat bread and some fresh dates. Turning to Khalid, he said, "Brother, you are welcome to some."

Khalid thanked him, explaining that he had left home too early for breakfast. He savored the first date in his mouth. It was more flavorful and richer than any date he'd eaten in his life.

"These are delicious. Are they from Meknes?" Khalid said.

"No, from Tafilalet. Indeed, they're exceptional."

He also partook of an offered chunk of bread, and he was surprised as he crunched the grains in his teeth. What a dream, Khalid thought. What does it all mean?

The crowd grew quiet as the standing onlookers in the back parted for two men. They strolled under the alcove toward the front, both dressed in finery like the men who had come out of Khalid's house that morning. They looked to be in their thirties, strikingly handsome, and one wore an ochre turban. He spoke first, his voice so sonorous that it could likely be heard out in the street. "Peace be upon you, my brothers. It is an honor to introduce my friend Ibn al-Khatib to you. As we know," the speaker continued, "in years past, great plagues raged through the world, from east to west. Not one of our families was untouched, God is our Protector. And yet, though the plague has lost its power, it returns every few years. And now it has appeared again in Marrakesh. We again grapple with its cause, for it could come to Fez."

"So what is causing it? Surely it is the will of God, no one can deny this. But is something more at work? My dear friend has investigated this question, and he consented to speak with you about his ideas today. I give you Ibn al-Khatib."

Chapter 16

Muscles Samir

Silence filled the courtyard as Ibn al-Khatib took a breath and scanned the crowd, smiling, his eyebrows raised. Khalid was enthralled; if this was a dream, it seemed completely real.

"In the name of God, the Merciful, the Compassionate," Ibn al-Khatib said. As he spoke, the crowd strained to listen. Even though his name meant "preacher's son," he spoke quietly, and the audience was riveted and motionless.

"You are no doubt aware that the Great Calamity has returned to this land, though for now, it is confined to Marrakesh. But this doesn't mean we are not threatened by its return. There are some who are convinced that these plagues are God's wrath in action, His way of chastising mankind for our evil ways. Others believe the plague is the work of the devil, God protect us from the evil ones. Today, I would argue that there is another reason that the plague returns from time to time, sparing some cities and attacking others."

"God is the All-Powerful; to this I bear witness. And whatever theory I may have, He alone knows the truth. Yet we know that God wants us to seek knowledge; to learn the truth about the world around us."

For the first time in his life, Khalid was drawn into a lecture. He'd always been a distracted boy in school. He had a hard time concentrating, what with all the pranks his friends played on each other, even during the most important exams.

But here, he was riveted by the talk, in this strange dream among oddly dressed men. And since he was dreaming, he told himself to just relax and go along.

"The great scientists of old believed that illness was caused by the humors in the air that traveled from one man to another. And why should this plague be different from any other illness? It is true that, in one form, it appears as lumps on the skin, and then it kills the victim within days, without other symptoms. So why do some people survive while others do not? We all know stories about those who ran from the plague and survived as long as they stayed out of the city. And we know that the sickness eventually passed, like a slow-moving rainstorm. Those who returned after the pestilence had passed were never afflicted. As for those who remained in the city, many were taken, without any apparent pattern.

"It is said by the Greeks that investigation of facts is the key to understanding. I had the good fortune to stay at an inn here in Fez ten years ago. My host was humbled and grateful by the fact that his children had survived that terrible time, and he now has many grandchildren. So I asked him what they did in his house during the plague.

"He said he didn't know, that somehow, miraculously, he and his children were saved—although not the whole family. As I stayed at that house for some weeks, I noticed that this fine house, which was high on a hill, had its own well. The family washed its clothes there, and they had their own hammam. And they also baked their own bread, so they did not make use of the neighborhood ovens. So I wondered if perhaps the plague was in the water, some evil humor in the *wadi* that flowed through the city. Yet I knew it had been clean for centuries. This did not make sense.

"Then my host mentioned that he had broken his leg in a riding accident and couldn't walk to the mosque for prayers. He and his sons prayed from home. Being a literate man, he taught his own sons to read, and they were not in school. The only people who left the house were the servants, who went to buy food in the markets. But once the plague came upon the city, they stopped even that. The family bought a great quantity of grain and kept to themselves. And nothing happened. They could hear the wailing of the neighbors. They would buy vegetables and meat only from their own house, picking out wares from the street-sellers who came by. They would lower a basket from the roof to take up the goods and send down money.

"So they survived for many months. Then, one day, my host's brother arrived from al-Andalus, and of course they could not turn him away. He stayed with them for a few days, and then he exhibited the signs of the plague and died within a week. Three others in the house died from it, and then it stopped. This story leads me to conclude that when the disease comes, it is carried by man. It is not a punishment from God. It is a humor that is passed in the air from man to man."

Heated conversations erupted throughout the crowd, and Ibn al-Khatib paused. Many people muttered invocations for protection from God. Others discussed what he'd said with their neighbors, shaking their heads and folding their arms. Ibn al-Khatib waited patiently until the silence returned.

"Do you believe it is blasphemy to say this? That the plague passes from man to man? We know that many things pass from man to man. Like the ideas of sin and greed. Like valuable kernels of knowledge, brilliant poems, and beautiful melodies."

At the mention of poetry, many heads nodded in the audience, and someone started to recite a poem that Khalid recognized. "My beloved came to me at dusk, as if she were the evening star on the horizon…" Gradually, most of the audience joined, including Khalid, in reciting the poem about secret lovers that was so famous even he knew it. It ended with the line, "he who sails the sea has no fear of drowning." The crowd laughed quietly as the speaker smiled and nodded, waiting for them to quiet down.

Khalid's jaw dropped in astonishment when he realized that Ibn al-Khatib must have authored that poem. It was a favorite of his, and a recital of those same verses had been made famous in a modern recording by the celebrated Lebanese singer, Fairuz.

Once the audience grew quiet, the speaker continued. "God gave us minds to think and tongues to speak, so we could share our knowledge. And because we breathe the same air and drink the same water, our humors mingle together. I would also argue that there is evil afoot in all the world, at all times. Yet why do we go for years without any news of the plague, even though merchants travel among our cities, carrying goods, sharing our food, living among us?

"Last year, to test my theory, I went to a village up in the hills, where the plague had returned. I moved there with my manservant and rented a house that had its own well and its own ovens. I stayed two months through the worst of their plague and was not afflicted. I lived apart from the local people, remaining in my home while I studied and wrote. And I bought produce only from the rooftop of my home. Once the illness seemed to have passed from the area, I began to mingle with the townsfolk, and nothing happened. I remained well.

"Despite my success, I did not know why it worked for me, and for my hosts in Fez. Then I started to think about other possibilities, and I remembered that each house where the plague was kept at bay had cats. Yes, cats. And those cats hunted and killed vermin to keep them away. So, my good friends, I submit to you today that I believe this plague is passed from house to house by humans, but also by the mice and rats. If we keep clean and we let the cats take care of the vermin, we may be saved. And now that the plague has returned to the Maghrib in earnest, we must prepare for it."

An elegantly dressed man stood and addressed Ibn al-Khatib. "But Sir," he said, "Given your theory, what should we do to prepare?"

"Indeed, that is the question of the hour, is it not," he said, pacing back and forth, his hands clasped behind his back. "First, if you can, move to the countryside as I did. Live simply there, away from people. If you stay in the city, I suggest you buy large jugs and fill them with water, covering the top with a cloth to keep out the vermin. Stockpile grain and keep that safe, too. Lock these provisions in a room where no one can enter, that's protected from the humors. And keep cats. Let them hunt the vermin in your homes. Of course, we must pray to the Almighty to protect us from the pestilence and to guide us in wisdom to find the truth.

"This cannot protect the whole city. My approach worked for me, and you can replicate it with your own family. But we know that commerce must continue. Travelers must come and go. Work must get done and crops must be sold. Given that, I assume that only one in 100 families will do what I suggest. This will save many homes, though not all. It is the only thing I can offer."

"But this makes no sense," the old man next to Khalid said. "How can putting aside water and grain and having cats protect us against the plague?"

"But he's right," Khalid said. "Disease is transmitted by microbes, by germs. They're carried by animals and humans. It's a known scientific fact."

Just as those words came out of his mouth, the men around him turned to listen.

"What did you say?" the man in front of him said, his eyes narrow and piercing.

Khalid said, "It's simple, really. Everyone knows that diseases are caused by germs. All you have to do is keep clean: wash your hands, drink clean water, wash off your food before you eat it, and keep vermin out of your house. It's common sense. Why, my mother washes everything three times before she starts to…"

The old man clutched Khalid's knee. "I beg you, hold your tongue. Such ideas are dangerous."

Everyone fell silent as four soldiers entered the madrasa, long swords drawn. They looked like something from the Crusades. They strode to the front, surrounded Ibn al-Khatib, and began to escort him out.

"O men, do as I say and prepare yourselves!" Ibn al-Khatib said, even as they led him away. "Silence!" one of the soldiers said.

"What's happening?" the old man asked.

"They've arrested Ibn al-Khatib," his son said. "The Sultan's men."

"God protect him," the blind man said under his breath. The crowd went completely silent as they watched Ibn al-Khatib being led away.

The sultan? Khalid thought. A learned man gets arrested for lecturing about science in Fez, which is ruled by a sultan? This is some dream.

The crowd began to disperse in a barely controlled panic. Khalid helped the old man stand up, and he rode with him and his son on the tide of the men pushing out onto the street. He wanted to ask them why Ibn al-Khatib had been arrested, but just then the call to the noon prayer began, and the men moved as one across the street into the Qarawiyyin mosque. Khalid could not get to his shoes and was swept along with the crowd.

The faithful converged across the street and moved into the mosque. As he did his ablutions in the courtyard, Khalid took in the enduring beauty of the mosque. The ceramic floor tiles were bright green, white, and black, glistening in the sun that shone into the courtyard. Hundreds of keyhole arches around them led to the prayer hall.

He joined the congregation that stood in lines on the massive carpets, the ritual prayer underway. At least this was the same. Leading the prayer that day was a tall wiry man with a light brown, almost reddish beard. Khalid was in the third row, so he got a good look at the man. Khalid was struck by the man's appearance, for he was distinctly European.

At the end of the prayer session, Khalid drifted toward the main door with the crowd. He started across the street to retrieve his shoes, but someone hit him in the stomach with such force that he buckled over in pain and fell to the ground. Rough hands grabbed his arms and lifted him up. He struggled to get free, but their grip was too strong, and they led him away, one of them clenching Khalid's head under his arm and holding it there as he struggled to walk. Two others held his arms as they propelled him forward, like a large animal being led to a slaughterhouse.

"Come along, won't you?" the guy who had him in a headlock said, his voice rough as a camel roar. "Now, no use making a fuss, for no one will dare defy me." The crowd melted away around them and people scurried off. Khalid looked up for a moment and saw the old blind man and his son. The son was explaining what was happening to his father, who wore a worried look as he stared ahead, seeing nothing, saying nothing.

"But Sir," one of the men said to the man who held Khalid. "He looks just like…"

"Exactly!" he said, standing still for a moment and grabbing Khalid's chin with his beefy fingers, turning it from side to side. "Strange, isn't it? Yet he's bare-faced, just like a little girl, and look how closely his hair is cut."

As they hurried him up the hill, Khalid was convinced they knew about his fight, and that they were taking him to the police. But they were going in the wrong direction, so his confusion grew, and it grew even more when he didn't recognize any of the shops. He prayed that this nightmare wouldn't last much longer. They turned down an alley and banged on a door until someone let them in. They led him inside a small building that stood on the edge of a great courtyard, then once inside, led him down some stairs to a series of barred cells.

"Here, my tender blossom. I hope this salon will suit you," the bald man said as his men shoved Khalid into a small cell. Straw was strewn across the floor. A single small window near the ceiling shed the only light. "You're our guest now. My name is Samir, welcome," the bald man said. The door clanged shut, and Samir padlocked it.

"But why?" Khalid asked. "What have I done?"

Samir crossed his arms and smiled, revealing one blackened incisor. "You appeared in the perfect place at the perfect time. You, my friend, are an opportunity. And I never pass up an opportunity, 'specially where the boss is concerned." The men turned to leave, and Khalid rubbed his neck, leaning his head against the bars as he watched them climb up the stairs and out into the courtyard, slamming the wooden door behind them.

"*Ya Allah,* I wish morning would come, and soon," he said to himself.

"Morning? It *is* morning, or it was recently," said a voice from the next cell over.

"No, I mean, this whole thing is a dream. And I'm about to wake up." You could say anything in a dream, he thought.

He was answered by quiet laughter that was more like snickering. "Yes, it's a dream all right. You just keep thinking that the next time Samir pays a visit. You tell him he's nothing but a ghost from your own imagination, or, better yet, call him a djinni, or an *afreet.* Then you'll wake up all right...in the next world!"

"Who are you?"

"I'm Badr, a *guest,* like you. Our generous host is Muscles Samir, henchman of Nimr al-Anmash."

Nimr al-Anmash. Spotted leopard, Khalid thought. Not a bad name for a thug.

"But I've never heard of him, and I've lived here all my life. How can that be?"

"You tell me, er..."

"I'm Khalid. Why are you in here?"

"Samir's trying to get me to talk. And you? What lucky circumstance brought you here?"

"Truly, I have no idea," Khalid said. "Yesterday I got into a fight with my girlfriend's new fiancé and the cops chased me, but I got away. I was just coming out of noonday prayers and Samir grabbed me. But it doesn't matter, I'll just play along until I wake up, since this is a dream."

"I've told myself that a hundred times as the whip caresses my flesh," Badr said. "He only comes at night, you see. So in the daytime, I can sleep. I suggest you do the same."

"What about food?" Khalid asked.

"If you can call it that. Moldy bread and lukewarm, watery soup."

"What about water?" Khalid asked.

"If you cooperate, they'll bring you a clay jug. If you don't, you'll go thirsty and hungry."

The dungeon's wooden door swung open, and Khalid heard footsteps on the stairs. He hid in the corner of his cell, hoping that whoever it was, wasn't coming for him.

Chapter 17

Two Gazelles

Many kinds of people wandered the streets of Fez, and like most boys who had grown up in the medina, Hameed knew all of them. He could discern the various manners of scholars and foreigners, the tradesmen, even criminals and charlatans. As for women, he could distinguish an Andalusian Jewish lady from a Tunisian aristocrat by her dress, her footwear, even by the way she walked while draped in her white haik. But Munir, the man he'd met at the madrasa and had later found passed out in the alley—he was a puzzlement. Sort of Frankish, sort of Maghribi, but neither one. He wore the clothes of a Fez nobleman, yet he had a unique accent that Hameed couldn't place. Munir had no mark of a family or profession. He wore a small gold ear hoop like a privateer or a slave, high on his earlobe. It didn't make sense. And, strangest of all, Munir didn't know where he was or what he was doing there.

Hameed was fascinated, and he wanted to solve the mystery of this man, so he had followed Ibrahim and Mike as they made their way from the madrasa through the city. Hameed was even more perplexed by Ibrahim, who was clearly Amazigh, but acted just as strangely as Munir. He studied the way they walked and talked. Everything about them seemed more than a little out of place.

He followed them all the way to the alley and saw them speak with an old woman. After they crossed under an arch, he approached the arch himself. But as he got close to it, the old woman stood up.

"Oh no, now there's one who's a little too curious," the old woman said to herself. "Have to take care of this right now." She clenched her fists and then her legs and arms stretched longer and she grew taller, arms and legs extending beyond the hem and sleeves of her caftan, until she stood ten feet tall. She raised her arms and started walking toward Hameed, roaring, "Go home, or the ghouls will get you!"

Hameed backed away as the giant lady kept walking toward him. She said, "I'm warning you, get out of here and don't come back!"

Although he ran off, the old woman's warning had the opposite effect than what she'd intended. He decided he would get to the bottom of this mystery. He would find out who those strange men were, and who the giant old lady was. As for her, she was obviously was some kind of djinni, or afreet, though admittedly he'd never personally encountered one before. He circled the block, trying to get to the other end of the alley by any other means. But he couldn't find it, and he got lost. Each time he returned to the alley, the old woman was there. She never moved. His obsession with finding out where Mike and Ibrahim had gone grew, and he vowed not to give up on this mystery until he had solved it.

Further investigation would have to wait for another time, however, for Hameed was late. He wandered back through the side streets, weaving his way up the hill and back to the madrasa. He hoped no one would notice he was missing, for he had duties to perform. He was expected to sweep out the students' rooms each day and to be available to help the headmaster of the madrasa. Now that he had turned twelve, the headmaster had given him a measure of independence, as long as he fulfilled his duties.

When Hameed was five, his father had gone on *Hajj* and never returned, and his mother succumbed to the plague a year later. From that day, he and his brothers had to fend for themselves, for they had no family in the city. His sisters went back to his mother's village, but he refused to leave Fez, and he was eventually taken in at the madrasa where, it was hoped, he would have a chance at a better life. He joined the *kuttab* school to learn and memorize the Qur'an, but he found learning to read too difficult. They let him stay in school, though, for he could memorize well. But he would never read, they were certain of that. He was illiterate, yet owing to his hard work and quick mind, he had been safe in the madrasa until recently, when a new supervisor arrived. The new man had it out for Hameed and his independent ways. Hameed had already had half a dozen thrashings for questioning things, and for doing things in new ways that somehow threatened his new boss.

His curiosity lit, Hameed returned to the end of the alley whenever he could. He was there in the shadows on the night Khalid ran through at top speed and disappeared up the hill. He followed Khalid to the house where he slept on the roof. And the next day, he saw Khalid get taken into custody by Nimr's man, Samir. He followed them as they took Khalid to the gangsters' villa, and he heard them lock him in a cell. The city's visitors always held fascinating mysteries, yet this djinni, and the people walking in the alley, were something different all together.

One day he got lucky. He came to the alley and noticed the old woman sitting cross-legged near the arch in a patch of sunlight, with her back against the wall, her arms crossed. Her head rested on her chin.

Once he was sure that the old-lady giant was asleep, Hameed crept down the alley with the lightest steps he could manage and tiptoed past her, watching her breathe. He stepped under the arch and stopped short. His ears were filled with strange noises. These were loud sounds, not animals exactly, but as loud as a donkey braying, but more mechanical and metal, like the sounds of soldiers marching by. When he inhaled, strange odors filled his nostrils. Something like gas, and the smells of a chemist's shop. This was an odd neighborhood indeed, he concluded.

Hameed stepped out to the main road, and he couldn't believe his eyes. Two young girls his age walked by, arm-in-arm. Instead of modest caftans, they wore dark blue sirwal as tight as their own skin. And their long hair swung from side to side. He was entranced. When they passed him, they noticed his stares, but just giggled. Apparently, they had no shame. Hameed was so bewildered that he blushed and turned away, sneaking glances at them only after they had passed.

"Those are the sweetest gazelles of the neighborhood," someone next to him said. A man, also wearing the same kind of blue sirwal, sat on a chair smoking a white tube. A cloud of white smoke surrounded his head as he smiled. "But don't get any ideas, they're my nieces."

"Of course not, Sir," Hameed said. He started to cough from the smoke and the very air itself, which seemed dirty.

"What is that you're smoking?" Hameed asked, once he stepped clear of the white cloud.

"Marlboro," the man said. When a bell rang inside the man's overcoat, he reached into it and pulled out a small silver object and started talking into it. Hameed watched in fascination as the man talked into this piece of silver metal.

"Sir, what is that, if you don't mind my asking?" Hameed said.

"Latest model, here have a look," he said, and turned it so Hameed could see bright-colored images, like dollops of ink on a page.

"And why do you talk into it?" The man handed it to Hameed, who held it up to his head but didn't hear anything. "There is no one there."

"Ha! It's a mobile, haven't you ever seen one?" Hameed shook his head. "So where are you from then, the moon?"

Hameed didn't know what to say or do. He handed the silver object back to the man and said simply, "I don't know, I think I'm lost." The ringing sound returned, and the man went back to talking into the silver thing.

Hameed walked on, drawn to the sound of music. It was pounding and so loud that it seemed like a wedding was taking place close by, but there were only a few people. The sound was coming from the upper floor of a riad. As he looked up in the sky above, he saw a bird flying so high he could scarcely see it. A long billow of white smoke trailed out behind it. He rubbed his eyes and looked again. It was gone.

He sat down on the threshold of a house and tried to make sense of things. He'd grown up in this very city. Why was it all new to him?

A boy about his own age came up the lane leading a donkey and cart piled high with wooden boxes of bananas, pomegranates, and grapes. The fruit looked fresh with no bruises, as it if had been chosen for the sultan's kitchen.

Hameed followed the donkey cart, hoping that something would fall off. He was feeling a bit hungry and had no coins. Soon, he was in the flow of the pedestrians caught in a slow current behind the cart. Hameed watched the other people and listened to them speak. Their accents were strange, yet these were clearly not foreigners. They could be his own cousins. Some of them spoke in the tongue of the Franks, and, for the first time in his life, he understood every word they said. He knew a few words of Frankish, but this accent was simple and clear to him, and Hameed was amazed.

Before he knew it, he was in the square outside the Mosque of the Qarawiyyin. Yet the emerald tile roof no longer glistened. The road was covered in marble stone, but the dirt and dust in the air filled every crack in the marble. Strange dark ropes linked the buildings around him, and there were white dishes on sticks atop the nearby houses.

His eyes were drawn to a yellow sign with crimson script. Without thinking, he read what it said, both in Arabic and in Frankish: "Sulaiman's Handmade Brassware." He wondered what 'handmade' meant. Were not all brass things made by the hands of artisans? After circling the perimeter of the mosque, he came upon another place, reading the sign, "Museum of Berber Antiquities." He stepped inside, and immediately two young men in crew cuts and sunglasses sauntered up to him. "Move along, kid. There's nothing here for you."

"Sorry, Sirs," he said, and only when he stood outside, looking at the sign, did he realize he was reading it. He was reading words. For the first time in his life, Hameed could read.

"Hah!" he said out loud, "I got it!"

No one passing by paid him any attention; so many of them were in strange clothes, though even the ones dressed like him ignored him. Taking advantage of his anonymity, Hameed wandered through the streets, reading every sign. He stopped at a bookshop and stared in awe at the paperbacks. He'd never seen such books in his life. But he was afraid to speak to anyone.

When the call to prayer started, Hameed realized he had to get back to work. So, out of habit, he followed the route along the western wall of the mosque and turned up Tala'a Kabira. On his way up the street, he was shocked that all the shopkeepers were different. Where was Abdullah, his friend whose father bound books? And the tailor shop he'd passed not an hour ago? His heart beat faster, and he started to run uphill, growing more out of breath with every turn in the road. And then, up ahead, he saw the minaret of the madrasa beckoning him. He looked up as he passed the water clock, the wonder of the city. But it was in ruins. What had happened? Like the others who slipped through the arch, Hameed imagined he was dreaming.

Returning to his home, he skipped up the front steps of the Madrasa bou Inania, but fear grew in him when he found that the door was shut. He banged on it, but no one answered. A brass plate indicated the hours of the establishment, which he could read, and he noted that it was closed until the next day.

Overcome by confusion, Hameed sat on the steps of the madrasa and watched the crowds of strangers pass by. He was growing hungry, and he could smell food from the nearby cafés and homes, but he had no money and he knew no one. Elbows resting on his knees, Hameed cupped his face in his hands and started to weep, hoping no one would notice. How could he be lost on the streets he knew so well?

"Well, it's about time!" Moustapha said. Ramses the cat sat in front of him, purring loudly, waving his tail back and forth.

"You stayed under the arch the entire day, from start to finish. Bet you've been up to no good. Go on, go inside and get some milk."

But Ramses wouldn't be shooed away. He sat still in front of Moustapha and purred. Then, as he did when he was curling around the feet of the maid who fed him milk, he started to meow and purr at the same time. His green eyes glowed, and he said, "Ghrrrrrrrrrrrr."

"So? Is that all you have to say for yourself?" Moustapha asked.

"Ghrrrrrrrrrrrrrrrrrrrrr," Ramses said again. Then he exhaled a puff of air from his nose in frustration. He started again, "Ghrrrrrrrrrrrrrrrrrrrrrr....hhhhalp." When Moustapha said nothing, he tried again, "Ghrrrrrrrrrrrrrrrrrrrrrr.....hhhhalp....Hhhhhaameeed."

"Help? You want help? Ramses the cat is asking me for help?"

Ramses rubbed his head on the djinni's chin, then sauntered toward the front of the riad and looked back, adding again, "Ghrrrrrrr....hhhaalllp."

"Cats are speaking now, are they? I can see why this arch is such a problem. Okay, I'm coming, I'm coming!" Moustapha slowly stood up and shuffled after the cat.

Ramses led Moustapha up the hill through the back streets, and, when they reached the madrasa, he sat down on the steps near Hameed, who was curled up on the top step, sobbing, his head in his hands. Ramses rubbed against Moustapha's legs and said, "Ghrrrr....Hhaaammeeed."

"Hameed?" Moustapha said. When the boy looked up, the djinni recognized him immediately. He was the lad who had tried to sneak through the arch. Apparently, he'd done it. Terror filled boy's face.

Moustapha reached out his hand and said, "Come with me, lad." When Hameed drew back in horror, having remembered Moustapha from before, the djinni said, "I see you managed to sneak by me while I was napping. Don't worry, we'll get you home. Now, don't ask any questions, just come along. You think you're in a dream, and well, you are. But to wake up you must follow me." Moustapha offered Hameed his hand. The boy took it and went along willingly. Ramses led them down the hill, again through back streets with little traffic. It was, Moustapha realized, a very effective shortcut to the alley, and he would make use of it himself.

As they walked, Hameed said, "Ma'am, you are a djinnia and…"

"No, I am a djinni. Just because I'm wearing a caftan doesn't mean I'm female. My name is Moustapha, so please call me that. I'm sick of 'Ma'am this' and 'Ma'am that.' Okay? Now, what were you going to tell me?"

"Samir's got him now, that young man."

Moustapha stopped and grabbed his arm. "You know something? Why didn't you say so? What has happened? There's one thing worse than an afreet for giving me a hard time, and that's an impudent boy. So speak, lad. What do you know?" His voice ended in a near-growl, as if he might turn into a lion in an instant.

Hameed's eyes had grown as wide as plates as he tried to pull away.

"You can't get out of my grip, no matter how hard you squirm, so speak."

"Let go or I won't tell you!" Hameed said. He was no idiot. He knew you had to bargain with a djinni to maintain the upper hand. At least that's what he'd always heard, but he was new at this. After all, this was his first face-to-face encounter with a real one.

"All right," Moustapha said, letting go of the boy's arm.

"That man, the one who ran down the alley last night. I followed him."

"And?"

"Samir has him. He locked him up in his jail."

"Who's Samir?"

"Muscles Samir, the henchman of Nimr al-Anmash."

"Nimr the gangster?"

"Yes. Nimr's in prison now, so Samir's in charge. I followed them when they took the man. He's there now, in the dungeon, at the back of Nimr's house."

Moustapha grabbed him again. "You little imp, how do I know you're not making this up?"

"I swear it's true. They just grabbed him coming out of the Qarawiyyin. Why are you hurting me? I thought you wanted to know?"

"Come on then," Moustapha said, pulling Hameed along. "Show me the place, and then I'll let you go back home."

True to his word, Moustapha took Hameed back through the arch, and, in turn, the boy led him to the great riad that had become the gangsters' lair. A venerable mansion falling into disrepair, it was surrounded by tall, crack-filled walls. Hameed took the djinni to the back alley.

"See those windows there? They open into the dungeon."

"I see," Moustapha said. "Thank you kindly for the information. Now, go on home and mind your own business. There's ten worlds of trouble for lads like you who push their noses into the affairs of gangsters. So help me, if I catch you coming through the arch again, I'll wallop you with the spiked tails of a hundred dragons. Go on now!"

Hameed started to run, relief coursing through his veins, and he didn't look back as he raced to the Madrasa, where he found everything just as it should have been. He said nothing about what had happened to him, sure that it was some kind of dream. But the next morning, when he was sweeping out one of the student's rooms, his gaze settled on a manuscript on the desk. Just as in his dream, he could read the words.

Chapter 18

Perfect Penmanship

The Arabic students toured the Roman ruins at Volubulis, a couple hours' drive from Fez. The air-conditioning kept the summer heat at bay, even though the sun was beating down with full force. Vistas opened up around them for miles in every direction.

Ibrahim introduced Volubulis as the bus turned into the site, which was filled with scattered arches, pillars, and the remains of stone walls. Once an opulent city ruled by King Juba II and the orphaned daughter of Cleopatra and Marc Antony, Volubulis overlooked a verdant plain where the Romans grew wheat, grapes, and olive trees.

Walking with the group among the ruins, Mike was drawn to some movement near a pillar off to one side. He caught sight of a short man darting among the ruins, as if he were following the group, and yet trying to remain hidden. Mike turned to watch him and was struck by the strangeness of his form. He was short like many older Moroccans, but hunched over. He wore the robes of a peasant, but ran from stone to stone and pillar to pillar with strange agility for someone so old.

What was going on? No one else seemed to notice him, and Mike instinctively knew he shouldn't point him out, in case he was hallucinating. The man waved his arms at him, grinning. Mike blinked and the man was gone. For the rest of the tour, Mike trailed at the back of the group, keeping an eye out for the strange man, but he was nowhere to be seen.

As the bus pulled away from the ruins, Mike glanced out the window and saw him again, jumping up and down, waving his arms and laughing. The man stopped jumping and pointed at Mike, then tipped his head back and laughed again. Mike quickly turned away, fearing that he was indeed seeing a spirit, maybe a djinni. The thought that djinn were real, and also among humans, made his stomach churn.

Mike mulled over the incident during their next stop at the nearby town of Moulay Idriss. Moroccans made a pilgrimage there to visit the tomb of the man for whom the town was named, who was considered the main founder of the City of Fez. The town's charming whitewashed houses could have been illustrations from a book of the *Thousand and One Nights*. It was considered a holy town, and there Mike saw no sign of anything out of the ordinary.

After lunch, the students were turned loose to explore the town. Maureen got into a fracas with a young merchant, accusing him of abusing an old donkey that he'd tethered next to the stall where he was selling trinkets. To Mike, it was obvious that donkeys, goats, sheep, cats, and dogs were only as well-fed as their human owners. People shared their poverty with their animals. But there was no reasoning with Maureen.

Meanwhile, the girls from Texas attracted their usual following of young men and giggling children begging for pens. "*Stilo, stilo*, Miss," they'd say, their hands stretched out for donations of western ballpoint pens. What did they do with all the pens, he wondered? Everywhere they went in the small towns and villages, the kids begged for pens. Maybe they sold them to each other.

Mike spent the time bargaining with an old man for a small figurine of a *hamsa*—a hand of Fatimah—that was carved from alabaster. He then rambled back to the bus as Ibrahim began herding the group. Even Mike was surprised at himself. For once, he wasn't late.

On the bus back to Fez, most of the students pulled out their books and quietly reviewed their Arabic lessons, for they had a test the next day. Mike had forgotten to bring his book, so he shut his eyes and drifted in and out of sleep, conjugating some of the new verbs they were learning in the past tense, then the present tense, and running through all the persons: I waited, you waited, he waited, she waited, we waited, they waited. When the bus reached the straight highway that crossed through miles of olive groves, he pulled out his journal and started to write out the conjugations.

At first, he didn't pay much attention to his writing, as he worked through the verbs. But then he realized that his hand simply *knew* how to draw the letters in perfect proportions. He'd been embarrassed by his Arabic handwriting, which was more like the awkward scrawl of an eight-year-old. But now the letters that looped in arcs below the line, like the *nuun* and *qaf,* came out in perfect half-circles. Yet they looked strange to him, since they weren't like the typewritten Arabic of his textbooks. He wanted to laugh out loud, but managed to keep it to a grin, letting his hand make artful arcs across the page.

Ibrahim came down the aisle, offering everyone Tangos, his favorite chocolate- and vanilla-filled cookies. He sat down in the empty seat next to Mike and glanced at his writing.

"That's unbelievable!" he said in a low voice.

"Yeah, I know. How am I doing this?"

"What's odd is that you're writing in the old Moroccan style. They call it Maghribi script." He took the journal and looked at it closely for a moment, then handed it back.

"Can you still write like you used to? Try it."

Mike took up the pen and tried to make his penmanship as poor as it had been before. It worked, although to him it looked strange and forced.

"Maybe you should write like this for class," Ibrahim said. "Otherwise, the teachers will start asking questions."

"You're right," Mike said. He was glad their Arabic teachers hadn't come with them that day. They were nice people, but it was hard to relax when they were around. Whenever one of the students tried to use their Arabic, they stood by and corrected each mistake.

"You did really well back there," Ibrahim said. "I overheard you bargaining with that old guy."

"Oh, you mean over that alabaster hamsa. Yeah, I did get a good price." He pulled the hamsa from his pocket and turned it over in his hands, then held it up to catch the sunlight.

"No, I mean your Arabic," Ibrahim said. "Did you realize you were speaking in perfect Darija?"

"Really? I didn't notice, I just started talking with the guy." Mike had enjoyed bargaining with the old man. He'd asked him how he carved the rock, then listened to the old man's account of fighting in World War II with the Allies. The old man reminded him of relatives back home, uncles and older cousins who had lived adventurous lives.

"You didn't see me, but I followed you. And I assure you, your dialect is absolutely perfect."

Mike was astounded. "Do you think it has something to do with..."

"Of course, what else could explain it? Won't your teachers be surprised on your next verbal exam?" Ibrahim got up and kept walking up the aisle, offering more Tangos to the students.

Mike smiled at the thought of doing well in class. Until then, no matter how hard he studied, he had never been able to do better than a C- on any quiz since he'd arrived in Morocco.

Then the song of the spice merchant popped into his head again. He wrote down the lyrics in his new script, remembering every line, admiring each clever rhyme. Then he drew five parallel lines across the page and sketched out the melody in notation, along with the tricky rhythm. He hummed the melody as he wrote.

Her eyebrows, arched like palm branches.
May I always sleep in their shade.

Chapter 19

An Unfortunate Resemblance

Later that day, Moustapha pulled Ibrahim aside and told him about Khalid being held in the gangster's jail. Ibrahim in turn recruited Mike's help, and, after dark, the two of them returned to the archway, dressed in their 14th century outfits. Moustapha led them to the back of the gangsters' villa and left them there. Careful to avoid being seen, Ibrahim and Mike climbed over the outside wall into the courtyard. A guard was curled up near the central fountain, asleep, facing the main house where candles burned brightly in the windows.

They crawled on their knees toward the door leading to the cells, then slipped through and closed the door behind them. They felt their way down the stairs, where Ibrahim turned on a small flashlight. In the first cell, a figure was curled up asleep. He was too small to be Khalid. At the second, they were startled to find Khalid standing against the bars as if he'd been waiting for them. He sighed and rolled his eyes when he saw them, signaling them to whisper.

"We'll get you out," Ibrahim said, pulling a chisel from his robe.

Khalid said, "No, they'll hear you. It's too dangerous."

"We've got to get you out of here," Ibrahim said. "These guys are bad news."

"What's that got to do with me?" Khalid said, shaking his head. "For all I know, I'm just dreaming this whole thing."

"No, you're not," Ibrahim said, handing the chisel to Mike, who was about to begin filing the padlock. "You're in deep trouble here."

"Don't use that," Khalid said. "You'll have better luck picking the lock."

Mike tried to open the padlock with his knife.

"Khalid, this is no dream," Ibrahim said. "When you were running away from the cops, you slipped under an arch, through a time portal, and back to the year 1374."

"Hello, is there someone there?" whispered the prisoner from the next cell.

"Shshsh," Khalid said. "Keep quiet. We may be getting out of here sooner rather than later, just don't say anything."

"Praise God," the man said. Ibrahim stepped to the cell next door. The prisoner was sitting up now. He was emaciated and sat shivering, wrapped in a wool blanket full of holes.

They heard the sound of voices and approaching footfalls.

"Hide, quick," Khalid said. "Give me your knife. I'm going to need it more than you." He took the knife and hid it in the straw.

Ibrahim and Mike slipped into the neighboring empty cell and crouched in a dark corner. The door at the top of the stairs swung open and crashed against the wall. Someone came down the stairs holding a torch to light the way. From the shadows cast by the torch, Ibrahim concluded one was burly while the other was small and thin, and wore an elaborate turban. The thin man belched and held his stomach with his hand. "This had better be good, Samir. I don't like being interrupted at supper." he said.

The men gathered at Khalid's cell. The guard held up the torch up to light Khalid's face.

"Remarkable," the thinner man said. "Simply astounding."

"As I was saying, Your Grace," Samir said. "He'd have to grow his beard for a few days, and we'll dirty him up a bit to make him look a little older, but otherwise, he could be the Boss's own twin. And all we have to do is get him into the prison and get the Boss out. That's where we'll need your help, Sir. And once the Boss is out of prison, we'll proceed with our plans, and no one will suspect a thing."

"What are you planning?" Khalid asked.

"Well, he sounds intelligent, and I'd add impudence to that, certainly," the thin man said. "I'll tell you, since, as of now, you're part of our plan, which is to rob the treasury of Qarawiyyin, become masters of the great city of Fez, and for Nimr to become sultan of the realm," he coughed and added, "God willing."

"God has nothing to do with this!" the prisoner called out from the other cell.

"Shut up!" Samir said. "Hold your tongue or we'll cut it out of you."

The men turned to leave, passing the other cell. "He still hasn't told you where the treasury is, has he," the thin one said as they began to climb the stairs.

"No, but he will. Believe me, he will. Any day now."

"If you don't have it out of him by the time Nimr's free, you can count on losing an appendage or two yourself."

When the door had shut, and they heard the men walk away, Ibrahim and Mike returned to the door of Khalid's cell.

"We'll get you out now," Ibrahim said. Khalid handed the knife back to Mike, who started in on the padlock.

"It's no use," Khalid said. "If what you say is true, that we're in the past, when we go back home, the cops will just arrest me, and I'll wind up in jail anyway."

Ibrahim couldn't believe what Khalid was saying. He tried to argue with him, but Khalid had given up, and was refusing to come.

"The knife isn't working," Mike said. "We need to get something else for the lock."

"Well," Ibrahim said. "Looks like you'll get your way, at least for now. We'll be back."

As they started to leave, Khalid said, "I know this makes no sense to you, but I feel safer here than back home."

"I don't care what you feel, we're getting you out of here."

When they were half-way up the stairs, Khalid called them back. "I need you to do something for me."

Chapter 20

The Scheme

Though he was exhausted from lack of sleep, Mike's heart pounded with happiness as he took the Arabic test. He knew the answers to all the questions with total certainty. The hardest part was writing his answers in his old, childlike script. Though he knew he'd completed the test before anyone else, he waited until half the class had finished to turn it in. Then he took a hot shower to try to revive himself.

Maureen was waiting for him when he emerged from his room in his bathrobe. Mike couldn't believe her audacity.

"So where were you last night?" she said. "What's going on?"

"Ibrahim took me out to a club. We were looking for a guy who makes ouds and hangs out in a couple of the discos outside the medina. But we never found him."

"And what time did you come in?"

"It was about 4:30. I think I got two hours sleep," Mike said. "I'm bushed."

Maureen shook her head as she left, and went to tell Dr. Charles that Ibrahim was keeping the program's worst student out at all hours.

"What's happened to Khalid?" Suhaila asked, looking back and forth from Mike to Ibrahim. The three of them met in a café in the new city, far from the medina. They had no trouble finding her, sitting alone on a red-leather swivel chair amid gleaming stainless steel fixtures. She was just as Khalid had described her, small and bird-like. She'd tucked her wavy brown hair behind her ears, as he said she would.

"Khalid's caught in an unusual situation," Ibrahim said.

"Is he in jail?" she asked, her eyes filled with worry.

"Detained, but it's not what you think. He just can't come to you now. We saw him yesterday," Ibrahim said. "He asked us to find you and to tell you he loves you, but that you must marry your fiancé. Khalid wants you to be happy, and he said your fiancé will provide you a much better life than he could."

She began to cry, trying to hide her tears from the other patrons in the café, mostly young people who looked like they were reviving themselves with espresso after being out all night.

"Is that all he said? Why doesn't he call me himself?" she asked, sniffling, wiping her tears and smearing her mascara.

"He's not free to use a phone now."

"Where is he?" she said. "Is he in prison? You've got to tell me. The police are still looking for him, and his mother is going crazy."

"Why? What does it matter to you? You're to be married, and you'll have your life. Don't worry about Khalid, he'll be fine."

"No, everything's changed. My fiancé called off the engagement when he found me in the café with Khalid. I'm in so much trouble. My father is furious with me. I don't know what's going to happen next. So why can't I see him?"

"It is too dangerous for you to know," Ibrahim said. "This is what Khalid wanted. When he can call you, he will. In the meantime, here's my mobile number. And please, don't say anything to the police, or even to his mother. It's too dangerous."

"When you see him," she said, composing herself, "tell him I still love him." After they left, she cupped her face in her hands, and her brown curls shook.

"You are from the future?" Badr asked, pressing his face against the iron bars of his cell, trying to get a glimpse of Khalid's face.

"Yes, Sir," Khalid said. "I'm from the year 1439 Hijri. I accidentally crossed through a passageway between my time and yours." Khalid assumed that Badr thought he was deranged and was humoring him.

Badr cackled. "Truly, I have seen some wondrous things in my life, but this is the ultimate, by God. Tell me, what is your Fez like?"

"Oh, our city is ever the same. The Qarawiyyin still stands, and the university, too. Can you imagine? More than 600 years from now, the faithful still come to pray and study in the same place, just as they do now."

"Praise God," Badr said. He was silent for a few moments, then he began to sob. "Then this means that Nimr will not succeed. If what you say is true, we must be strong, you and I. And I must be strong. I've felt myself wavering these last few days. You've given me hope."

Badr began to pray aloud. Khalid listened at first, then joined with him, tears streaming down his face. Badr believed him, which made him accept the fact that the mess they were in was real.

After a while, Badr cleared this throat. "But surely, young man, have you not improved upon anything in daily life?"

Khalid sat up and scratched his arms, strangely resigned to letting the lice and fleas feast on his flesh. He smiled. If Badr only knew. "Yes, we have made a few improvements. For one thing, we make our cart tires out of a flexible thing called rubber and we fill them with air, which makes a cart ride much smoother."

"By heavens, that is something."

"And nearly everyone can read and write, too."

"Praise God, that is truly a wonder."

"How long have you been here?" Khalid asked, knowing he'd cause trouble if he talked too much about the future.

Badr coughed. "Two weeks, I think."

"And is no one looking for you?"

"No. I took leave from my post at the mosque, and I was going to visit my brother in Midelt. No one but my colleagues at work knew of my plans, and they don't expect me back for weeks. Since I'm delayed, they will assume that family business has detained me. The gangsters must have been watching me for a long time, for they kidnapped me shortly after I left the city."

"How could they kidnap you, a mosque official, just like that?" Khalid asked.

"My dear young man, you have no idea. The city has lived in fear for years, owing to Nimr and his men. They terrorize every merchant, demanding a monthly sum that increases each year. If someone doesn't pay, or is late with their payment, their store is burned down, then their house, and then they're killed."

"But what about the police? Doesn't anyone fight them?" Khalid asked, knowing that the medina's maze-like streets and complicated relationships would make it easy for a brilliant bully to wreak havoc.

"What police? All of them, from the night patrols to the market inspector and weighmaster are paid off by Nimr's gang. In fact, everyone either pays or is paid off. But until now, they've left the university and mosque alone."

"So what changed? Why would Nimr try to take over the mosque now?"

"When Nimr's men attacked the Sultan's own caravan a day out of Fez, the Sultan had him arrested and imprisoned. He's being held at the citadel just outside the walls of the old city. But locking up the gangster hasn't helped. Samir and his henchmen have stepped up their harassment of merchants and travelers. The mosque's imam, Ibn Murad, is a good man. He prays for help every night, praying for God to rescue the city from these evil men. He is not alone, either. The men of his order, he is a mystic you see, they are fearful and do not act."

"But why would Nimr try to take the mosque?"

"If Nimr takes control of the treasury of the mosque and university, he will be able to depose the Sultan, for the lifeblood of this city is the mosque."

"What's in the mosque treasury that's so important?"

"The endowments."

"You mean the sums that old ladies leave to the mosque when they die, for the upkeep of the poor?"

"Aha, I see that some things *have* changed in your time," Badr said. "In *this* time, the pious leave great sums to Qarawiyyin. You must know that a woman named Fatimah gave her personal fortune to found the university and mosque, setting an example that generations of Fezzis still follow. Every week or so, someone dies in Fez, leaving some of their wealth, usually in gold and property, to the mosque. And it is my job to count it, keep track of it, and protect it. And, God have mercy on me, I am now held by these thugs who would learn its secrets and rob the city of its most important treasure."

"But doesn't the Sultan protect the endowment? Surely, he must send guards to help."

"While it is inconceivable that anyone would rob the mosque treasury, guards would only call attention to its location, which is a secret. Besides, this is a Muslim city, and until now we all thought such a thing would be beyond anyone's wildest nightmares."

"So they must be stopped." Khalid said. "But how?"

"I don't know," Badr said. "If only I could speak to the imam, to Ibn Murad, he would know what to do."

Khalid remembered the imam he'd heard preach. "I think I saw him at prayers. Is he tall, with a reddish beard?"

"Yes, that's him. Though he is modest and lives the simplest of lives, he has great wisdom and touches the hearts of many. May God protect him."

"If I can get to him, or if my friends can, what should we tell him?"

"Tell him of their plans, and that I'm captive. Besides me, he alone knows where the treasury is located. I fear my strength will not withstand Samir's torture, and I will reveal its location. They already took the key from me."

"They've tortured you?"

"Behold the work of Samir and his men." Khalid drew close to the common wall joining their cells and recoiled at the sight of Badr's right hand, which he had extended out of his cell. It was swollen with infection, and the thumb and index finger were missing.

Chapter 21

Lower Thy Wing

"Never!" someone shouted from inside one of the gangster's cells. Ibrahim was relieved it was not Khalid's voice. He and Mike were lying on the roof of the building next door, listening.

A long agonizing scream followed, then a cell door clanged shut. Moments later, Samir and two of his men emerged from the dungeon and crossed the courtyard. "When we get Nimr out tonight," Samir said, "he'll have another go at the son of a bitch. Meanwhile, prepare Khalid. Everything's in place. We'll move him late tonight, after the moon sets."

"Khalid, are you all right?" Ibrahim asked, whispering through the high barred window at the back of his cell.

"Yes, I'm fine. My neighbor Badr here, however, is in bad shape. They're torturing him."

"OK, sit tight. We brought a hacksaw. We'll get you both out, *God willing*." Mike began sawing at the bar with a hacksaw he'd carried in from the future.

"We have to get to the Qarawiyyin as soon as possible," Khalid said. "We have to warn the imam there, Ibn Murad. So far, Badr has kept its location secret, he's being brave." Then Khalid leaned back and looked up at them, wildness in his eyes. "Hurry up, will you? They've cut all the fingers off his right hand, and still he keeps silent."

"Young men," Badr said from the next cell. "If something should happen, recite this verse to Ibn Murad. It is our secret signal of danger.

Lower thy wing to the Believers who follow thee.

Ibrahim repeated it and said, "We'll tell him, but hopefully there will be no need, for you will see him soon, God willing."

Mike kept sawing at the bar, but it wasn't working.

"We met Suhaila," Ibrahim said. "Her engagement is over, and she still loves you."

"What did you tell her?"

"That you couldn't see her now, but that you would find her later."

"Yes, all right, feed them some gruel!" Samir's voice boomed from the top of the stairs. The gangsters were returning.

"He's coming back. It's no use, Ibrahim!" Khalid said. "Just go to the imam right away; there's not a moment to lose!"

"Don't give up hope, Khalid," Ibrahim said. "We'll get you out somehow."

Even as his rescuers disappeared and his tormentors returned, Khalid smiled, relishing the words he had just heard. Suhaila still loved him.

It was still hours before the late-night prayer, so Ibrahim and Mike circled around the mosque's walls, taking their time. Few people were in the streets, which were lit by the moon and candlelight from upstairs windows. As he thought through their situation over and over again, Ibrahim couldn't help but be amazed that so much of the old mosque remained intact in the 21st century, that generations of Fezzis had maintained the same double doorways of cedar wood.

"Ibrahim," Mike said, stopping short in his tracks. "Do you see that?"

"What?"

"That *thing*."

"No, what?"

"It's like a ghost, about 30 feet in front of us. It's round, glowing orange like a pumpkin. And it's turning around. You don't see it?"

"No. Listen, don't worry. They said you might see things like this, after what happened at the gnawa night."

Mike rubbed his eyes and looked up. "It's gone now. I've been seeing things here, and even at Volubulis. It's been driving me crazy."

"It's okay, just try to ignore them." The two of them found a quiet alley where they sat in the shadows, listening to the strange sounds of the sleeping medieval city, their thoughts with Khalid.

With the late-night call to prayer, the faithful approached the mosque in silence, as if they were sleep-walking. Ibrahim and Mike joined the others, removing their shoes, taking part in the ablution ritual at the fountain. The mosque was lit with just a few lanterns. Both men were deeply moved by taking part in a late-night prayer session 600 years in the past, a ritual unchanged by the centuries.

They crossed the vast carpeted prayer hall toward the front of the congregation, which at that hour was not very big. A group of men sat at the front, wearing matching tunics. They were carrying green turbans under their arms.

"They must be members of a Sufi order," Ibrahim said to Mike, then elbowed him and directed his gaze forward, for the imam had entered the prayer hall and stood in front. He was taller by at least a foot than any other man in the room. He looked French, or maybe Spanish, with his long face and pointed red beard. At prayer's end, the worshippers turned to greet each other, saying, "Peace upon you," and it was over.

They waited for the imam as he spoke to some of the worshipers, then followed him as he walked up the hill through the quiet city streets. Ibrahim wondered what it would be like to have this daily duty, walking to and from the mosque five times a day, with such an important public service to perform at the city's biggest mosque. He led them to a residential area, then went through a great wooden door. Ibrahim couldn't tell whether behind that door stood a sumptuous palace or a honeycombed warren of small, cramped rooms. They would just have to take their chances.

They waited a few minutes. Some young men, looking like those from the madrasa, emerged from the house deep in a discussion of geography. In all likelihood, it was some kind of hostel, which was a lucky break.

After paying off the houseboy on duty, they stood at the door to Ibn Murad's room. Ibrahim knocked.

The door swung open, and Ibn Murad stood before them, bareheaded, wearing a patchwork robe of brown wool.

"Excuse our interruption," Ibrahim said. "But we have a message from Badr the Scribe."

Ibn Murad beckoned them in and shut the door. He motioned for them to sit with him on the woven rug. It was, along with the simple mattress covered in wool blankets, the only furnishing in the room. Several thick leatherbound books were stacked against a wall. A copy of the Qur'an sat open on an ornately carved wooden bookstand, the only luxury.

"Lower thy wing to the Believers who follow thee," Ibrahim said.

Ibn Murad put his head in his hands. Then he looked up, sighed, and said, "God forbid. He has come to harm, has he not? May God protect him."

Ibrahim said, "I'm sorry to tell you that he is being held and tortured by men of Nimr al-Anmash."

"Allaaah, no," Ibn Murad said, his head bowed. "He is our most trusted servant in the mosque. That he should be taken by those dogs..."

"Badr sent us with a message, Sir. Nimr is going to break out of the citadel tonight. He and his men are planning to rob your treasury. That is why they have Badr captive. They have his key, and they're torturing him to find out where the *sunduq* with the endowments is kept. He warns you to move it as soon as possible."

"And how much time do we have?"

"A few days at most. Nimr will move fast once he gets out of prison."

"But how will they get him out? He's in the Citadel, after all."

"They also hold an innocent young man who looks exactly like Nimr, who happens to be our friend. They will put him in the prison in Nimr's place, and no one will suspect anything."

"But if I move the treasury now, too many eyes will see it, and we will be even more vulnerable. It is in a place so hidden, so secret—a place chosen generations ago. Only Badr and I know its location. No. I will trust in Badr's courage. God will give him strength to keep silent."

"But Sir," Ibrahim said, his eyes growing round in amazement at Ibn Murad's denial of the danger. "Nimr's men are known for extracting information. They will stop at nothing until they get what they want."

"Badr has always been faithful, God give him strength. If Nimr and his men come for me, then it is God's will."

"Should we alert the Sultan?" Ibrahim asked. "Wouldn't his men want to keep the sunduq and the mosque's wealth safe?"

"No, this wealth is not the property of the Sultan, nor of any one person. Only the institution of Qarawiyyin owns it. Generations of citizens, rich and poor, have given to the endowment, and they continue to do so only because they know it stays in the hands of the pious."

Ibn Murad closed his eyes and began to pray. Ibrahim and Mike followed his example. After a while, Ibrahim opened his eyes and found Mike staring at him. They shrugged their shoulders at each other and waited, careful not to disturb the imam.

"My sons," Ibn Murad said as he stood up. "I will continue to pray on the matter. If you have more news, you can find me at the mosque. We must give the appearance of everything being normal, or they will know we are aware of their plans. So I beg for your discretion. God deliver us from the evil ones. May God give Badr strength and courage."

"So far," Ibrahim said, "Badr has plenty of that. He has not divulged anything. And he is paying for his silence one finger at a time."

"I was afraid it might have come to this," Ibn Murad said, his eyes closed. "May God preserve him from evil and deliver him to safety."

Chapter 22

The Citadel

Ibrahim and Mike returned to the gangsters' riad. They climbed onto the neighbor's roof to assess the situation, fearing they were too late. They could hear Samir talking with his men in the jail.

They didn't have to wait long before Samir and his men brought Khalid out of the dungeon into the courtyard, his hands and feet shackled. They had dressed him in a prisoner's loincloth, like the prisoners Ibrahim had seen being led through the medina. Samir's men pushed him onto a donkey cart and made him step into a large burlap bag, which they pulled over his head. They tied the opening with rope and made him lie down between two other bags. Samir opened the back gate, and the cart rolled out of the courtyard.

Ibrahim and Mike scrambled down from the roof to follow. They kept a safe distance, moving along the alleys and roads behind the cart. The cart made its way to the northern wall of the medina, then to a great stone building set on a higher elevation, just outside the city's fortified walls. Torchlight blazed at the front gate, where two men stood guard. One of the guards spoke to the cart driver and went through a small opening in the prison door. Within moments, the double doors opened, and the cart disappeared inside. Ibrahim and Mike waited in the shadows, their thoughts on

Khalid and his fate. After a while, the cart reappeared. The guards questioned nothing, waving the driver along.

The two men hurried back to the gangsters' riad, hoping to get there before the cart returned.

"Badr, can you hear us?" Ibrahim asked, whispering into the cell from the window opening. "It's Ibrahim and Mike."

"Yes, young men," Badr said, his voice weakened. "I am still here in this world, though I believe it will not be for long. Did you find Ibn Murad?"

"We did, but he says he can't move the sunduq. If he were to do so, everyone would know where it is, and that would be a greater risk. He prays for you, and we told him that you are keeping the secret courageously."

"I swore to protect this wealth, even in the face of death. I, like all the clerks before me, have taken this oath. And I will fulfill it to the end. But I fear that if they don't get the secret from me, they will try to capture him. And what a catastrophe if they succeed." After a few moments of silence, Badr moaned, then said, "God willing, I will be released from this hell, and soon. Now go, before Nimr comes to pay me a visit, *fi aman Illah,*" he said, committing them to God's care. They answered his blessing and left.

Khalid could not imagine how anyone could survive in such a place. He thought the gangsters' jail was bad, but the Citadel was much worse. With his one free hand, his right, he managed to keep the flies out of his mouth and eyes. He crouched against the wall on the hay-covered floor and watched the rats saunter past. The smell of urine and feces was so overpowering he'd blocked his nose with his arm. He'd only been in the Citadel for a few hours, but he doubted he had the stamina to survive for long.

Not a word had been spoken to him since he'd left the gangster's cell. Once inside the prison, Samir had let him out of the burlap bag. Before him stood a tall man with a ruby ring that blazed in the torchlight. The man gasped in astonishment when he saw Khalid's face. "It is indeed quite remarkable. He could be his brother. The master will be amused."

They led Khalid down a series of dark hallways, passing no guards. They stopped at the doorway of a cell where a prisoner sat against the wall, where his left arm was chained. When he looked up, Khalid was shocked, for it was as if he was seeing himself. There was no doubt who it was. Nimr stood and smiled as he held out his shackled arm. The man unlocked Nimr's arm and put Khalid's in its place.

"You are my long-lost brother, it seems," Nimr said to Khalid. "And now you're going to rot in prison, a pity. Perhaps, someday, when I am ruler of this place, I will find a use for you. That is, if you survive. You look rather weak to me. Believe me, you will not grow strong on the food here. So good luck to you, my dear brother." The cell door shut, and they were gone.

Khalid said nothing, still in shock that the transfer had taken place so easily. He wondered how many people had been paid off. He listened to the night sounds of the prison. Men snored and moaned, and some spoke, either in their sleep or from insanity. Who wouldn't go crazy here, he wondered.

Hours later, someone carrying a lantern approached his cell, and two men opened its door. A black man entered and glared at him, then placed a wooden bowl of some kind of soup in front of him, along with a tin cup of water. He had bruises on his wrists and arms, and the sleeves of his robe were torn.

Behind him, a man with the lantern stood back, observing, as the black man backed toward the door, still staring at Khalid. The boss was better dressed, in a gray robe, and he had a simple black turban on his head.

"I'm not Nimr," Khalid said. "They've switched me for him."

The black man's eyes grew wide as he paused for a moment. Then he looked down and continued backing up.

"Silence!" the boss said. "Or perhaps you enjoy lashings." Khalid shook his head. "I thought not. Keep your mouth shut then. Not one word." The men left and Khalid brought the bowl to his lips and spat it out. It tasted of filth. He smelled the tin cup of water and took a small sip.

"You are worthless, worthless, do you hear me?" Nimr said. Badr laid on his side, his robes in tatters, as an infectious fever raged through his body. Khalid had tried to bandage Badr's hand through the bars, using fabric he tore from his own clothes, but Badr knew that God would take him soon, no matter what Nimr did to him.

"You think you're some kind of noble servant. No, you're not. You're a filthy nobody, and you're going to tell me where that sunduq is." Badr was too weak to respond. "Samir, you're an idiot. You've ruined him. Now he's dying, and he can't even talk. He's worthless to us now. I'm through with this dog. Get rid of him."

"But he's a servant of Qarawiyyin. You can't just..."

"Yes, I can. It doesn't matter who he is. Just finish him off."

It was a mercy from God that the Samir's men left for a few minutes, for Badr's infection ran its course before they came back for him. He lay alone in his cell, feeling his heart race, while his eyes burned, and his limbs throbbed. He prayed for both release and forgiveness as he struggled for his last breaths. Then he knew he had to give in, consigning his soul to the Almighty in prayer. With tears streaming down his face, he prayed out loud at first, and then silently. Over and over, he said the prayer he had learned from the imam for ministering to someone facing death. "O God, forgive me my sins and cleanse my spirit and bring me into Thy presence." At some point, the pain lifted away, and he let himself slip into unconsciousness. It was not long after that his spirit floated out of the prison over the city, and he could see his beloved Qarawiyyin in the starlight.

Samir's men put his body in a burlap bag, loaded him on the mule cart and, once the gates of the city were opened, took him out of Fez and buried him in a village cemetery that held most of Nimr's victims.

As the sun rose, Nimr stood at his window, gazing over the courtyard and beyond, to the city glowing yellow, savoring his regained freedom. All those months in prison, he'd begun to accept the possibility that he would never see the sunrise again, that he would die in prison at the whim of the Sultan, as his father had before him. Or perhaps the Sultan would exile him to the desert like his grandfather, never to return to his beloved Fez. But now, thanks to his mysterious twin brother, he had the treasury of Qarawiyyin and control of the city nearly within his grasp. After that, given his allies within the palace, he could conceivably become Sultan, the very embodiment of Fez itself. And he would never be imprisoned or exiled again.

Most importantly, his name, Nimr al-Anmash, would go down in history. He would become a legend of Fez. His descendants would be the proud scions of a respected lineage. His thoughts returned to his young son, living in safety, hidden in a mountain village with his wife, Safia. One day, he vowed, his son would return to Fez in splendor, and his own legacy would be assured.

Chapter 23

Something Just Clicked

"Please come to my office. I'd like to speak with you for a few moments." Dr. Charles had been running this Arabic program for three years, and he had only recently begun to feel that he'd tailored the program to his satisfaction. And now this had happened.

After closing the office door, Dr. Charles told Mike to sit down and said, "We've got a problem. And I want you to be completely honest with me. If you are, there won't be any trouble," he said, pacing on a tribal carpet behind his desk. "How did you do it?"

"Do what, Sir?" Mike asked, realizing what the meeting was about. This wasn't the first time he'd done something unexpected, so far out of the usual that he had been suspected of wrongdoing. Like the time he'd composed a jazz suite in high school and the teacher accused him of plagiarizing. And when he'd written an essay about Sufism in college that the professor suggested he'd copied from an old text.

Dr. Charles stopped pacing. "You know what I'm talking about. Yesterday's test." He handed the test papers to Mike. "How did you suddenly ace it? Until now, you've been getting straight Cs and Ds on every quiz. Who helped you cheat? I won't tolerate this in my program."

Mike glanced at the A+ written on the top sheet, then to Dr. Charles, whose eyes demanded an answer. What could he say? Even he couldn't explain it.

"Something just clicked," he said, which, in a way, was true.

"Something just *clicked?* Well, I'm glad to hear that. And I'm going to let you prove it. I have another test for you. Take this one, right now." He handed Mike a piece of paper and pencil.

Mike read over the questions first. Once again, he knew every answer. Yet he could tell there was material on this test that hadn't been covered in their classes yet. He wrote his answers slowly in his old childlike script. To further allay Dr. Charles' suspicions, he made two subtle mistakes that a non-native speaker might make. He took his time reading over his answers and corrected some. Then, with a calculated look of doubt on his face, he handed the paper back.

Dr. Charles made Mike wait while he read through each answer. When he discovered Mike's mistakes, he smiled, then forced the smile into a frown. He laid the paper down and braced his hands against his desk, looking up at Mike. "Not perfect, but excellent indeed. I apologize for my suspicions, but I hope you understand."

"Of course, Sir," Mike said, wondering where this was going to lead.

"I'd like you to meet with your teacher and me today after lunch. We must discover how you have reached this breakthrough, since it's truly spectacular."

Dr. Charles' mind was filled with the ramifications of Mike's success. If he could develop a system that would duplicate his improvement, he'd be famous. "The Khamis Method" would revolutionize Arabic teaching and maybe other languages as well. Like many Arabic teachers, he dreamed of a breakthrough that would ease the process of learning the language.

"I hear you've been absent a lot these last few days and nights," Dr. Charles said. "Off having adventures at all hours with Ibrahim, I understand. From now on, stay with the group more. Part of this program's process is group study and group learning. We need you to be fully present and well rested. Need I remind you that parts of Fez are dangerous? Be careful—even Ibrahim has limits." As he walked Mike out of his office, Dr. Charles said, "And I hope you won't mind that we'll be videotaping you in class so we can document your dramatic improvement."

Chapter 24

The Guilds

"Don't worry about Dr. Charles. I'll make sure you don't get in trouble," Ibrahim said as he and Mike crossed under the arch into the past. They walked onto the main thoroughfare, strolling along as if they had nothing better to do but go for a walk.

A commotion drew them into a small side street. Men were shouting and women were screaming. Ibrahim thought a fire had broken out, so they started running toward the sounds, only to find a crowd gathered below the body of a burly man who was hanging from a rope tied to a beam that crossed the street. His hands were tied behind his back, and a man was cutting the rope to lower him to the street. Women wept.

"What happened?" Ibrahim asked a young man whose eyes were filled with fear.

"Nimr al-Anmash's men," said a coarsely featured, unveiled woman who took in the scene with a greedy curiosity. "Couldn't pay back his debts, so they made an example of him, right in front of his own family. They only left five minutes ago. God curse them and their cruel ways."

Ibrahim tasted bile in his mouth as he fought back nausea. The woman said, "They took his wife and children, and they'll make slaves out of them. That's what they always do, sons of dogs. They've left his parents penniless. And, since they've confiscated their property, the old folks are without a home, too."

"But won't someone go to the police or the Sultan's men?" Mike asked.

"Whoever does that will be next," she said.

"Come away now," Ibrahim told Mike. "There's nothing we can do here."

"Won't someone bring Samir to court for murder?" Mike asked. "Don't they have courts or judges?"

"If it's anything like our time, no witnesses will come forward. And, without that, the judges can do nothing."

They walked on, climbing up the medina's sloping lanes. Ibrahim was desperate for ideas that might save Khalid, and he always thought more clearly when he walked. After a while, they started working their way back down the hill. They needed help, but they had nowhere to turn. The two of them were no match for powerful gangsters. They strolled through the side streets and alleys where craftsmen plied their trades. Just as in the modern day, the air was filled with the din of hammers and saws, and the clinking and clanking of tools on metal. There were blacksmiths, brass workers, wood turners, and weavers—all hard at work.

They came upon a blacksmith's workshop. Young men carried bundles of heavy iron rods and stacked them onto a cart. The men were strong and worked as a team without saying anything.

That's when Ibrahim had an idea. "Follow me," he said, "and don't say a word." Ibrahim led Mike deep into the backstreets with resolve until they reached a warren of carpenters' workshops.

Unbelievable," he said. "Carpenters still work in this same area in our time. And they're still one of the most powerful guilds. They organized a strike in the 1980s that shut down the medina, then spread to the entire city and paralyzed it for weeks."

As they explored the workshops, hammering and sawing filled the air. Ibrahim breathed in the smell of freshly cut cedar. His jaw dropped at the sight of logs of *thuya* wood stacked to the ceilings. In modern times, it had become so rare that the government kept strict control of its harvest.

In his work, Ibrahim was always judging men's characters. He scoured the market for someone who looked like they would be both trusting and trustworthy. He finally approached a man who had just concluded a deal with a wood supplier.

"Sir, can you please direct us to the head of the carpenter's guild?"

"Certainly. And do you know him?"

"No, but I need to ask his opinion on something. What is his name?"

"Kamal Abu Bashir. Follow me, Sir. I'll take you to him." Ibrahim was surprised at his genteel manner, more refined than the modern-day carpenters he'd met.

The man led them to a large carpentry shop at the back of the souq. It was teeming with men chiseling designs of leaves and arabesques into moldings that would later grace the city's elegant homes. Ibrahim thanked the man who had directed them and asked for Kamal.

One of the workers brought them deeper into the shop, leading them to a man who was examining some lengths of wood.

"Yes, that's me, who's asking?" Kamal had closed his fists on his hips, and from his height of over six feet, which towered above everyone in the room, he looked down with an undisguised smirk. Ibrahim remembered how badly his approach to the leather poof craftsman had gone, and he knew he would have to do better this time.

"We'd like to discuss some serious business," Ibrahim said. "Is there somewhere we can speak in private?"

"Serious business. Well, it better be, with you interrupting us all here," Kamal said, looking around the room at the carvers who had stopped working to listen. "Now back to work all of you, stop gawking!" He led them to the back of the shop and into a quiet side room, where he beckoned them to sit on a bench under an open window.

"You are head of the guild?" Ibrahim asked.

"Yes, I suppose you could say that."

"And are you aware that Nimr al-Anmash has escaped from prison?"

"How?" Kamal asked, his eyes glinting with alarm as he clenched his jaw.

"He replaced himself in prison with a double, who happens to be our friend. We also heard that Nimr and his men are planning a great robbery."

"And just who is bringing me this news, and what does he expect me to do about it? You look a bit familiar," Kamal said, "but you are definitely not from around here, are you? You look like you've been living in a cave for a few years. Not much muscle, yet no sign of refinement either."

"Please excuse my lack of manners. I am Ibrahim, and this is my friend Munir. As you guessed, we are visiting from abroad, from the east," Ibrahim said, hoping that would be enough detail. Did he really look that bad? He felt his biceps to make sure he had the muscles that were usually there.

"So, assuming you are telling the truth, which I don't necessarily believe, then what is it to me what Nimr does?"

"He's planning to take over the city. Would that matter to you?"

The guild master shut his eyes and clenched and unclenched his jaw. "Listen, and listen carefully. We do not interfere with him," he said. "Let me be more specific. We *cannot* interfere with him."

"But why?" Ibrahim asked. "They're common thugs! Just an hour ago we saw their handiwork—a hanging in the street."

"The man probably couldn't repay a debt," Kamal said. Ibrahim nodded, and the guild master said, "That is how they settle big debts. And I suppose they took the family and house in payment. We are powerless against them. They're squeezing the city into a vise. All we can do is make our payments and stay out of their way. We hope and pray for the day when he'll be defeated by God's own hand."

"But he must be stopped!"

"Stop him from what? He already controls much of the city. He'll take what he wants, whenever he wants."

"But what about the guild, and your business? How do you protect yourselves?"

"Simple," he said. "We pay, very dearly indeed, every month."

"What if they threatened the mosque, Qarawiyyin itself?" Ibrahim said.

Kamal lifted his gaze to Ibrahim for a long moment then said, "Even if they attacked the mosque, we could to nothing to stop them. We pray for God's help. The Sultan is weak, and we citizens have no means of fighting back. If we were to lose, our families, our livelihood, and our lives would be destroyed. We prefer to endure. Besides, as long as we can meet our payments, they leave us alone. It is a question of outlasting him. We've survived great plagues. Now, we're enduring this evil pestilence, knowing that the Almighty will end it. But until then, we are trapped and can do nothing."

He went on, "Whoever is sending you to inquire about this, tell them we are powerless. God alone is the Victor, and God alone can save us from these evil ones. And I advise you to watch out, for you never know who's in Nimr's pocket. Even in our own guild, I suspect several men are in league with them. But if you must ask around, I'll give you the names of some men who can be trusted."

Ibrahim took the names and tried the leather workers, the blacksmiths, the weavers, and the butchers. Each gave the same answer and warned the two men to hold their tongues about Nimr, that even speaking about him put them in danger.

Having been rejected at each guild, the two men walked back toward the arch as the city grew dark. Mike swore he saw the donkey laden with gold jewelry again, and he shook his head to get the vision out of his mind by thinking of supper back at the riad.

A man stepped out of the shadows and spoke to them, saying "Follow me." The fellow turned down a side street, and Ibrahim and Mike followed. Behind them, Hameed, who had been trailing the two men all afternoon, followed the followers.

Chapter 25

The Sons of Fez

Ibrahim weighed the possibility that the man might be from Samir's gang, but they had to take the risk, and if he began leading them toward Samir's lair, they could always run. Before long, though, Ibrahim's apprehension grew as he lost his bearings. Owing to his many visits to Fez, he believed he could always find his way based on the way the streets ran along the city's many hills. But that night, he became completely lost.

A few minutes after Ibrahim gave up trying to orient himself, the man led them into a small square and knocked on a wooden door that was carved with eight pointed stars and crescent moons and decorated with gleaming brass studs. An old man carrying a candle answered, and he gestured for them to enter. No words were spoken as he led them along a low-ceilinged hallway that opened onto a large carpeted room, where about fifty men sat cross-legged in a circle lit by a few candle lanterns. Without a word, they made room in the circle for the newcomers.

Ibrahim found several familiar faces; guildsmen they'd spoken to earlier, including Kamal, head of the carpenter's guild. Most of the men had their eyes shut, as if in meditation, but Kamal looked Ibrahim in the eye and squinted at him, as if trying to bore into his soul. He was clearly suspicious.

Ibrahim and Mike joined the meditation. After a few minutes, Ibrahim grew calmer, noticing his pulse and breathing had slowed. Mike nearly fell asleep, he was so relaxed.

Someone spoke. "We welcome you to our brotherhood." Ibrahim opened his eyes to search for the speaker. He was a middle-aged man, dressed as the others, in black robes and a dark green turban.

"Thank you," Ibrahim said. He introduced them both to the group.

"Do you know who we are?" the man asked.

"No, not at all."

The man smiled. "That is as it should be, for we are a secret brotherhood, the Sons of Fez. This is our gathering place, our *zawia*. To all but our brothers here, it does not exist. My name is Hamza, and I am the mu`allim, the leader of the group."

A Sufi order, Ibrahim thought, wondering if they could stand up to a gang.

"You have news of a threat against Qarawiyyin. You may speak freely here. Please, tell us what is happening."

Ibrahim told them of Nimr's plan, and that Ibn Murad had been warned that he was in danger, but chose to leave things in God's hands. And that the guilds had said they could do nothing.

"Tell me, young man, do you have a plan to stop the robbery?"

"No, Sir. We do not."

"And it is the two of you against the gangster Nimr al-Anmash?"

"Yes, but until this moment we were the only ones who knew of their plot. Except for Ibn Murad, of course." He declined to mention Moustapha, in case they took a dim view of djinn.

Hamza waited a moment for Ibrahim to add more, but when he didn't, Hamza said, "If you wouldn't mind leaving us for a few minutes. Please wait in the next room."

"So these guys are Sufis?" Mike asked, as he and Ibrahim sat in a cushioned alcove in the hallway.

"Yes. I've never heard of this order, but Morocco has always been home to many mystics."

"A secret Sufi order, wow." Then, remembering the seriousness of the situation, Mike said, "If they're Sufis, that means we can trust them, right?"

"We don't have much choice. Now they're probably deciding whether to help us. And if they don't, we'll be out on our ears, right back where we started. Even if they do want to help, I wonder how a group of Sufis can possibly go up against such a nasty gang." Ibrahim said, thinking of the modern-day Sufis he knew in Morocco. They lived quiet lives, apart from politics. Some, like his uncle, spent months in solitary meditation. But then he remembered that in ages past, some Sufi groups wielded great power behind the scenes and even led rebellions.

One of the younger men appeared and led them back to the main room. They took their places in the circle.

Hamza said, "This crime against Qarawiyyin must be stopped. If you agree to keep our identities and our very existence secret, we will help."

"Agreed," Ibrahim and Mike said.

"Good. Then let me introduce you to our brothers." Each man came from one of the city's many guilds, and by the time all the men were introduced, Ibrahim couldn't think of a single guild or trade that wasn't represented. He began to have hope, for these men had knowledge of practical affairs, not just contemplation. If only they could come up with a plan.

"Spend the evening with us," Hamza said. "We will dine later, but first we will partake of the spirit and ask for guidance."

With the mention of food, Ibrahim realized he was hungry, and he wished they would eat first and meditate later.

"Please follow along with us, as you wish, and God willing, we will find answers."

The circle of men closed their eyes. After a few minutes of silence, Ibrahim heard the men rustling around and opened one eye. Several of them were holding frame drums of various sizes and were settling back into the circle. They placed the drums face down on the ground in front of them. The sheikh began to chant, "*Allah hai, Allah hai,* God is alive, God is alive, exhaling hard on the 'h' of *hai.*" Everyone began to repeat it in unison. They took a deep breath between each repetition and leaned to the right then left as .one

Ibrahim grew light-headed. He was only half-aware of the frame drums picking up the rhythm. The men stopped chanting, but they kept swaying from side to side as the rhythm sped up. Ibrahim got so dizzy he leaned back and collapsed. Two men moved him onto a row of cushions along the wall. Meanwhile, the others kept on. They stopped only to return to quiet prayer and contemplation, before chanting again, using different phrases that praised God's power.

Mike was instantly caught up in the rhythm and the ritual. Someone handed him a frame drum and he joined in playing. He opened up his heart, and the spirit of the group and their devotion moved around and through him. He felt he was one of them, as if he had known them before. He had no worries about Ibrahim, who was, they told him, in a kind of contemplative trance.

In fitful dreams, Ibrahim relived the last few days. He heard Ibn Murad refuse to take action, Suhaila's tears, and saw Moustapha's wrinkled face. What was he supposed to do? His mind ran in circles. At last he fell into a deep sleep, and his anxious thoughts dissolved into nothingness. He woke when someone nudged his shoulder.

"Sir," a young man said. "It is time to eat." The young man offered him a cup of cool water. Ibrahim sat up and gulped it down.

The men made room for him at a long, low table that had materialized in the room while he was asleep. Though they didn't speak at all during the meal, Ibrahim felt drawn to these silent strangers. They ate like his grandparents used to when he was a child, dipping their right hands into the couscous and balling the food up in their fingers before popping it into their mouths. Mike was seemingly in his element, Ibrahim noted, having taken to this method of dining with ease.

The silence allowed Ibrahim to turn back to his thoughts. Laila and the boys were so far away—across the centuries and the continents. He never imagined he would be this far from home. In every journey, on every tour, he reached a point where he knew he was farthest from home, and, from that moment on, he was turning homeward. It was a strange law of the road that he'd discovered after leading so many tours. And even though he'd traveled seven centuries into the past, he sensed he still had to travel further before he could turn toward home.

He wished he could call Laila and explain everything, asking forgiveness for ignoring her calls and abandoning her during her pregnancy. Then he willed himself to leave his emotions behind, to focus on the task at hand.

After eating, the men sat back and drank mint tea. Between thoughtful silences, they proposed ideas. Some suggested confronting the imam and convincing him to let them move the treasure to safety. Others wanted to hunt down Nimr and return him to prison, revealing the plot to the Sultan. Through it all, Kamal kept pointing out that the risks were too great if their plans should fail, and that everyone knew how much corruption was found among the Sultan's own courtiers. Hamza insisted that above all, they had to preserve the secrecy of the brotherhood.

"We've got to talk about weaponry," one of the men said, and Hamza nodded for him to continue. "Our situation is not helpless in this regard. As swordsmith, I know how sharp the gangsters' blades are. They are professional fighters, and as we all know, heartless murderers. So if we get into a fight with them, you might think we're doomed. But we won't be. First, of course my brother and I will supply what blades we can. But each of us must also bring tools from our trades, and wield them as expertly as a sword. You, blacksmith, bring a heavy iron bar. Tailors, your sharpest scissors. And think of how to use them, God forbid, if you have to. Perhaps attach the scissor blades to a stick to make a spear. If you are summoned, bring your sharpest and most deadly tools. And use your wits! Take advantage of momentary opportunities, and above all rely on God's help. We are on the side of good here. God will aid us."

A silence followed, during which the men contemplated the odds that would be against them if they had to face an army of fighting swordsmen. Hopefully it wouldn't come to that.

In the end, they decided to monitor Samir's gang closely, so Hamza instructed the men to set up watches in various parts of the city. They were to rotate their watch hours so that no one at their shops would suspect anything was going on. Ibrahim and Mike were part of a group that would keep watch over the gangsters' house. Everyone was to stay put at their watch, and if anything happened, to alert the others immediately.

"Our strength is in our secrecy, our cleverness, and the element of surprise," Hamza said. "To summon us," he said to Ibrahim and Mike, "you need only do this." He pursed his lips and whistled a little phrase like a birdcall. "Our ears are everywhere in the market, and you will be heard. And, if you hear the whistle, meet at the back of the main prayer hall in the Qarawiyyin. Yet be discreet, and do not cause alarm among the people."

Kamal raised his hand and said, "These two newcomers, you've given them the most important job. Shouldn't *we* be the ones watching the gangsters?"

"While we are not an army," Hamza said, "We are a brotherhood and we work together. Since I am the mu`allim here, you'll follow my orders. That goes for everyone here, including you two," he said, nodding at Ibrahim and Mike. "If there is any news, give the signal. Otherwise, there is no need to move at all, stay at your watch positions. The most important thing is that we have our eyes and ears on everything. Also, do not bother the imam. He is a busy man, and unless we have a real and direct threat, leave him to his work."

Ibrahim and Mike waited outside Nimr's villa for two days, and nothing out of the ordinary happened. Mike could only join after lunch, for he had to go to classes each morning. Ibrahim had convinced Dr. Charles to allow Mike to accompany him on his market duties in the afternoons, to sharpen Mike's local dialect. He brought Ibrahim lunch each day. Two others from the order spelled them each evening, when Ibrahim and Mike would slip back through the arch, happy to get a hot shower, supper, and a cup of tea.

Chapter 26

A Haik and A Proof

Barbara and Maureen were quite aware of Mike's absences. A couple of times, he had entered the first morning class at the last moment, looking like he hadn't slept or showered. They discussed what he might be up to, disappearing with Ibrahim every afternoon in the souq.

When Maureen confronted Mike about it directly, he had an answer ready. "Ibrahim asked me to help him buy musical instruments. We're visiting various instrument makers, checking out the quality. I play them and give him my opinion. He's doing a lot of bargaining and says it's a new direction for his business back in the States, so it's taking a lot of time." He and Ibrahim had rehearsed this answer, assuming the other students would be curious.

Although at first they were satisfied with this answer, Barbara and Maureen grew doubtful. Mike never said anything about the instruments, and not one oud or drum entered the riad. At lunch each day, Mike ate his meal quickly, then disappeared upstairs and was out the door of the riad before the others had finished eating.

Barbara and Maureen planned to follow him, yet when the day came, Maureen told her to go ahead on her own. Maureen was suffering from her allergies, and the medications had made her sleepy.

Barbara dressed in a caftan, as she sometimes did, and went to classes. No one remarked on it. At lunch, she sat in a corner near the stairs that led to her room, and she excused herself before Mike usually did. Putting on a headscarf, she snuck out of the riad and waited for Mike. Just a few minutes later, he darted out the front door and turned down the alley, the very alley they were forbidden to visit. He was dressed simply in a light grey djellaba, with a white turban wound around his head. This wasn't the usual fancy garb he'd been wearing.

She walked to the corner and looked down the alley, surprised to see Mike having a conversation with the old beggar woman. She was standing up and talking to him, her back straight as if she were in perfect health. What was going on? He handed her a plastic bag, probably lunch, which she set on the ground. Then with a cloth bag slung over his shoulder, he walked with the old lady down the alley. She spoke with him in earnest, waving her arms and pointing fingers at him. Barbara couldn't understand what was happening, and her curiosity was only piqued further.

Barbara stepped out and walked behind them, keeping close to the alley wall, in case they turned around to see her. She slipped through the archway and moved ahead, just as Mike and the old woman reached the far end of the alley, still in animated conversation.

Fearing they would turn back and see her, Barbara hid herself, stepping into a doorway along the alley. She stood tight against the door frame which happened to be deep, and managed to push herself into the shade. Sure enough, she could hear the old woman coming back toward her. She was muttering something under her breath, and walked right past Barbara, unaware of her presence.

Barbara stayed there for a minute, then slowly peeked down the alley toward the arch. The old woman had sat down in her usual place. She was devouring the food Mike had brought her. She was facing away, with her back to the alley, still muttering between bites. So Barbara took a chance and stepped back out into the alley. She had to hurry if she was to catch up with Mike.

She made it to the end of the alley, but didn't know which way to turn. She would have to take a guess. Well, usually, when she went to the market, she went uphill. That was where all the shops were, since the riad was downhill from a lot of the major sites. So she turned left and started walking, looking for Mike.

She sensed she was in a strange neighborhood, an enclave of some kind. The men dressed like Mike, and the women wore the old fashioned white haik, drawn around their bodies like an over-the-head shawl, some holding the edges with their teeth to cover their faces.

For some reason, her own costume started to attract attention. Men stopped to watch her pass, and one woman, with two children in tow, jerked her head in shock when she saw Barbara. She stood still, grabbed her children, and turned their heads into her skirts as Barbara passed. *Wow, this must be a really conservative place*, Barbara thought. What was wrong with her outfit? It was a modest, violet-colored caftan, and her headscarf was a deep purple. Nothing was showing at all. She stopped to adjust her scarf, so that the ends covered her chest, and continued on, looking everywhere for Mike.

"She's a stranger, that's for sure," said a merchant sitting on a bench outside his shop of brass trays. "Maybe she's from the Frankish countries."

"Ah yes, but even in that northern country, isn't it wonderful how palm trees sway gracefully." The two men laughed.

Barbara was angry at their comments, but then she came to the same realization that Mike had when he first crossed under the arch. She understood every word! Even the nuance of what the second man had said. Yes, he had objectified her, but it was a compliment to her gracefulness.

She kept walking uphill, and she started to take in the smells, sounds, and the talk of the people around her. *This is the most incredible part of Fez I've seen yet*, she thought. Resigning herself to having lost Mike, she turned down a quiet alley where bolts of fabric were leaning against the wall outside some shops. She paused before each shop, delighted by the unusual fabrics. There were woven cottons with fantastic stripes, and they were all, she was sure, in natural dyes. The merchants stared at her, and she ignored their reactions, assuming they weren't used to seeing foreigners in this part of town. She nodded to them in silence, not wanting to upset them.

A woman was on duty in one shop, so Barbara greeted her. "Good afternoon, Ma'am," she said in her best attempt to be polite, while using her local dialect.

"And to you, my lady. What brings a Frankish woman out on the street alone like this?"

"Is it taboo for me to be here alone?" *How did my words flow out so easily*, she wondered, *and how did I know the right word for taboo?*

"Excuse me for saying this, my lady, but yes, it is not correct, except for in the morning when women do their market rounds. And then, they are always chaperoned. In the afternoons, ladies of Fez rest at home. I think you must be new to our city."

"Yes, I am a student here, learning your language and culture."

"A Frankish woman studying here? Well, that *is* a wonder. If there is anything I can help you with, I'm at your service. My name is Lalla Maha."

"And I am Barbara, er, Basma. May I ask, are these fabrics woven here?"

"Of course, my dear Basma," she said. "My family weaves all our fabrics, and we ladies do embroidery, too."

Next time she would bring Maureen, who would go wild for these fabrics. She longed to linger, but she started to feel uncomfortable when the woman said, "Now, if there is nothing further, I suggest you return home. Come back with a chaperone. It is not fitting for one like yourself to be out unaccompanied. In fact, wear this haik. I have an extra. We ladies must be modest."

Maha proceeded to envelop Barbara in a traditional haik. She began by folding the large rectangle of white cotton around Barbara's waist, creating two bunches of fabric, one on each side of her waist, then tying a cord to each bunch and hanging the cord behind her neck. She wrapped the rest of the fabric around Barbara's head and pulled it around front to cover her completely. Then she showed Barbara how to hold it close—Barbara was not about to hold it in her teeth.

Feeling embarrassed and duly reprimanded, Barbara retraced her steps back to the corner of the alleyway. She marveled in the strangeness of the neighborhood, and the outfit she was wearing. She looked forward to bringing Maureen there soon.

Barbara walked toward the archway, noticing that the old woman was asleep, her head resting on her chest, her breathing slow and regular. Barbara did not want to disturb her, so she slowed down as she got close to the archway.

Just then, Barbara had to sneeze. She tried to stifle it and managed to let out only a dainty "choo!" But it was enough to wake the old woman, whose head jerked up.

"Noooooo!" the old woman jumped up and yelled in a decidedly masculine voice. "Human female, step back. You cannot approach here. This place is forbidden." And she started to grow taller, her arms getting longer and reaching out beyond the sleeves of her old pink caftan.

Barbara said, barely able to get the words out, "But I'm a student at the riad. I need to go to my room."

"You're a *what?*" the old lady said, more in a growl than a voice. "Who are you? What are you doing here?"

"I'm Barbara O'Neill, and I'm studying at Dar Surour. I was just out for a walk after lunch."

"How did you get past me?"

"You were talking with Mike. I was going to walk with him…"

"You mean you were trying to follow him, don't you?"

"Well, yes. I suppose I was."

Moustapha reached out and grabbed Barbara by the arm, gripping her hard with his enlarged hands. He pulled her forward through the arch and pushed her along, then stood blocking the archway.

"Oww!" Barbara yelled. She managed to recover her balance, and, when she turned back, the old woman had returned to her normal size and was sitting on her usual piece of cardboard box.

"Sit down, right now," the old woman said. "You're in a lot of trouble. Right *now*, I said." She thumped her fist on a spot next to her on the cardboard.

Barbara sat down.

"Where did you get that haik?"

"A woman gave it to me."

"And her name?"

"Maha. Her family are weavers and cloth merchants."

"I suppose you created a scene, being dressed as you were back there."

"Well, a little bit, but the streets were quiet."

"And thank heaven for that."

Barbara didn't know what to say. Who was this old woman? What was happening? A few moments ago, she'd looked more like an ogre from an old folktale, with a booming voice and her hairy arms grabbing and shoving.

"So, Miss Barbara. Did you notice anything unusual there, in that neighborhood?"

"Well, it was conservative. Even dressed in my caftan and head scarf, they acted like I was being immodest. The most remarkable thing was that I understood every single word they said. And not only that, I could speak *darija* quite fluently."

"I see," the old lady said. "Listen, young woman. Things are not as they seem here in this alley, and that is why you were told not to venture here. This is serious business. You must never return here, never go down this alley again."

"But what about Mike? Why does he get to go there?"

The old woman started speaking like an ogre again, "No, listen to me. You. Will. Not. Go. There. Again."

"Peace be upon you." Neither Moustapha nor Barbara had noticed that a local woman had come right up to them and was standing over them. Barbara shaded her eyes to block out the sun so she could get a look at her. The woman looked familiar, but she couldn't place her at first. She was wearing a striking turquoise caftan and a matching headscarf tied up artfully like a turban.

"And upon you be peace," Moustapha answered.

"Are you all right? Is this foreigner bothering you?" the Moroccan woman said.

"What do you mean, bothering her?" Barbara asked, again she was amazed at her newfound language ability.

"You speak Darija?" the woman in blue asked, standing back in shock. It wasn't just Barbara's words that surprised her, but her Fezzi accent.

"Well, there are words coming out of my mouth, aren't there?" Right away, woman in blue started laughing.

Barbara assumed she had said something wrong, which was her usual experience. But the woman smiled and shook her head. "Sorry to laugh, it's just that you sound exactly like my aunt. How did you learn to speak our dialect so well?"

Before Barbara could answer, they heard a snarling noise coming down the alley from the modern side toward the arch. It was some kind of huge dog, galloping with its mouth open, showing two rows of huge white teeth.

The woman in blue screamed and hid her face with her arms. Barbara jumped up, and they ended up hugging each other. "I'm so afraid of dogs," the woman in blue said. Barbara pulled her in closer and backed them both up to the wall.

"Halt!" Moustapha yelled, standing up in front of the creature. It slid to a stop in front of him, then crouched while lolling its head from side to side, snapping its jaws.

"You're not going through. Not now, not ever."

The dog growled, crouched lower, then jumped right over Moustapha's head and ran through the arch.

"Nooooo!" Moustapha yelled, running after it half-way down the alley. By that time, it had turned the corner and was gone. Moustapha shook his head and walked back, muttering, "What a bad dog. That horrible creature never heels, never obeys. What a mess I'm in." All this, he said in his male voice.

"Who are you? Human or djinn? Male or female?" the woman in blue asked. She was no longer afraid, but standing tall, hands on her hips. Barbara remembered her just then, from the gnawa night when Mike was in a trance, she was the one who commanded the spirit to leave him. She was showing that same air of authority, even though she was afraid of dogs.

"Moustapha of the Mountain, I am called. And yes, I am a djinn. And you, I have seen you before at the riad."

"I am Shafiqa. Indeed, I came here when there was a gnawa lila, and there was trouble with one of the students. But what are you doing here, er, Moustapha of the Mountain? Why are you in this alleyway, dressed like an old beggar woman, yelling at this American woman?" She looked at Barbara and said, "Sorry, I don't know your name."

"Barbara."

"As I was saying, why were you bothering Barbara? I came down the alley because I thought she was bothering you, and in fact it was just the opposite. Spirit, answer me, I demand it. And tell the truth."

"The truth?"

"Yes, I commanded you tell the truth."

"Then sit down, both of you, and listen. Now that you have demanded the truth, I will tell you both. For Barbara here has discovered it through her own curiosity. And you have commanded, demanded—or whatever you did just now—and I must answer in truth."

The two women sat down, their eyes boring into Moustapha's face as he looked straight ahead.

"As I said, I am a djinn of the male persuasion. The Powers that Be have assigned me to watch this arch, to keep all humans on the side of the arch where they belong. For on the other side of that archway is another time. It is the year 775 *hijri,* or 1374 to the Europeans. This arch must be destroyed, for the spirits—djinn, ogres, ghouls, and other devils—are trying to go through and cause trouble. The biggest problem is that the spirits from the past want to move to the present day and stay in this time. I cannot stop the spirits, as you have seen. My job is to keep the humans in their correct time."

"But Mike is there."

"And he's not the only one. Mike, Ibrahim, and one named Khalid are all in the past. I have to get them all back, and then we can destroy the arch. Until then, it is imperative to keep you here in your own time. Do not, under any circumstances, cross under the arch. Do you hear me?"

"Where are they?" Barbara asked. "Why don't they come back? I see Mike and Ibrahim every night at supper, but come to think of it, I haven't seen Khalid in days."

"It's a complicated story."

"Remember, now, the truth," Shafiqa said. She grew more suspicious as Moustapha told them about Khalid being held, about the gangster Nimr, and about the plot to rob the treasury.

"You do weave a fanciful tale, I will say that much," Shafiqa said. "And how can I even be sure you are telling the truth?"

"I can tell you," Barbara said. "It really is different over there. Everything is so quiet, and the people are dressed in a completely different way. And strangest of all, I became fluent in Arabic, just like that, in an instant, when I went through the arch. How could that happen?"

"Maybe you stumbled upon a conservative neighborhood. There are such places, in the back alleys here and there."

"But that doesn't explain..."

Shafiqa stood up. "*Djinni,* I don't believe you. So I am going to see for myself. Don't block my way. You know as well as I do that I have the right to walk as I wish, for I am human. You have no power over me." With that, she stood up and stepped under the arch, her head held high.

Barbara wondered whether the locals in that old neighborhood would bother her, being dressed like that, without a haik. Barbara stood and followed her under the arch. "Here, use this haik," she said, unwrapping the white cloth from around her shoulders.

"No, my dear, you keep it. I am dressed just fine." Barbara stood still, about to turn back, when Shafiqa added, "Why don't you come with me. I know just where to go to prove that the djinni here is lying." Barbara raised her eyebrows and stepped in with her. Together, they strode down the alley in the past, ignoring Moustapha's calls.

Shafiqa's confident stride soon slowed to a dazed walk. She was indeed shocked at what she saw, as she led Barbara toward the heart of old Fez, the Qarawiyyin Mosque. The moment she saw its outer wall, looking newer and with a grandeur that had faded by the 21st century, tears welled in her eyes. She stopped to feel the walls, and the two of them peered inside a window opening to see the faithful walking by on the same mosaic tiles Shafiqa had known all her life.

"But how is this possible, dear God? What is the meaning of it?"

Barbara said, "So you think it could be true?"

"Somehow, maybe it is. Dear God, help me understand this strange but beautiful scene before me."

The afternoon call to prayer began. Instead of the usual amplified voice, one muezzin with a rich baritone sang out in the most beautiful way, directly above them. Both women were stunned by the clarity of his voice. They looked up and could see the head of the muezzin leaning out of the minaret above them, his hands cupping his ears.

Barbara said, "Go ahead, go to prayers. I can wait over there." A stone bench sat in full view of the outer wall of the mosque. It was set in a small discreet alcove built right into the wall.

"Are you sure?" Shafiqa asked. Barbara nodded.

"I will never forget this kindness. I will come to you straightaway after prayers."

As Shafiqa walked away, Barbara sat down and pulled her haik close. She witnessed people from the past that she could never have imagined—men, women, and children streaming into the mosque for prayers. They were of all classes—from wealthy merchants to craftsmen and even servants. During prayers, everything was quiet in the streets, except for the chirping of some sparrows in a tree, the branches of which spilled over a nearby wall. No one joined Barbara on the bench, and, as the minutes passed, she felt more confident. Looking up three stories, she saw an old woman sitting at an open window gazing out over the skyline.

Shafiqa felt she was walking in a dream as she did her ablutions and joined the throng of women in their prayer hall. Tears streamed down her face as she moved as one with the others, bending, prostrating herself, greeting her neighbors with a nod. She wondered at the accent of the prayer leader, and in fact the accents of all of those around her. They spoke in the unique way that Fezzis do, but so archaic and antiquated. What if this really was the past? She was afraid to speak to anyone and remained silent as she absorbed everything around her. She prayed for wisdom and courage.

After prayers, Shafiqa found Barbara waiting for her, and, without a word, they walked back, carefully retracing their steps to the alley, where they found Moustapha at the alley corner. He waved to them, but acted the part of a beggar woman in case anyone was watching.

Once through the arch, they sat down again, and Shafiqa spoke.

"I owe you an apology. This is truly the most wondrous thing I could imagine, this arch."

"Wondrous, but it is also extremely dangerous and must be destroyed."

While the women were gone, Moustapha had decided that it might be better to recruit these two to help him, rather than fighting and arguing with them. He explained the situation to them, sparing no detail.

"Things are about to come to a head. And I may have to leave the arch for a while, so I could use some helpers. Would you be willing?" The women looked at each other and nodded. "Then you must swear not to let anyone else through the arch. And you must swear not to tell anyone else about it."

Both women agreed to help. Barbara would keep to her classes as usual, and they would both meet Moustapha after lunch.

As the two women returned to the road, Barbara turned to Shafiqa and said, "This whole situation is totally bizarre, isn't it?"

"I'll say it's bizarre," Shafiqa answered. Barbara started laughing.

"What's so funny?"

"You're speaking in English." Shafiqa stopped and cupped her hand over her mouth. Before that moment, she had never spoken a word of English in her life.

Khalid, meanwhile, was growing more anxious each day of his confinement, wondering what had happened to Ibrahim and Mike and whether the robbery had gone off as planned.

At night, the prisoners in the other cells talked in hushed voices, so as not to bring the guards. No one spoke to him, and he had kept silent, trying to learn as much as possible by listening. He assumed they all knew he was just a placeholder for the gangster, an unlucky nobody whose number had come up. He learned that Ibn al-Khatib, the scholar he'd heard lecture on the plague, had been jailed for heresy. The other prisoners said it was a political rival who had him jailed, and assumed that someone would eventually pay off the authorities to secure his release.

The bread was stale, and, if he was lucky, the watered-down stew they fed him once a day might have a small piece of meat in it. But Khalid forced himself to eat everything and to drink as much liquid as possible. Surprisingly, he didn't get sick. He also had enough strength to do a daily exercise routine, but he could feel himself growing weaker. The caloric intake was inadequate, and he'd soon be as skinny as the other prisoners he'd seen being walked past his cell in shackles.

Khalid began to doubt that he would ever get out of the prison and return to his own time. How would Ibrahim and Mike ever find him? For the first time in years, he began to pray, and to think about his life up to that point.

He thought about the time portal. Who had built it, and how could such a thing exist right in his own city? These musings always brought him back to his shame at having turned his back on learning while he was growing up. He vowed that, if he ever got home, he would continue his schooling. Ibn al-Khatib's lecture had lit a fire in his imagination. He realized that man's knowledge of science had changed the world. And now he had experienced time travel. If he had, how many others in Fez had done the same? Would he ever have a chance to find out?

Chapter 27

A Generous Tunisian Donor

"Excuse me, Sir. A believer from Tunis would like to speak to you. He says he wants to donate to the mosque." The eagerness in Amin's eyes hinted that this might be a man of great generosity. As second clerk to the imam, Amin had been working hard to fill the shoes of Badr, the chief clerk who was away on vacation.

"You may bring him to me," the imam said, rising from his favorite sunny reading spot in the courtyard. He was always pleased to accept donations on behalf of the Qarawiyyin, for donors supported not only the mosque itself, but the university and many poor families in the city. From its beginnings, the Qarawiyyin had relied on personal gifts, both large and small.

The imam sized up the two men as Amin led them over. There was the man who was likely the donor, more richly dressed, and another, perhaps his assistant. They were no doubt Tunisians, given the way they wrapped their black and white turbans. The wide sleeves of the donor's robe glistened with a sumptuous silken weave. He had the quick eyes of intelligence and a well-trimmed beard. His teeth gleamed in a wide smile that, for a moment, unnerved the imam. The man looked vaguely familiar; Ibn Murad decided he must have seen him at prayers.

"Peace be upon you, and the mercy and blessings of God," the imam said, bowing slightly, his right hand on his heart.

"And upon you, O Ibn Murad, servant of God."

"Please, join me in the office, where we can speak in private. Amin, can you arrange for some refreshment?"

"Yes of course, Sir," Amin said before hurrying away, his woolen cloak catching the air behind him like a cinnamon sail.

"So you are from Tunis, I'm told."

"Indeed. I have been here on business for some weeks, and, like many before me, I am deeply impressed with the Qarawiyyin."

The imam led the two men along the edge of the courtyard and beckoned them inside a small room that opened onto it. They sat with him on low cushions that ran along its walls. Leather-bound accounts and ledgers filled built-in bookshelves above them. A low wooden table along one wall groaned under more volumes.

"We welcome you here, Mr. ..."

"Naeem al-Tunisi, dealer in the carpets from the mosque's namesake city, Kairawan. I have concluded our business in Fez, and I wish to donate a portion of my profits to the mosque and university to support your great works."

"Praise God, we would be most grateful. It is generosity such as yours that keeps the Qarawiyyin going, and how fitting that your business links us with our founders' home city."

"Sir, if you don't mind, I want to get directly to the point. We would like to donate the sum of 10,000 riyals. We can bring it here as early as tomorrow if you wish. Unfortunately, our business affairs require us to make haste back to Tunis. We must leave the city in a few days, so time is of the essence."

The imam took a quick breath. This was a fantastic sum indeed. Not only would it fund the operations of the university for a year, plenty of money would be left over for other good works, and perhaps even a good contribution toward fixing a section of the mosque's roof. Yet he had a problem—only he and Badr knew the location of the treasury. This sum of money would require additional help. It had to be counted and moved to safety.

The imam said, "And how would you bring the funds to the mosque?"

"My men and I will bring it here in a wooden chest, which you can keep if that is easier."

The imam readily assented, and the men agreed to return the next day with the donation. Amin returned with a servant who served them a sweetened lemon drink, and the men conversed amiably. The imam enjoyed hearing his visitor's impressions of his journey and news of the community of Kairawan.

That night, the imam hardly slept, praying for Badr: for a miracle, and for his courage. He was such an upright young man. The imam hated the thought of him being tortured. But he told no one of his predicament, for the mosque always maintained its independence, and he was not willing to risk losing that. This was a matter that stretched generations into the past, and, God willing, it would continue long into the future.

The next morning, the imam drafted Amin to help him with the transaction. They would take the donation to the treasury and would take care of counting it later. Ibn Murad acknowledged that it had been foolish not to allow Amin to be more involved in the treasury operations before this. But the most important thing was to get the funds into the safety of the treasury, as a sum of money that great would be a temptation to every gang of robbers in the city.

As soon as the markets opened, Ibn Murad had Amin check out the donor's story. And indeed, at the carpet market there had been a new shipment of Kairawan carpets sold by one Naeem al-Tunisi, who matched the description of the man who had visited them.

When the day progressed and the men did not return to the mosque, the imam began to wonder if they had changed their mind. It wasn't until an hour or so before sunset that Amin led the two donors and their men back to the office. The men accompanying the donors carried a large wooden trunk with long handles. With each step, they struggled under the trunk's weight.

"Please excuse our tardiness; we were detained in the market. If it's possible, we would like to take care of the transaction, then we would be honored to join you for the sunset prayers."

"Of course," the imam said, welcoming them once more. The men deposited the trunk in the middle of the room. The trunk being so heavy, he realized it would be impossible for him and Amin to move it to the treasury.

"Our chief clerk is absent at this time, so I'm afraid I cannot even count your generous donation. We will have to take care of that when he returns."

"But Sir, at least we would like you to see the riyals, so that you know we are men of good faith."

"Of course, certainly."

Naeem unlocked the top of the wooden chest and lifted its lid. It was filled nearly to the top with gleaming silver riyal coins. With his right hand, Naeem scooped up a handful and let them slip through his fingers.

"Your generosity is beyond anything we have experienced here in many years, Sir," the imam said. Naeem scooped up another handful of the coins, and they made a delightful clinking sound as they fell back into the trunk.

The imam had been mentally weighing the risks, and he made a decision. "If you don't mind, we're short staffed and would appreciate it if your men could help us deliver the chest to our treasury. I rely on your utter discretion of course."

Naeem smiled. "I am a trusted confidant of our governor, and I can assure you that your trust in me is well-placed. However, I do not want to put you in an awkward position." He was silent for a few moments, gazing out in the courtyard. "My assistant and I have no need to accompany you. We can wait here. If you lead them, my men can be blindfolded. That way, no one among us will learn the location of the treasury."

The imam and Amin led the two men carrying the chest through the back streets of Fez. As agreed, some distance from the mosque, Amin tied blindfolds on them. Passersby didn't notice, because they pulled the voluminous hoods of their burnooses down over their faces. And the trunk itself was disguised as a load of fabric. Naeem and his assistant had been instrumental in helping with the disguise, telling the imam that, in commerce, one often had to create such illusions for secrecy.

Ibn Murad led the way. When they arrived at a door that looked like it led to an ordinary household, he had them stop while he unlocked it. Once inside, the imam lit a lantern and led them across a small courtyard that led to another locked door, which he unlocked. They walked downstairs, then along a long hallway before climbing another set of stairs, only then arriving at the treasury room itself. The men carrying the trunk were sweating, but they didn't complain.

"Here, you may leave the trunk right here," the imam said. The trunk bearers remained blindfolded, but Amin's eyes grew large at the sight of the treasury. Generations of donors had given all manner of riches. There were stacks of wooden crates and precious leather boxes, as well as a mountain of vellum documents tied in scrolls, and rows of small burlap bags that appeared to hold gold and silver coins.

They returned to the mosque, and the donor and his men stood in the front row at the sunset prayer. After bidding the men farewell, the imam returned to the office to take a simple meal and rest before the early evening prayer. Something glinted on the floor in front of him as he entered with his lantern. It was a few coins that Naeem must have dropped. The imam held one up to the light. Something wasn't quite right. Looking at it more closely, he saw a large chip in the silver, with copper underneath showing through. His heart beat faster as he turned it over. It was some kind of counterfeit, a silver coating with mere copper underneath. In that instant, he knew he'd been duped.

He stood up and shouted, "Amin! Come quickly!"

Chapter 28

Tools of Their Trades

"Something's not right," Ibrahim said. "We've been here for hours and haven't seen any sign of movement. I know we're supposed to stay and keep watch here, but something is going on, and it's not happening here." The sun dipped behind the hills, and the call to the sunset prayer rose around them from a dozen mosques.

Since morning, Ibrahim, and later Mike, had been watching the front entrance and side alley of the gangster's house. Disguised as poor men from the countryside, no one paid them any mind as the hours passed.

As the evening fell, Shafiqa approached the two men. Moustapha had asked her to make daily walks to check on the lookout.

She was about to pass by them when they heard the signal. At first it was far away, then it grew closer. Noting their reactions to the sound, Shafiqa withdrew to a safe distance, but within earshot. She watched as one of the younger members of the Sons of Fez found them. "Nimr and Samir," he said, trying to catch his breath, "they've been seen at Qarawiyyin. Something's going, on and we're all to meet there."

As they started down the hill toward the mosque, Shafiqa following discreetly, listening as the young man explained that one of the guildsmen had seen two men carrying a heavy trunk out of the souq. They were disguised and dressed like Tunisians, but when they spoke, he recognized their voices. He had followed them to the mosque and raised the alarm.

At that point, Ibrahim, Mike and the guildsman sprinted to the mosque while Shafiqa made her way back to the arch to tell Moustapha.

At the Qarawiyyin, Ibrahim and Mike knelt down on the carpet in the last row, still out of breath. Inside, nothing seemed amiss. The imam led prayers as usual, and, at the end, he greeted some members of the congregation.

One by one, the Sons of Fez gathered on the carpet under a designated keyhole arch, posing as a study group. Kamal's eyes blazed as he sat down. He said to Ibrahim through clenched teeth, "And you never saw them leave their place?"

"No, nothing happened at all. They must have left early in the morning."

Just then, the imam hurried by, followed by another man who was trying to keep up. Ibn Murad frowned as he strode, leaning forward like a ship sailing into battle.

"Let's follow him," Ibrahim said, standing up.

"But the *mu`allim* told us told us to leave him alone," Kamal said. "And what if nothing has happened yet?"

"If we keep our distance, he won't even notice us. Think of the alternative—what if there is something happening, and we do nothing? Then who will answer to the wrath of the mu`allim, and the entire city?"

Resigned to Ibrahim's logic, Kamal organized the men to follow at a discrete distance in groups of two and three; the dusk gave them cover.

Ibrahim walked in front with Mike and Kamal. In the lamplight and firelight, they watched the imam shake his head and wave his right hand as he spoke to his friend, who didn't appear to be older than twenty.

The men in front kept the imam and his companion in sight, signaling the others to stop when the two men paused at a corner. Ibrahim and Kamal snuck up close enough to hear them.

"God help and deliver us," the imam said, gripping the wall and holding his head up as if he were about to faint. "They've got two guards out front. God knows what's going on inside. And we are defenseless. It was my mistake, taking them there. God forgive me, this is my fault. I should have listened to the warnings. They were right."

"Warnings from whom?"

"Two young men warned me, and I ignored them. Now we need help."

"Sir, we are here to help," Ibrahim said, stepping forward to stop them. "It's me, Ibrahim, the one who came to you."

Amin jumped in surprise, and his eyes grew wide. "You've been following us? Who do you think you are?"

The imam took his arm. "No, it's all right. Praise God you are here. I was wrong to ignore your warning. But how can you help, you are only two or three? How can you stand up to these thugs?"

"We are a dozen at the moment, and we can muster many more."

Ibrahim waved the others to come forward so they could be seen. The imam explained what happened; how he had been duped by two men pretending to be generous believers from Kairawan. "And now, around this corner and down the street, two of their men are guarding what was until now the secret entrance to the treasury of the Qarawiyyin. God help us, the thieves must be inside right now, robbing the treasury. Years of work to keep it safe and secret were for nothing."

"And was the trunk quite heavy?" Kamal asked.

"Why yes, yes it was."

"Well then, perhaps they hid someone inside the trunk— someone small. And they must have had others trailing you to learn the location."

The imam closed his eyes and rubbed them with his long fingers, as if trying to gain a greater understanding. "Yes, I suppose that is how they did it. And I was so naïve."

Kamal said, "No sir, you are not naïve. Rather, you are a pure-hearted person who is not prepared for the treachery of such vile men."

Ibrahim walked to the end of the street and peeked around the corner. Two men were standing guard at an otherwise inconspicuous old door. Both were large and well-muscled, and each carried a sword. He went back to the others.

When the younger man described the two would-be donors, Ibrahim was certain they were indeed Nimr and Samir. "And did one of them have a mole on the right side of his face?" he asked.

"Yes indeed. It was almost beneath his right ear."

"That, O Shaikh, is Nimr al-Anmash himself. And he's done it, he's broken into the Treasury of the Qarawiyyin, just like he promised," Ibrahim said.

"We must alert the Sultan's guard," Ibn Murad said, then paused. "And yet, I hesitate. God forgive me for saying this, but these days the throne is as corrupt as the gangster himself. Well, not the young Sultan, but those around him. And there is no time."

The imam looked down and closed his eyes in what was obviously prayer.

When he nodded his head and opened his eyes, Kamal said, "There is another way, Sir."

"But how on earth could you and your friends stand up to them? You are not armed, are you?"

"Sir, we are the Sons of Fez."

"So you *do* exist. *Mashallah,* then it's true." The imam looked from man to man in wonder. Ibrahim had assumed that the imam would know of them. They really *were* a secret society, even to the leader of the spiritual community.

"Yes," Kamal said. "And we are armed with the tools of our trades. We are many, and if you need us, we will fight to defend you, the mosque, and the city. Just give us the word."

"But what is the plan? You can't just start a brawl in the backstreets of Fez without the Sultan's men appearing."

"Give us a moment," Kamal said.

The members of the order huddled. Ibrahim and Kamal sent two men to summon the mu`allim and the rest of the order. A quiet consensus formed around a plan: once enough men arrived, they would overcome the guards and make their way silently inside to confront Nimr.

Amin asked to join the men in the fight.

"But have you any experience in such things?" the imam asked.

"Yes, I have," he said, pulling a dagger from his robes. "Badr instructed me to always come armed in case something like this were to happen. It is my duty, Sir."

Ibn Murad explained the layout of the treasury. After they entered the interior courtyard, they would find a door leading to a long stairway that headed down, then another to a short stairway that led up. At the top of those stairs was another door, which led to the treasury room itself. It was far underground, with no windows and only the one door providing access.

Within fifteen minutes, two dozen order members had gathered, the mu`allim among them. More were on the way. All had arrived in near silence, and the two guards down the street remained unaware of the army gathering just around the corner. Cloaks opened in the faint lantern light to reveal swords, hammers, saws, crowbars, daggers, ropes, and chains.

"Leave me alone!" Hameed squirmed as one of the men held him by the arm and pulled him forward to the mu`allim.

"I know him," Mike said to Ibrahim. "That's the boy who helped me when I got sick at the madrasa." He was astonished by the coincidence, unaware that Hameed had been trailing him and Ibrahim for days.

"Are you a member of this order?" Ibrahim asked.

"Well, I…"

"He certainly is not," the old man Hamza said. "This is most unsatisfactory."

"Please, I can fight, believe me. And I won't tell anyone."

Hamza stood before Hameed with his hands clasped behind his back. "And what is your full name, young man?"

"Hameed bin Sulaiman."

"Your father's trade?"

"He, well, he was a stonemason, but he went on the *Hajj* when I was young and never returned."

"Do you know this boy, Sharif?" Hamza asked, turning to the stone mason.

"No, I don't. But about his father, yes, I remember the story…"

"I know him, Sir," Mike said. "He works at the madrasa, helping the students."

"I see," Hamza said. "So that is where we should return you. But it seems you know too much. Therefore, for the time being, you'll be spending the evening with us."

But Sir," Hameed said, turning to Ibrahim. "I can run faster than all of them, and I can fight better, too. I know every inch of the medina, and..."

"No indeed, Hamza is right," Kamal said. "You are too young to fight, but not too young to help. Perhaps we will need you later."

And with that, Hameed stood back, controlling his smile. They might need him later.

The imam handed the treasury key to Amin and said, "God be with you. He alone is the Victor." The mu`allim took the imam by the arm and the boy by the hand, and they disappeared into the dark, walking to safety. The men were unaware that Shafiqa and Barbara had followed them all the way to the Sons of Fez's secret zawia.

Once the imam and mu`allim were out of sight, Ibrahim and Kamal conferred for a moment, then nodded to the others. It was time. The guildsmen removed their turbans and rewound them into a *shesh,* the style of Tuareg men, drawing the fabric end across their faces in disguise. Mike copied Ibrahim, who did it slowly so Mike could get it right.

On Kamal's signal, they whispered "*Bismillah,*" "In the name of God," each to himself, and the two bladesmiths crept around the corner, their swords at the ready. When the others created a diversion, the bladesmiths rushed toward the guards.

Chapter 29

The Treasury

The bladesmiths jumped out in front of the gangsters, and one of them shouted, "Drop your weapons!" The gangsters, who were clever fighters, were surprised, but they leapt into action, rushing at the guildsmen, who unfortunately had no fighting experience. Blades were raised and the clanging began, but it quickly became clear that the gangsters would have the upper hand. Just then carpenters rushed forward with clubs of gnarly thuya wood and managed to knock out both gangsters by hitting their heads from behind.

As Ibrahim, Kamal, and Mike neared the door, four more gangsters jumped on them from a nearby rooftop. They had long knives, but more tradesmen swarmed upon them, wielding crowbars, chains, shovels, and knives. The four gangsters managed to fight their way to the edge of the crowd and disappeared into the darkness.

"Let them go," Kamal said. "The treasury's our first priority. We have to get inside."

Kamal shook one of the guards. When he came to, Kamal held a dagger to his throat and asked, "Is Nimr still inside?"

Not getting an answer he repeated he question, and the guard nodded.

"Where are they taking it?" Kamal said.

"Taking what? You think Nimr tells me what he's doing? I'm just a lookout," the man said, his deep voice as rough a grindstone.

"Liar!" Kamal said, pricking the skin of the man's throat. "Where are they taking it? Answer me now, and you'll live to see another day. Or you can keep silent, and this will be your last moment on earth. Your choice."

After a moment's thought, the man said, "God curse you. The tanneries. I swear before God, the tanneries."

Kamal tied the man's hands, then gagged him. He turned the prisoners over to four older guildsmen. "Blindfold them, then take them both to the house near the zawia. We'll deal with them later." He gave instructions to gather more men with weapons at the plaza around the Qarawiyyin and to wait for word there.

The treasury house door was unlocked. Ibrahim glanced inside, and, finding the courtyard empty, he beckoned the men to enter. On the far side of the courtyard, the door stood open, and through that door they could hear men shouting. But it was faint, from somewhere far inside.

"It's Nimr," Kamal said. "I'd know his voice anywhere. Ibrahim, you and I go first. Everyone else, behind. Amin, stay back and, after we're through, lock this door and make your way back to the mosque and wait for us there. Whatever happens, lock this door!"

The men entered the far door and took a long staircase down, and then began to climb up the second, shorter set of stairs. They stopped outside the doorway at the top of the stairs, their weapons at the ready. The door was slightly ajar. The vault room was lit with candles, and the shadows of men filling bags danced across the walls. They were ransacking the place: opening trunks, rooting around for valuables, and throwing scrolls through the air like circus jugglers.

"Hurry up, you idiots!" Nimr shouted. We don't have much time, the Sultan's night watch will be along soon!"

"But master," one of the gangsters said, "The smallest things are usually the most precious. Let me finish looking in these bags."

"Never mind those, what matters is grabbing the most obvious things and getting out of here. Now hurry up!"

"I count eight of them," Kamal said to Ibrahim. "With the element of surprise, I think the twelve of us can take them." Then, a bit louder, he told the others, "Wait for my signal."

Kamal's nod set everything in motion. The tradesmen rushed into the vault room. If Nimr was surprised, he had no time to show it, for the weapons flew in the air: crowbars, clubs, spears, swords, and blades clinked and clanged against the gangsters' swords and knives. Ibrahim swung a long pole with pointed spearhead like a sword, but then realized that, if he used it like that, it might just be snapped in two. So he jumped back and a young blacksmith handed him a crowbar, one of two he was carrying. The ripe odor of sweat and fear filled the air.

Ibrahim watched the young blacksmith raise a heavy crowbar, and hit it hard against the blade of a gangster's sword. The young man yelled, "You maggot-brained swine!" and pushed his opponent to the floor. "How would you like to be shod like a filly?"

"By you, son of a gelding?" the gangster said, rolling out from under him and jumping away. But the blacksmith swung again, and his opponent cowered.

Though the gangsters were the better fighters, the tradesmen's assortment of unconventional weapons were a clear advantage. And while the sword makers weren't great fighters, their blades were the sharpest in the city. It was the biggest fight the gangsters had faced in years.

The men fought while standing ankle deep in vellum documents that had been tossed aside, amid overturned boxes and small chests that once held valuables. Coins and pieces of jewelry that the robbers had missed were scattered among the pages, glinting in the torchlight, but no one saw them in the midst of the fight.

Mike fought side by side with the others, using his fists and dagger to keep the pressure on some the gangsters, though he inflicted no wounds.

Kamal charged toward Nimr, roaring, his axe held high.

"That one's got a bit of a temper, wouldn't you say?" Nimr said as he stepped aside and let one of his henchmen hold Kamal off. Kamal got away from his grip before he could be wounded.

A burly builder swung a long chain and managed to wrap it around the waist of one of the gangsters, but the man twirled around to unwind it, then rushed his opponent. Kamal rushed him, swinging his axe and hitting him in the shoulder. His victim collapsed, the first to fall in the fight.

The Sons of Fez were not violent men, and seeing one of their own inflict a serious blow caused some to stop for a moment to look. Unfortunately, the robbers took advantage of their pause and started toward the door. Ibrahim saw them grab Amin, who had been standing wide-eyed at the back. He had disobeyed Kamal's orders and followed them into the vault. Another gangster stabbed a slow-moving young carpenter who held only a hammer, and he fell to the ground.

That's when Ibrahim felt a knife at this throat, and a tight grip on his arm. They had him! Ibrahim struggled, but the men's hold was strong. They dragged him away, along with Amin. Nimr led the way.

Mike watched in horror, frozen in fear, as Ibrahim was taken away.

"After them!" Kamal yelled, and the guildsmen, with Mike in the rear, chased after the gangsters and their two hostages.

Nimr laughed as his men slammed both doors behind them. "Farewell, fools!"

The tradesmen opened the door, only to find that the stairway was starting to fill with smoke. There was no other way out, so they felt their way along the stairs, their eyes burning, until they found the source. Nimr had thrown a torch into the stairway, expecting it to ignite the building, but it was sending up more smoke than flame.

One of the carpenters broke through the far door with his axe, and they stumbled into the courtyard, coughing. Though Nimr had gotten away, at least the tradesmen knew where he was going—the tanneries.

"Look, Kamal," one of the young men said. "It's Amin's key. He must have dropped it for us on the way out."

Two of the guildsmen arrived behind them, carrying the wounded carpenter who was moaning, blood dripping from a wound to his abdomen. Kamal ordered them to carry him to the home of a physician who was also a member of the group. Then, after locking the treasury door behind them, Kamal sent one of the blacksmiths to muster more guildsmen, while the remaining men, eight in number, set off down the dark streets toward the tanneries, their thoughts focused on the fight to come, and on their comrades' fates as prisoners of Nimr al-Anmash.

Mike tried to imagine the terror Ibrahim must be feeling. And how, Mike wondered, could the Sons of Fez defeat these gangsters? How could a group of tradesmen stand up to ruthless killers and torturers?

Mike had never been in the military. Aside from the usual fights he'd had with boys in his neighborhood, he'd never faced battle. And this was unlike any fight he could have imagined. Seeing men badly wounded brought the bloody reality of battle to him for the first time. This was no computer game. There was no high-tech way to attack. There were no bombs, and no guns, and they didn't even have a real plan. They were relying on God, their wits, surprise, their makeshift weapons, and on luck. Soon the rhythm of the men's quiet and determined march quieted his thoughts, and he focused on what lay ahead.

Following the imam, Hamza, and Hameed, Shafiqa and Barbara took careful note of their route to the zawia. And, owing to Shafiqa's keen sense of direction and knowledge of the city, they found their way back to the arch with ease.

"God help them all," Shafiqa said as they sat with Moustapha in the alley.

"And we're going to need His help here, too," Moustapha said. "If things get out of hand in the world of humans, the conflict in the world of djinn and demons will be stirred up into a blazing fire. Now, you two, you must keep yourselves safe. Keep to your regular routines as if nothing was wrong. There is nothing you can do now."

"We can pray," Shafiqa said.

"Well, of course you can, and you must, both of you," Moustapha said. "You know, after wearing this costume and living in your female world somewhat, I will admit that I have wondered these last few weeks what mankind would be like if women were more clearly in charge of things."

Both Shafiqa and Barbara were about to echo the sentiment, when Moustapha stopped them. "Yes, I know in modern times female humans do have more power and influence than before, but there are some battles that would be too dangerous. You must stay out of this one. It is not for the likes of you, so go home to safety and pray."

Shafiqa and Barbara returned to their rooms: Shafiqa to her simple mattress at her aunt's home, and Barbara to her room at the riad. Maureen was snoring, having fallen asleep while reading a classic English murder mystery. The book was open on the floor, where she had let go of it when she'd drifted off.

Barbara didn't want to sleep, so she read by flashlight, but her eyes eventually closed, and the flashlight fell onto the mattress.

Shafiqa began a prayer ritual she had learned from her aunt's order. It was an ancient prayer, and she repeated it until her eyes grew heavy and she too fell asleep and her prayer beads slipped from her hand to the floor.

Chapter 30

The Tanneries

The guildsmen reached the tannery district, forced to move forward in pairs as the alleys narrowed. A blacksmith who walked at Mike's side led him along, and they trailed the dim forms of the men in front of them. No one spoke. There was starlight, but the moon hadn't risen, and the warehouses and shops were all shut tight.

When they came to a small open space, they stood still to let their eyes adjust. There was no question that they had nearly reached the tannery itself, for the pungent odor of solvent assaulted their nostrils. Mike was amazed that it smelled exactly the same as it did in modern times.

Led by the tanners in the group, the guildsmen moved through one last alleyway and slowly entered the central tannery area. Shadows had been created by a dim light of some kind, which shone down on them from high above. Kamal stepped to the front of the group. Then he crouched down and crept ahead along the walls, minimizing his profile and keeping to the shadows. He peeked around a corner to survey the situation, then waved for the others to follow.

When Mike reached the others, in full view of the tanneries, he noted how little the area had changed over the centuries. Just as in modern times, it was jammed with circular vats of various sizes holding solvents, dyes, and rinses. The buildings surrounded them in a seemingly haphazard way, like a child's arrangement of building blocks. His eyes were drawn to an open doorway, lit from the inside, on the third story of one of the buildings. A set of stairs weaved back and forth from the vats up to the open door, where two men stood guard. Nimr himself paced back and forth inside the open doorway. There was no way to know whether the hostages were in there.

A handful of guildsmen climbed a staircase in the shadows, out of sight of the guards, and scrambled onto a nearby roof. From there, they made their way onto the roof of the building where the gangsters were holed up, and waved to Kamal. On his signal, they pounced, taking on the two guards. Blades flashed and fists flew. Kamal sent more men charging across the vats and up the stairs. They scattered at each landing to find strategic places to fight.

Hearing the commotion, Nimr stepped outside. "Samir, we have some guests!" Samir joined him to watch. "So, it seems fighting is new to you," he said, watching three of the tradesmen circle one of his guards. He laughed, and the guard lunged at one of them with a long knife. The guildsmen blocked him, and another stabbed him in the back. He fell to the ground. The second guard backed down the stairs fought back, but he too was knocked by a punch and fell off the stairs onto a pile of dried skins.

"See how they're veiled, afraid to show themselves!" Samir said to Nimr. More of the gangsters' men streamed into the area and charged the guildsmen. Nimr apparently had his own army.

Mike's heart sank when he realized they were outnumbered. Then, out of the darkness, dozens more turbaned and veiled men emerged, jumping into the fight alongside the guildsmen. Reinforcements, just in time. A battle ensued, with each man wielding the tool of his trade.

Mike's hopes bolstered, he moved behind Kamal toward the foot of the stairs below the gangsters' lair. Mike fought with his fists and dagger as they worked their way through the melee. Mike noted with satisfaction that each of Nimr's men was battling with at least two guild fighters. Mike stabbed at least one in the gut. He couldn't believe this whole thing was happening.

"Why do you even bother fighting, fools?" Nimr shouted from his perch at the lit doorway. "You know I'll own this city by tomorrow night, and I will be your new ruler. I'll have you all killed, along with your wives and children. Are you such idiots that you don't realize this?"

Nimr obviously hadn't learned who they were, these beturbaned fighters defending the treasury. Ibrahim and Amin had kept their identities secret. Even though the Sons of Fez didn't have the best weapons, the guildsmen had everything at stake: their lives, their families, and the city itself. They fought for their very lives. Meanwhile, through all this, Nimr and Samir stood at the door, shouting orders as their men fought on around them.

Keeping to the shadows, Kamal and a few others, including Mike, climbed up ladders and stairways, edging toward the two gangsters. Mike tried not to think of how Nimr and Samir would revel in killing them all if given the opportunity.

"Enough!" Nimr said to Samir. "This is ridiculous, let's be done with this nonsense. Bring the Amazigh, the tall one. Bring him outside."

Samir led Ibrahim, who was bareheaded, bound, and gagged, to the stoop outside the door. He held a knife to

Ibrahim's throat and led him down the steps toward the vats. No one stepped in to interfere, for they were all too busy fighting. Mike's anger burned, but he felt paralyzed. He didn't know what to do.

Nimr asked, "What color would you like this one to be?"

Samir looked around. "Saffron. Yes, that would look nice on his skin, don't you think?"

"Hurry it up then," Nimr shouted, waving his hand toward some vats that looked more like ochre in the torchlight. "Show these men what fate awaits them if they continue to defy us." Samir nodded, then shoved Ibrahim into the vat and held his head down with both hands. Ibrahim kicked and squirmed, but with his hands tied, it was clear he wouldn't last long.

Mike's anger exploded in an instant. Without a word or signal, he and Kamal rushed up the stairs at Nimr. When Nimr held up a dagger in defense, Mike lunged at him and Kamal knocked the knife from Nimr's hand. Together they grabbed Nimr's arms and twisted them behind his back. Kamal held his blade at Nimr's neck. Mike was surprised that none of Nimr's men approached.

"You son of a dog," Kamal said to Nimr. "Tell Samir to let him go."

"What's that, my little sister?" Nimr said, struggling and eyeing Mike. "You're clearly deluded if you think your girls here are a match for my men." Mike and Kamal tightened their grip on his arms, and a drop of blood trickled from Kamal's dagger.

Down below at the vat, Samir was momentarily distracted by Nimr's capture. Taking advantage of this, two guildsmen ran straight at him and pushed him into the vat with Ibrahim. They kept Samir submerged, pushing down on his head until others set a heavy wooden plank on it—the sort the tanners used as a walkway. Samir thrashed and fought the men holding him in place, but his strength was no match for theirs. Ibrahim stood up in the vat, coughing through his gag. His hands still tied, he stood at the far edge of the vat. A guildsman stepped forward to loosen his gag and untie his hands. Ibrahim pulled himself out of the vat.

Everyone stopped to watch Samir. To the Sons of Fez, this was an unexpected triumph. It felt like justice was being handed down at last. Samir was being drowned, and the great Nimr was held at knifepoint.

"You idiots, get them off me!" Nimr called to his men. "They're nothing but a bunch of—"

"Whoever we are, you'll never know!" Kamal said, loud enough for all to hear, including Nimr's men. "We are the men of Fez, and we've had enough of you and your men. We're taking back our city." The gangsters' men stopped fighting. His few words planted doubts in their minds, doubts about these men who had the advantage over both Samir and Nimr. Then, one or two at first, then the rest of Nimr's men turned and fled into the night.

"Come back, cowards!" Nimr shouted. "These men are no match for us. We have the treasury! We control the city! Traitors, you'll pay for this!"

Kamal nodded at Mike, and the two of them started to lead Nimr down the stairs toward the vats.

"You are powerless over me. I am Nimr al-Anmash! You think you can get away with this? My men will take revenge on each one of you and your families. The Sultan's ministers are in my pocket! You'll never be safe, and my curse will follow you for generations!"

Nimr struggled, but the men held him firm. One of the guildsmen pulled Mike aside and took his place. "This is *our* fight, not yours. You need not bloody your hands."

Mike stood back as Kamal and the other guildsman took Nimr down the last of the stairs and shoved him into a vat of blue dye.

"You'll pay for this!" were Nimr's last words as they pushed his head down and held it under with long, heavy wooden boards. He struggled, just as Samir had, but after a couple of minutes, the bubbles stopped coming to the surface, and he stopped moving. The guildsmen stepped back in silence. "That was for my brother Salim," Kamal said. "And for my father, God rest his soul," said the other.

The Sons of Fez watched the two bodies floating, motionless, in the vats. It had happened so quickly, it hardly seemed real. After a minute or two of silence, the guildsmen hauled them out and laid each of them on a wooden plank.

"For once, it's me getting you out of trouble," Mike said as he slapped Ibrahim on the back.

"Yeah, and I think it's fair to say, I owe you one."

"Let's just call it even." Then they almost hugged, but Mike held back, owing to the fact that Ibrahim was still dripping in dye. They laughed and shook hands instead. Mike used a sleeve to wipe the traces of dye that had dripped into Ibrahim's eyes and mouth.

They turned to see Kamal run back up the stairs. He found Amin tied up inside the torchlit room. Amin led him to a back room where Nimr and his men had stashed the stolen treasure. It was too risky to carry it back through the streets that night, especially with the gangsters' own men likely still about. So

Amin stayed there along with a handful of armed guildsmen, awaiting instructions.

The men outside agreed to burn any clothing with traces of dye, so that they couldn't be traced to the tanneries. Then, in exhausted silence, they disappeared into the night, leaving eight men who lifted the heavy boards laden with the corpses onto their shoulders and started up the hill toward the citadel. Kamal, Ibrahim, and Mike were among them.

The men struggled with their bulky cargo through the twists and turns of the back streets. They were alert in case Nimr's men attacked them, but it never happened. Instead, the city was eerily quiet, and they encountered no one.

After trudging uphill for a while, Kamal said, "Let's rest and catch our breath." Sweat dripped off his forehead onto his nose. He was a strong man, but carrying the body-laden board was a challenge, even for him. They sat down in the dark.

Kamal sat near Mike and Ibrahim. Eyeing Mike, he said, "You were quite a fighter back there. I misjudged you both from the start, and I owe you an apology."

"Thanks. You and your men, you were all impressive," Ibrahim said. Then he brought up the subject of Khalid.

Kamal shook his head. "Trying to spring him tonight would be mad. Even in the best circumstances, it would take a lot of palm-greasing, and then you'd need a team of *real* fighters. And think of the situation we have here. First, we're about to leave the city's most dangerous gangsters on the steps of the prison. At dawn, they'll be discovered, and the place will be swarming with the Sultan's men, trying to figure out what happened. Second, your friend is better off where he is, for, in the morning, the authorities will learn that Nimr's cell is occupied by an innocent man. Lastly, we just can't risk it.

We must disappear and our order must remain secret. Remember, the Sons of Fez don't even exist. Secrecy is the only way we survive."

Ibrahim hated to admit it, but Kamal was right. It would be suicidal to try to get Khalid out that night. Yet Ibrahim didn't trust that everything would go smoothly the next day, or that Khalid might not somehow be implicated in the gangsters' scheme. In the end, Ibrahim had no plan. He would have to ask for the imam's help. But no matter what, he vowed he would not leave Khalid behind.

After a grueling hour, the men reached the open square just below the citadel. They set the bodies down and studied the situation. A single torch lit the front entrance, which stood at the top of a winding cart road. For some reason, there were no guards visible—they must have been taking a break. The guildsmen would have to move quickly. On Kamal's signal, they lifted the bodies for the last time and, using their remaining strength, they struggled up the hill to the steps of the prison. They laid the two boards, propped up head-first across several steps, so they would be noticed in the morning light.

Kamal said, "Hopefully the wild dogs won't get to them before they're discovered. We do want them to be recognizable."

Relieved of their cargo, the men returned to the safety of the streets below the prison and bade each other farewell. Ibrahim, Kamal, and Mike walked back to the zawia, and the rest of the men went to their homes. Pride and wonder swelled in Ibrahim's heart, and he was sure the others felt the same. Not only had they survived, but these humble tradesmen had defeated the city's worst gangsters. Fez should be proud to call them her sons, even though they could never take credit openly for saving her.

Hamza, Ibn Murad, and Hameed welcomed the men back at the zawia. Upon hearing of their ordeal, the imam was generous with praise.

"Young man," the imam said to Ibrahim, whose skin and clothes were now colored in different shades of saffron. "I think you've quite a tale to tell."

"We all do," Kamal said. "Thank God for the bravery of all the 'Sons' and our friend here." He put his arm around Mike and clapped him on the back.

They got cleaned up and shared a hearty meal. Ibrahim was about to bring up the issue of Khalid, but he was interrupted by knocking at the front door.

Hamza frowned and looked around the room. "Who could it be?" he asked as he rose. He put an ear against the door and called out, "Who is it?"

"Moustapha! I need to speak to Ibrahim. It's urgent!"

"One moment," Hamza said, turning to glare at Ibrahim. "A man named Moustapha is asking for you. You promised you would not disclose our location."

"I assure you, I never told anyone," Ibrahim said. "You must believe me. Moustapha must have followed us. But he can be trusted. He's with us. Let me go outside and talk to him. That way, your identities will remain secret."

Ibrahim stepped outside, relieved that this particular visitor wouldn't be admitted. He would have had a hard time explaining a pink-robed old woman named Moustapha.

Chapter 31

Haqud Returns

As soon as the door closed behind him, Ibrahim grabbed Moustapha's shoulders to give him a hug, then realized how strange it would be to hug a djinni. Instead, he gave his bony shoulders a friendly clap. "We did it! We defeated Nimr and Samir."

"Indeed, that is excellent. But you still have to get Khalid out of prison."

"Do you have any ideas? And if not, why are you bothering me? You realize you're getting me in a lot of trouble here. This is supposed to be a secret place."

"Oh, I have my ways of finding out secret things, I'm a djinni after all. I'm here only to warn you that the danger is not over. It's just beginning." Moustapha lifted a bony finger to the heavens. A hot shifting wind rose around them, and the smell of sulfur filled the air.

"You must stay here the rest of the night," Moustapha said. "Don't try to come through the arch. There's to be another battle tonight. This time, the djinn are fighting. It's been building each day among the spirits who defied God by coming through the arch and refusing to return. Tonight the demon star Algol is aligned with Mars. Therefore, once the moon rises after midnight, the spirits of this time have decided to claim their place in your time. You can be sure they know you defeated Nimr, and also know of our intention to close up the arch. As to who will win, only the Almighty knows.

"The old spirits want to live in your time, and those from your time want to stay where they are. Modern-day djinn and ghouls have it much easier, because you modern humans are so naïve. Djinn can slip around here and there without being noticed. And, on top of all this, the ancient spirit Haqud is active in the city again, just as I feared, stirring up trouble. He more than any being must be kept from your time, for his evil and power are unbridled, and, in your time, he would be extremely dangerous since you modern humans are so unaware of these matters. So I beg you, stay inside tonight. Bolt the doors and windows. Especially because you have that young man Mike with you. Things could get out of hand, and he is still vulnerable. Haqud may try to find him and use him somehow. The zawia is the safest place for him, as it is for all of you. In the morning, come through the arch as early as you can. Then we must destroy it. God willing, I will be there when you return—that is, if I survive the night."

"Why, where are you going? Are you not staying at the arch?"

"Alas, I have been told my duty is now to stop Haqud. So I must leave you humans to your own devices, at least until the morning."

"But what about Khalid?"

"Well, I don't have *all* the answers. That is up to you. You've got to figure out a way to get him out. As for me, with God's help, I will be at the arch in the morning to assist."

"Sounds like we'll both need God's help, my friend," Ibrahim said, as Moustapha scuttled away, his long dress dragging on the ground behind him.

"Friend! Bah!" Moustapha muttered. "No djinni was ever true friend to human." His laughter echoed as he disappeared around the corner. Ibrahim stood alone in thought for a few minutes, his eyes beginning to itch from the smoke that rode the rising wind.

Back inside, Ibrahim made the excuse that the inn where they had meant to stay couldn't accommodate them, and, as he hoped, Hamza invited them all to stay until morning. There was no question that the imam would stay there in safety, since the gangsters' men, even though they'd scattered, might still be abroad somewhere in the city.

Ibrahim took Mike aside as Hameed eavesdropped in the shadows.

"Moustapha says the djinn are battling tonight. We can't go back until morning."

"A djinn battle?" Mike asked. "Can we watch from the roof?"

"No indeed," Ibrahim said. "Especially not you."

"And what's that supposed to mean?"

"The spirit that possessed you, Haqud, is in the city tonight. Moustapha says you might be vulnerable to him."

Mike said nothing in response. In the last few days he had been recalling more from the gnawa night, as if he were seeing the ceremony in snapshots. He remembered feeling hot and sweating profusely. And there was a woman yelling at him, so close to his face that he could smell her cardamom-scented breath. Ever since, he'd seen and heard strange things and most nights had been filled with terrifying horrors. Perhaps this was why.

The men stayed up for a while, reliving the events of the last few days. When the winds began to blow and howl, wind-whipped sand began to seep through the windows, Ibrahim and Hameed pulled the shutters tight and bolted them.

Most went to sleep on cushions in the main meeting room, but Ibrahim was wide awake. He lit a single candle and sat up listening to the raging storm. He watched Mike sleep fitfully nearby, turning over and over. Sometimes, Mike muttered, but not in any language Ibrahim knew. Mike would grow more agitated, thrashing his arms and legs, and he'd start moaning. Then Ibrahim would lay a firm hand on Mike's shoulder, asking for God's help. Only then did Mike's limbs go limp, and he would sigh and fall into a calm sleep.

Eventually, Ibrahim dozed off, his exhaustion finally catching up with him. But he woke with a start when he heard what he thought was a lion's roar. He opened his eyes and saw Mike straddling him, his fists clenched and his eyes as big as eggs. Ibrahim rolled onto his side as Mike roared again, then started punching and clawing at him with his fingers. Ibrahim fought back and called for help. "He's possessed, someone's taken him!"

The men pulled Mike off of Ibrahim, but he kept thrashing his arms and shouting gibberish. Only this time, his eyes were aflame, and he was frothing at the mouth, his spittle flying everywhere. He ran to the front door and tried to get out, biting one of the men who held him back. Someone or something was banging on the shuttered windows, as if trying to get into the room.

"Here, bring him here!" Hamza shouted, beckoning them to an interior door with no windows.

Six men carried Mike as he writhed and shouted and spit. In one movement, they pushed him inside the room and shut the door; locking it with a heavy bolt. Mike screamed and howled inside. The men listened from outside the door, breathing heavily from the sudden unexpected exertion.

"He's possessed," Ibrahim said. "This happened before, with some gnawa."

"Gnawa?" Ibn Murad said. "What is gnawa?"

Then Ibrahim remembered that, in 1374, there were no gnawa in Fez; they didn't arrive until two hundred years later. "It's probably the evil spirit named Haqud. He has been possessed before, and now the evil one is back. Can you help?"

"Oh yes, I have heard of this one. He is a scourge of evil indeed. God willing, we will do our best," the imam said. He stood before the closed door and said in a loud voice, "Haqud!" Lightning struck nearby, and everyone jumped in surprise. Ibn Murad began to recite the Throne Verse, a famous Qur'an verse about the power of God.

Ibn Murad opened the door and stepped inside, all the while reciting the Throne verse. He nodded and the men closed the door behind him. He kept reciting that and other verses, louder and louder, even though Mike kept yelling. Finally the imam shouted, "In the name of God, I command you to leave, Haqud. Be gone! In the name of God, there is no God but God!" and the yelling stopped. Then he prayed. "O God, heal this man's soul and cleanse it of the traces of the evil ones, and protect him from them. Fill him with your spirit and with your strength. Only you are the Healer, the Protector, the Forgiver." The men stood by, silent, waiting.

After a few minutes, Ibn Murad came out with his arm around Mike. Mike stood quietly, his arms limp at his sides, his head hanging down in shame.

"I'm sorry," he said. He looked up at them, all the fire and rage gone from his face.

"Come, my son," the imam said, leading him to the main room. "God bless you and protect you. Don't worry, you'll be all right, God willing. Take some water. Then recite the *fatiha* and pray." Mike sat down facing Mecca and started reciting quietly along with the others, who joined him.

Later, as the men returned to their cushions and places on the carpets to sleep, Hameed pulled on Ibrahim's sleeve. "Can I speak to you alone, Sir?"

"Not now, I need to rest, and so do you."

"No really, Sir, it's important." Hameed said, jerking on Ibrahim's sleeve again.

"Isn't there someone else who can help?" Ibrahim asked.

"Has to be you." Hameed had chosen Ibrahim, and this was his only chance to speak privately with him.

Ibrahim relented and let Hameed pull him down the hall to a quiet corner.

"What is it?" Ibrahim asked, expecting the sort of night terrors his young sons experienced. He put his arm around Hameed and mustered an exhausted smile.

Hameed said, "I know who you are, and I know where you come from."

"You what?"

"You are from another time. You, Khalid, and Munir. All of you. And I have been there, to your time."

"Well, that's simply nonsense. Yes, we are from far away, but what you say, that's impossible."

"No, it isn't. I've been following all of you through the medina for days. I have watched you fumble your way here and there. One day, I went through the arch, and I visited your time. I have seen the girls walking with no haik and their tight indigo sirwal. I have seen those little silver talking boxes they use. So don't tell me I'm imagining it."

Hameed was relieved to get it out—he'd wanted to share his knowledge with someone ever since he'd realized what he had done when he crossed through the arch. But, until then, he had been smart enough to keep quiet. Yet after he'd told Ibrahim everything, the man just stood there, closed his eyes and rubbed his forehead. Hameed wondered if he'd made a mistake in speaking up.

"So what if it's true," Ibrahim said at last. "What do you want me to do about it?"

"I want to go with you and live in your time. I can work, I can do anything. But I want to stay with you."

"Well," Ibrahim said, "I don't know if you can. You know that Moustapha's job is to keep that from happening. We're supposed to stay in our own times."

"I know Moustapha won't let me, but I've already been through, and I know I don't want to stay here. Please, help me get over. I can work at the riad, I'm even willing to go to....school," he said, knowing he could do it now that he could read.

Ibrahim sighed then said, "I'll think about it. But for now, let's get some sleep. You and I, we'll talk in the morning." Ibrahim started to leave the room.

"Sir, one more question. I must know—can you tell me, what year is it, in the time when you live?"

"The *hijri* year 1439, which is 2018 to the Franks."

Six hundred years, Hameed thought. That is very far away indeed. And yet it wasn't so different, really. Fez was still there, the Qarawiyyin, and the medina. He drifted off to sleep, smiling as he dreamt of returning to that strange world of theirs, filled with music, beautiful girls, and silver talking boxes.

Mike was stretched on a cushion, his hands clasped behind his head, listening to Hamza and the imam talk. Oblivious to the storm raging outside, the two men sat near him in an alcove off the main room, conversing by the light of one flickering candle. They were discussing Sufism, and Mike remembered that Ibn Murad was some kind of Sufi himself, a member of another order, and therefore a kindred spirit.

As he listened, Mike was sad, for Ibrahim had explained that much of what they had experienced might vanish from their memories once they left Fez. He was already mourning that loss, trying to burn in his memory his night at the secret zawia among these wise men. He tried to memorize the way the men dressed, moved, and spoke, as well as the food, the smells, everything about old Fez. Perhaps, if he were hypnotized when he got home, it would all come back to him, and he could talk about it while under hypnosis. He could make a recording of it. *That's it*, he thought. *I just have to make sure I do it.*

Mike slipped in and out of sleep, turning things over in his mind. He had a strange metallic taste in his mouth, like sulfur, no doubt from that evil spirit. And as he slept, he heard the sounds of battle, of strange voices crying and screaming. The singing of the gnawa, and the ringing of the qaraqib filled his head.

Ibrahim still couldn't sleep, and sat up listening to the storm rage. He jumped when a clap of thunder struck nearby. Rain pounded against the shutters of the salon. It was coming down in torrents. *O my God*, he thought, *what if the wall gets washed away and the arch falls in.* Yearning for home filled his heart. More than at any other time, he feared he might never see Laila and the boys again. He wanted to run out of the zawia straight through the archway to get back, but he knew he couldn't leave Khalid and the others behind. He bowed his head and began to pray.

Chapter 32

Spirit Storm

A thunderclap woke Barbara from her sleep. She sat up, confused. The wind howled outside, rattling the window and shutter by her bed. Was she at home in her own bed? No, she was somewhere else. The room was stuffy, and there was smoke and grit in the air. Then she remembered. This was Morocco, and she was at Dar Surour. Then the rest came back to her—the portal, the fight to save the city, and Moustapha's edict to stay inside.

She picked up her pocket flashlight and jerked at another loud clap of thunder. Her roommate was still sound asleep, facing the wall, a huge pillow over her head.

Barbara had to get up and see what was going on. She pulled a caftan on over her pajamas, then zipped on her orange hooded rain jacket. She stood outside their room on the second-floor walkway that overlooked the courtyard and shined her flashlight around. Rain was pounding into the courtyard fountain, and the floor drains appeared to be backing up. If the rain kept up like this, the student bedrooms on the ground floor would be flooded. She made her way down the stairs and stood under the balcony, watching the edge of the ponding water creep closer to the bedrooms.

Another thunderclap startled her, and she ran to the kitchen door. She banged on the door and yelled, "Is anyone there?" knowing that was unlikely in the middle of the night.

After rapping on Ibrahim's door and getting no answer, which she expected, Barbara woke the residents on the ground floor. The arched colonnade around the courtyard kept the students dry, except for their feet, as they carried pillows and blankets to the second-floor salon. Soon, most of the ground-floor residents were asleep on the carpets, snoring as loudly as before despite the storm.

Barbara, however, was too energized to go back to sleep, so she stood on her balcony and watched. Ever since she was a girl, she would stay up until she knew a thunderstorm had passed and that she was safe. The rain kept coming, and the thunder and lightning, too. Even when the rain let up for a minute, the wind howled on, and the heavens kept booming. This was like no storm she'd ever experienced.

An orange light in the sky drew her to the roof. The rain had stopped, but the wind whipped her hair across her face. As she looked to the sky, she saw clouds glowing gold, blue, and red, as if each one shielded a full moon. And in the clouds, she could see things—flying things. Her stomach churned at the sight of nine winged centaurs, flying in a V, waving scimitars in the air. They vaulted across the sky into a cloud and were gone. A dozen fireballs arched above, flashing and booming. A winged donkey, bedecked in golden jewelry that jangled in the wind, flew by, chased by a clawing ghoul. The clouds themselves filled with rising flames and billowing smoke. Hundreds of odd creatures churned in the sky, fighting each other. The sky lit the city with the color of flames. Barbara wondered whether there was a fire somewhere far away in the medina.

Barbara leaned over the wall and aimed her flashlight down, amazed at the river running in the alley from the past to the present. Apparently, the storm was happening in the past too. Moustapha was there, standing near the arch. He looked up at her and waved for her to come to the alley. Barbara stopped in her room and pulled on her jeans and donned her flipflops. Then she made her way to the side door and out into the alley.

Moustapha's eyes glowed in her flashlight's beam. "Come, quickly!" Barbara rushed to his side.

"See those boards over there, the ones lying there. Bring them here, one at a time. I can't move, or else I would have done it myself. Hurry up! No time for dilly-dallying!"

Barbara did as she was told. The first board was heavy, and she had a hard time dragging it through the mud.

"Stand it up here, where I'm standing. We have to hold the arch in place, to keep it from falling down. The rain has washed out more of the wall, and the arch might collapse so we have to support it. Now, I'll help you with the rest."

One board at a time, they propped up the arch. Just as they finished, the clouds opened up again and rain pummeled them. Moustapha grabbed Barbara's hand and pulled her over to the side of the alley. They stood at the marble threshold at the side door to the riad, protected from the rain.

"Thank you, my dear. Stay here and make sure—make absolutely sure—that this arch doesn't fall down. Many lives depend on it. As long as you keep the arch open, you'll be safe. No matter what happens, keep it open until I return. And stay on this side of the arch! Now, I must leave you, to join the battle. As you can see", he said, pointing to the heavens, "the djinn, ghouls, and demons are fighting, and I'm supposed to stop the worst one of them all. In fact, they put me in charge." Moustapha jumped into the air and hovered for a moment a few feet off the ground, glancing back at Barbara, before he shot straight up into the sky and was gone.

The rain pounded on, and she leaned back, shining her flashlight occasionally at the arch. Water rushed down the alley and was soon a foot deep, still well below the threshold where she stood. At least the water was warm. She wished she had a pair of boots, not just flipflops.

The wind grew to a howling crescendo, and the orange light from the clouds illuminated everything. Barbara was overwhelmed and closed her eyes, leaning back on the metal door, until someone touched her arm, and she jumped in surprise.

It was Shafiqa, stepping into the doorway. She was wearing a rain slicker over her caftan, and held a child-sized umbrella over her head.

"What's going on?" Shafiqa shouted over the rain, closing the umbrella.

Something exploded in the sky above them, and the woman instinctively put her arms around Barbara and pulled her back, as flaming rocks showered down. Over the din of the rain and thunder, the sound of rhythmic clapping and the qaraqib of the gnawa clanged away for a few seconds, as if there was a ceremony nearby, then it stopped.

"What is happening?" Shafiqa asked again, more to herself than anything.

"Moustapha said we have to keep the arch open, no matter what. He's afraid it might fall down if rain causes the wall to collapse."

"Where is he?"

"Fighting the spirits. He said they put him in charge of this battle, whatever it is."

"Moustapha? In charge?" They both shook their heads. "God help us," Shafiqa said, then began to pray, with her eyes closed and her hands raised. She spoke so softly that Barbara couldn't make out her words. With the flaming rocks still pummeling the alley, Barbara leaned out very briefly to check on the arch.

After a while, Shafiqa said, "So are those boards really secure?"

"They're holding so far. Thank God you came. I couldn't do this alone."

With a gust of hot wind, a dozen flaming horsemen swooped down into the alley and galloped through the archway. Just behind them, ghouls shaped like fanged fish slithered by in chase. A great owl, the size of a winged horse and made of gleaming silver, soared through the arch from the past into the present. As it ascended into the sky, its wings screeched and cranked as its metal feathers caught the wind. The great bird glowed orange in the light of the flames.

Shafiqa prayed louder. "O Almighty, save us from evil, keep all things ordered, all things as You Command. You alone are the Victor."

She grabbed Barbara's arm. "Please, pray with me." At first, Barbara couldn't shut her eyes. She stared in wonder at the strange beings coming and going. Then, overcome by the sight, she closed her eyes and prayed along, drawing comfort from Shafiqa's warm grip on her arm.

After a while, the heavens went quiet, and a steady but a normal rain began to fall.

"Do you think it's over?" Barbara asked.

As if answering her question, the sky opened up again, and it began to hail, and the rain became a hard torrent. The water in the alley grew deeper by the minute as it rushed by them, nearing the level of the stoop where they were standing. They looked out and both concluded that the boards would give way at any minute.

They stepped from their dry perch and fought the rushing water to get to the arch. When they reached it, they felt each board, then, stood downstream and held the boards in place in the torrent. The water reached Barbara's knees. She didn't want to think about what might be flowing past her legs and concentrated on holding tight.

They heard men shouting down the alley, and three Chinese figures in long robes approached, colored jade in the light of their green lanterns. They waded from the past under the arch, very close to the women, a gargantuan dragon of the same hue lumbering behind them.

"Don't look at them!" Shafiqa shouted. "Just shut your eyes and keep them closed. No matter what, don't look and don't let go of the board. Hold on tight."

Barbara did as she was told. The rain turned to hail again, and then came the explosions. They heard the galloping of horses, the screams of men and women, the rage of lions and elephants, and the pitiful shrieking of children. To try to drown out the sounds, the two women repeated, "God alone is the Victor."

Chapter 33

The Battle of the Djinn

With the rain stinging my eyes, I flew over the medina looking for one spirit only: Haqud. I passed over the Andalusian quarter, which had all its shutters pulled and doors bolted. Why they waited until then to give me the power to go after him—well, their ways are beyond me. Above the mosques and shrines, all was at peace, for the djinn always avoided them. The rain fell into the courtyards of these sacred places, but evil stayed away.

Water rushed down the streets and flowed into the riverbed that bisected the heart of the city. The ghouls and spirits flew all around me, battling each other. Just as I'd feared, old spirits of the evil variety wanted to take the place of spirits who live in the modern-day. The present-day spirits had been crossing to the past, but most returned, satisfied to stay in their own time. Life in the 21st century was just too enticing to the legions of the past. They could cause so much more mayhem, disrupt so much more than in the old days. With all the mechanical wonders, and with electricity—itself a kind of djinni, really—how much trouble they could cause! And the airplanes—a djinni's paradise. But I saw no sign of Haqud.

I returned to the arch and flew through to the past. A fire raged on the hilltop, at the Citadel, where the human Khalid was imprisoned. Great pillars of flame jutted out of its towers.

How could a stone building burn like that? In the middle of the storm, men were running from the prison, scattering in all directions. Some were already fighting, swinging boards and rushing at each other with knives. "God help us, Haqud is at work here no doubt," I said out loud, as if someone were listening. "Who else but he would open up the prison and let convicts run loose?" I flew low over the crowd, but I didn't see Khalid anywhere. "God protect that fellow, for he's in deep now!"

Returning to my high-altitude scan of the city, the spirits battled all around, but I had no time to engage with these minor mischief-makers, and I gave them a wide berth. Still, I was unnerved by the sheer magnitude of the battle. A giant bat flew by me, a female demon astride it. Her eyes were lit by the fires and she chomped her fangs, no doubt looking for a meal of some unsuspecting human.

How was I supposed to find Haqud, anyway? That nasty devil could take any form. My answer came soon enough.

"What is that stink?" I asked myself. Many spirits had a peculiar idea about personal grooming, but this was just disgusting. I covered my nose with a sleeve, turning in a circle to scope out the source of the smell.

I didn't realize that, about fifteen feet below me, a giant fiddler crab hovered, its skin a dark blue-grey. It waved the larger of its pincers back and forth like a sword, waiting for someone to accidentally come within range. It smelled putrid, like something dead at the seashore. "Zhzhzhzhzhzh," it said. When I finally saw it, I jerked up into the air and then circled. The crab waved its larger pincer and said, "Moustapha the Guardian, old lady, prepare to meet your end!"

"What in the name of heaven are you?" I asked, laughing. "Spirit of Stinking Beach?"

"Zhzhzhzhzh, you have a sense of humor, even at the moment of your death. How zhzhzhzh charming. But you don't know me? I know you. Now isn't that nice, I have the advantage."

"But why would I care who you are, Prince of Putrid?"

"Oh, you care, for I am the one you seek. There's no need to keep it secret, I suppose. I am Haqud." When he spoke his name, a tremor rumbled through the city.

"Lord, it is him," I said to myself. How could I defeat this thing? And where were all the friends and allies I had been promised? Would I have to fight him alone? I wiped my eyes, for it was still pouring rain, and the lightning and thunder kept up all around us. I would have to act quickly.

I zoomed straight up in the air, and the crab pursued me, having grown to ten times its original size. It was waving its pincers, which had grown long and tentacle-like. An unfortunate flying serpent got in the way, and Haqud snapped it in two, his horrible mandibles pulling the massive, still-writhing pieces of serpent toward his mouth. He gobbled it up in a few greedy bites.

Taking advantage of the crab's distraction, I got away. By then, my blood was boiling. I was sure I'd been set up again, put in a position where I could not succeed. Flying close to the ground, I hoped to camouflage myself, and to figure out how to find help. I returned to the arch, relieved to see it was still standing. The two women were holding it up with the boards. But then, there was Haqud descending and shrinking in size, and aiming to fly through the arch into the future.

"No!" I shrieked, racing after the crab. Haqud flew through, within inches of Barbara and the woman in blue. They were still cowering when I got to them.

"Whatever you do," I said as I passed, "Watch out for that crab. He is the worst of them!"

They nodded, speechless, their eyes wide with fear.

I followed the crab as it flew from rooftop to rooftop, with its sickening snicker zhzhzhzhzh, knocking down satellite dishes and cutting electric wires with its pincers. Sparks flew, and the power went out in its wake. Wires dangled and writhed in the wind and rain.

"I do like it here," Haqud said, obviously aware of my approach. "So much more to *do* in this time. There's no end to the possibilities."

"No, this is not your time. Your kind was dealt with long ago, and humanity has rejected the hatred you try to sow in their hearts."

"Oh, is that so? My legions tell me otherwise. Humans have so much pride. They have invented machines that connect to the ether—and they think they have power over distance and nature, as we do. Their arrogance is misplaced, for *we* have the might to destroy them at any moment. And who's to say that what they have devised is not evil to begin with? Even I could scarcely have conceived of their flying machines, and how they send pictures and ideas through the air."

"So why would you want to destroy it all?" I asked, trying to keep Haqud talking while I racked my brain for a plan.

"Destroy it? Who said anything about that? No, my dear old woman, I don't want to destroy it. I want only to control it, at first anyway. For by controlling these machines, the systems that these proud men have invented and now rely on, I will control the earth. At last, thanks to them, it is within my reach."

"But humans won't bow down to a stinking blue crab. Are you crazy?"

"Hah! I can take any form—the form of a man or woman, beautiful, handsome, charming and rich. I can buy their affection, and they will give me control. And once I have control, well then, I will slowly kill them off. The world has had enough of humankind. It is *our* turn. Let them die, by the hundreds, the thousands, the millions. It will be a pleasure to watch them succumb to my plagues, to fight each other and destroy themselves. And afterward, the earth will be free of humans, at last, zhzhzhzhzhzh!"

I was half listening to the crab ramble as I scanned the horizon, trying to figure out what to do next. When the crab flew off toward the airport, I followed, dread filling my djinni heart. All around me, good and bad spirits and ghouls battled on. It was a free-for-all. I had never seen so many spirits, so many strange beings shooting slime, lightning bolts, rocks, and fire, and it was all I could do to avoid getting hit.

By the time I caught up with him, the crab demon had grown to a hundred feet tall. He was chopping the wings off of airplanes, bashing in windows of the airport terminal, and throwing flight-line vehicles around in the air, all the while laughing like the maniac devil he was. He set off fuel tanks, and he laughed as they exploded one by one.

"How am I supposed to deal with *this?*" I asked. Then I heaved a heavy sigh. "All right, I'll have to ask then." In a quiet voice, I said, "I summon you, good legions of Fez! Those who obey, who believe in the One God, who obey Him in all things!" After a minute or two, in which nothing happened, I flew high in the air and hovered over the medina and repeated my summons, this time louder. You see, like many human males, I am reluctant to ask for help.

"If you hear this, and choose to take the side of the Right, and Good over Evil, come to the airport. For an ancient spirit is among us, trying to take control of the earth and destroy us all! I call upon you all—from the meekest to the haughtiest! Come and fight, for your good deeds will be rewarded."

I waited, scanning the city below, and was relieved when the good legions began to appear. They rose out of the *hamamaat*, the wells, and the cisterns. They squeezed out of the sewers and rose up from the cemeteries. Those who were already fighting left their combatants. They gathered in the stormy sky like a ragtag flock of strange birds and flew toward the airport, following my lead.

Some of the djinn started shouting, "She's coming, Aisha is coming, look out!" I turned to see—flying toward me, cleaving a path through the other spirits, larger than any of these minor djinn—none other than Aisha Qandisha, the most famous djinnia of all Morocco, her husband Hammu Qaiu at her side. Their skin was luminescent gold like a candle flame. Both were in the form of winged camels with human heads, and they wore helmets of gold. Their golden hooves flashed with electricity.

"Ma'am, Sir, thank you for your assistance," I said, bowing as they drew near.

"So, old lady, where is this great evil one?" Aisha asked. "You summoned us, now let's get it over with. We've been fighting all night, and now this. He wants to move in on our territory, does he? Hah!"

A couple of gas tanks exploded, and everyone turned to see Haqud crushing airplanes into piles of twisted metal, laughing with glee at each blow from his mighty pincers.

Aisha said, "So, old lady, what's your name?"

"I'm Moustapha of the Mountain."

"Okay, Moustapha, we will help you, but there is one condition to our help."

I was not at all surprised at this, for Aisha was famous for her cleverness. "And what would that be?"

"After we get rid of him, you must obey us and only us," she said.

My temper exploded like a firecracker. I flew toward them spinning like a corkscrew and stopped not three feet from her. "Now see here, do you know who you're dealing with? It so happens that I am personal friends with your great-great-great-great-great-great grandmother Aisha. She would be appalled at you for asking such a thing of a God-fearing djinni. Hold your tongue from such nonsense. Have you no shame?"

Aisha's eyes burned bright green. "You do not fear me? I am Aisha Qandisha, and I wreak havoc on all of Morocco! I am the Royal Troublemaker, the Cunning Confounder, seeding discord in marriages, in families, and in the souls of men and animals. And you do not fear me?"

"No. And I have it on good authority that for the last fifty years or so, you have been thoroughly out of control. And you control your husband as if you own him. The Good Legions have had enough of your shenanigans."

The other djinn, too afraid to say anything, nodded tentatively in agreement.

"Do you not fear that we will join forces with Haqud?" Aisha said. "If we did, there would be no stopping us. Our influence could spread far beyond Morocco and the Maghrib. All would know our names, and all would fear us."

"Sure, go ahead. You are welcome to the putrefied crab. Together, you can stink up the world. And together, you can face the wrath of God Almighty." I immediately regretted my outburst, for Aisha was famous for her unpredictable behavior. At that moment I questioned, rather unfaithfully, whether God and his righteous ones would indeed interfere, or whether they, too, were tired of humanity's dominion over the earth.

To my horror, the husband-and-wife djinni pair flew toward the crab in a huff. I pursued them and waved the others to follow. My helpers gathered in a crowd, hovering above the airport, but far enough away from Haqud to be safe. I wondered if my temper might have just lost the battle. Why ever had *I,* of all djinn, been put in charge?

Aisha and Hammu joined Haqud. They knocked over light posts, broke windows, and overturned vehicles. The crab paused to watch them.

"And who do you think you are?" the crab asked, scuttling over to them. "And just what do you think you're doing?"

"Aisha Qandisha and my husband Hammu Qaiu, at your service," Aisha said, kneeling as camels do, folding one leg seemingly backwards.

"At my service? That's right, you are indeed, as are all these sniveling spittoons of spirit who are hovering around me like cowards. And what do you want? What do you have that I need?"

"We want to join you."

"Zhzhzhzhzhzh," the crab said, scuttling toward them. "Why yes, perhaps you can join me...*in a meal!*" Haqud lunged toward Hammu Qaiu and grabbed him around his middle. He drew Hammu near to his pendulous eyes to get a better look. "I do so enjoy camel, but usually I have it roasted. Yes, you would serve me well, camel."

And with that, Haqud started to pull the camel toward one of the burning oil tanks. Aisha roared, "Nooooo!" and flew straight for the crab's smaller pincer, trying to distract him.

In that instant, I suddenly knew what to do. I flew around and approached the crab from behind. Landing on Haqud's back, I grabbed at one of his eyes, which stuck out from his head on long, finger-like appendages. When I yanked at his eye, the crab dropped Hammu Qaiu, then tried to reach me with his pincers.

"Come on, help me here!" I said to the famous djinn pair.

Aisha and Hammu flew to his side and yanked on the crab's other eye. The crab howled and whirled in a circle, his pincers waving in the air.

Pop! I uprooted one of its eyes, and Haqud roared in fury. Aisha pulled off the other one, and then the rest of the djinn horde descended upon the crab, tearing it apart piece by piece. When the crab went limp, several managed to rip the thumb off its larger pincer. The crab knew it was finished, but in defiance it railed on, "I am Haqud, and my hatred is stronger than all of you! You'll see, for it lives in men's hearts! You can never destroy it!"

I said, "But we *are* destroying you and your hatred. You are finished on the earth. Enjoy your welcome in hell, Prince of Crabstink."

I carried Haqud's eye to one of the fuel tanks, still in flames. I dropped it in, satisfied at its sickening sizzle. Piece by piece, the others followed suit, and soon there was nothing left of the crab. Another earthquake, this one weaker, shook the city and set off car alarms in the airport car park.

The victorious djinn let out a great cheer. "All hail Moustapha! All hail us!" Then they surrounded Aisha Qandisha and her husband. Several strong djinn were holding them in place, in case they tried to get away. I approached to see what was going on.

"Why are you holding them? They helped us, didn't they?" I asked.

"For decades, we've had to put up with them. We've had enough of their meddling," one of them answered. "If the crab hadn't attacked them, we'd be fighting against them right now!"

"Well, perhaps I have been a bit too high-strung," Aisha said, looking down. Her husband nodded. "And…just maybe I have…. overstepped my bounds and meddled in things."

"Uh huh," the djinn said, nodding.

"Kill them, they're traitors and they can't be trusted!" one fierce-looking djinni said, looking to me.

I held up my hand. "No, we will not kill them." I had no such orders from my higher-ups, and I knew it would be wrong. "Aisha and her husband come from a long line of good djinn. As Aisha now realizes, she has overstepped her bounds. And now, she has seen what becomes of those who would align themselves with evil. We will let both of you live, but only on one condition."

"Yes, Moustapha. We have no choice but to obey," Hammu said. "And I speak for Aisha as well."

For many years to come, I would relish that moment. "From now on," I said, "you will stop seducing men, setting husband against wife, and causing trouble. From now on, you will act as you were raised to—that is, to protect humans from the evil ones."

"But I'm Aisha Qandisha," she said. "I have this reputation. If I don't cause trouble, who will?"

"There is enough trouble and evil in men's hearts to go around. As for you, you've made foolish choices, and you are lucky to be alive. And now, you and your husband will behave. Do I have your word then, both of you?"

The other djinn were awestruck by this moment, for Aisha had been lording it over all of them for decades, and they could scarcely believe things were about to change.

"Yes. You have our word."

"Then go. And remember, the legions of the good are watching you."

With that, Aisha and her husband flew away toward the north, and the sea.

The others started to disperse, but I stopped them, saying, "We're not through yet. We've still got to get all the djinn from the past back through the arch by dawn. Haqud was the worst of them, but we have to get them all back, or kill every last one of them."

We scattered over the city, and, working in teams, forced the djinn from the past back through the arch. The good djinn knew they had to return, and they did. As for the evil ones, once word spread that Haqud had been killed, it all happened rather quickly. That's not to say I didn't actually have to fight. We fought and chased djinn from the past, and herded, even pulled them through the arch to their own time. I set up a special team just to keep any from trying to sneak back through to the present.

Toward dawn, I surveyed the brightening sky as the good djinn departed for home. Somehow I, Moustapha of the Mountain, had defeated Haqud and led the others back to their proper haunts. No one would dare call me lazy again.

Chapter 34

Morning

Barbara opened her eyes to the early morning, every bone and muscle in her body aching. She was shivering and wet. How could she have slept like this, curled up in the alley, holding a board in her hand, her back resting against the wall? And then it came back to her, more like a vivid dream than a memory.

"Aha! You did well, my little pomegranate." Moustapha was crouched next to her smiling. Shafiqa was still with her, asleep nearby, also clutching a board.

Moustapha helped Barbara stand up. Her knees and ankles cracked, and her back was sore. She stretched her arms and twisted at the waist, her body coming back to life.

"Now, young lady, look up at the sky and you can still see them. The legions of the djinn. These are the victors, returning to their homes."

The sun's first rays lit a huge billowing cloud. A hundred or more beings flew toward it; winged horses with demon riders, flying camels and dragons, and flaming meteors that spun and sent smoke billowing behind them in curlicues, great purple iris-like plants that flapped their petals like wings.

"Wasn't it a fantastic night?" Moustapha asked with more pleasantness than she had yet seen in him. "Why, I myself killed three demons with my bare hands. And praise to the Almighty, evil is defeated, at least for now, for we killed

Haqud." Moustapha looked down at the front of his pink caftan. It was stained with blood and with blotches of what looked like yellow and green paint. "Demon blood," he muttered. "I'm going to have a hard time getting that out."

"What's that?" Barbara said, pointing to a scaly lizard the size of a canoe, lying on its back in the alley, just 20 feet from them.

"A spurling. Took care of it a while ago. In fact, it should..." and, as Moustapha said those words, it faded and disappeared.

"What happened—it's gone!" Barbara said.

"It died; that is its way."

Barbara's thoughts finally sorted themselves out into words.

"But where are the men? What's happened to them? And Khalid?"

"God willing, all will be well. They are still in the past. And, if all is as it should be, they will return today."

"And the arch?"

"If God wills it, the arch will come down today."

Before she could ask more questions, he said, "You two did your jobs well indeed, but there is nothing to be done now."

"Shafiqa," Barbara said, kneeling near her and nudging her gently.

"No, let her sleep a few moments longer. She, like you, has worked hard. Now, you go along to your room and get some rest."

"Well, I might change and get some breakfast, but I won't sleep, and I'm not missing this day for a million dollars." She walked down the alley and entered the front door of the riad, sneaking by the door guard, who was snoring as he slept in one of the cushioned alcoves in the lobby.

Moustapha stretched and yawned and said to himself, "If I were a human, I would surely take a nice deep nap. Oh, when will I be able to sleep again in my dear mountain bed, high in the sweet cedars?"

Moustapha turned to Shafiqa. She was by then wide awake, laying on her side. She sat up and stretched.

"Good morning, Sister," Moustapha said. "You have done well, and you have my thanks."

"So you admit that two women helped in the battle and that we made a difference?"

"Well, yes, I suppose I do."

"Then, you are welcome. It was an honor." Shafiqa put her hand to her heart and nodded.

"Since your work is done, you may return home and rest."

"Well, I do have one request. And you will grant me that, I'm sure, in thanks for our work."

"There is always a string attached, is there not, when a human is concerned?"

Only acknowledging his barb with raised eyebrows, she said, "I want to go to the woman who founded our healing order, to see her, and to listen to her speak. She was alive in the time of Ibn Murad. I have recited her prayers since I was a girl. And if she is there, in the same place as always, I will be with her in the same room. I cannot imagine a greater gift. Then, God willing, I will return."

"And return you must, Sister, for the arch will be broken in a few hours, and then you must stay where you are, either here or there. There will be no chance to travel back through, after the arch is gone, and you would never see your family again."

"Then I will go now, and God willing I will be back before the noonday prayers." With that, Shafiqa dropped her rain jacket and umbrella and swept through the arch down the alley, nearly at a run, her exhaustion, hunger, and thirst forgotten.

"Before the noonday prayers!" Moustapha called after her. Then he shook his head and muttered, "Yet another mortal to keep track of."

Ibrahim had never welcomed the dawn prayer as he did that day. When they gathered on the roof of the zawia, Mike was already there. He'd been up early, listening to the *adhan*.

Who could forget that morning when Ibn Murad led their small group in prayer? Afterward, the men looked out over the city. Everything seemed intact, though the night's storm had caused some flooding.

One of the guildsmen brought the news that the Citadel had caught fire, and all the prisoners escaped. Amid the chaos, the Sultan's guards found the corpses of Nimr and Samir. So far, no one had taken credit for the deed. The authorities knew nothing. The Sultan's men were busy rounding up escaped prisoners. Ibrahim and Mike exchanged knowing glances of hope that Khalid would turn up unharmed.

The messenger added that the wounded carpenter would survive. The stab wound had missed vital organs; he had been lucky. He turned to the imam and said that Amin had kept the treasury safe at the tanneries. The imam nodded with a smile.

"Sheikh," he said, addressing the imam, "You can feel that the people are no longer afraid, and that it's a peaceful morning. Yet they were asking why the imam was not at the mosque for dawn prayers."

"I think it's time to return to Qarawiyyin," Ibn Murad said. "Do you agree, Hamza my brother, that the way is now safe?"

"Yes, Sir."

"Then, my friends, please accompany me to the mosque. Together, we will give thanks to the Almighty for saving the mosque and our city."

As they prepared to leave the safety of the zawia, Hamza approached Ibrahim and Mike, and clapped his arms around their shoulders. "You are a true Son of Fez," he said to each one, "and you are our brother forever. You are always welcome in our circle."

When it was Mike's turn to be hugged, tears filled his smiling eyes as he said, "I will never forget you and all the brothers, and your courage."

It seemed the entire city of Fez had gathered at the Qarawiyyin Mosque for the noonday prayers, including the Sultan himself, sitting in the front row with his ministers. Hamza led the group from the zawia to an open space. All around them sat the men with whom they had fought in the tanneries, looking straight ahead, wearing the subtlest of smiles. Ibrahim and Mike relished the moment, hoping they would retain this memory for a long time. Then someone shoved himself between them and knelt down. It was Khalid, wrapped in a cloak he'd been given when he took refuge during the night in a quiet alcove of the mosque. Still kneeling, they wove their arms together in hearty but silent hugs, disheveling their cloaks and knocking their turbans askew.

After prayers, Ibrahim, Mike and Khalid said goodbye to their new friends one more time and set out at last toward the arch. When they reached the alley, it was all the men could do to keep from running through it. Ibrahim's eyes teared up at the sight of Moustapha, sitting in his usual place on a new piece of cardboard, for he was sure only then, that he was truly turning toward home.

Khalid's heart swelled to bursting as he stepped back through the arch. He teared up, too, remembering the fear that he would never get back home. Now he breathed in the smells of modern Fez. Gone was the ever-present wood smoke. Instead, he smelled a whiff of cooking gas. He spied a little boy struggling to carry a kitchen-sized canister along the street at the end of the alley. He could hear classical Moroccan *Andalusi* music playing quietly from a nearby window, punctuated by a jackhammer at a jobsite somewhere in the neighborhood.

"Welcome back!" Moustapha said as the three men stood still, taking in the change in atmosphere.

"So you did it, Moustapha," Ibrahim said. "You got him."

"Indeed I did, with some help. And now, we just have to take down the arch."

Khalid smiled at Moustapha. He still couldn't get used to the idea of this old woman being a djinni.

During the storm, the arch stones had been washed clean. The malachite keystone shone a brilliant green for the first time in centuries. On either side of it, stones of lapis, red jasper and turquoise set the arch off like a necklace. The men pushed at several of the stones, and not one of them seemed loose. Then they got to work setting two long boards in an X across the opening, and they leaned other boards against them vertically to block anyone from passing through.

That was when Khalid remembered his cellphone, watch, and clothes. He'd left them on the roof of his house, in the past. Moustapha grew agitated and explained that Khalid had to get them back, for if they were found, history might be changed. The men moved the boards to let Khalid through the arch to the past. Once through, he took off in a run, his robes flowing behind.

"But what about my blue gandoura?" Mike said, remembering he'd traded it at the tailor's shop when he first stepped through the arch.

"Not to worry," Moustapha said. "I retrieved it, and your other garments. It's all in your closet."

Chapter 35

Sisterhood

After Khalid ran through the arch to the past, Moustapha wrung his hands and looked to the sky. Where was that woman, Shafiqa? She was late, as it was well past the noonday prayer.

"I have to look for someone," Moustapha said to Mike and Ibrahim. "Stay here, and don't let anyone but Khalid through in either direction." Moustapha pulled up the hem of his long caftan, stood on his toes, and jumped up into the air. "Absolutely nobody, got it?"

"Yes, yes, of course," they said. And with that, Moustapha sailed over the houses and into the sky.

Moustapha was certain he knew where Shafiqa would be. By 1374, her order was a well-established Sufi sisterhood. He hovered over the towering rooftop of a house that stood high on the hill, a beautifully appointed riad with a rooftop garden. He flew in closer and hovered behind a potted hibiscus bush. Shafiqa was sitting in a circle of women. Tears were running down her face as she gazed lovingly at an old woman who lectured them, dressed in turquoise. Moustapha noted there were Frankish women there, too, even one dressed in the style of a Spanish nun.

The old woman spoke in classical Arabic. "And did the Almighty not instruct us all to seek wisdom? And to do good in the world? And do we not look to God for strength in all that we do? Therefore, my sisters, we must also look to each other and not be bound by what others tell us are the limits of friendship. I enjoin you to look to your hearts and to plant the seeds of goodwill and friendship. And to pull the weeds of hatred from your souls. For it is the spirit of love, which God created, that drives all mankind. And when it is harnessed for the good, we can all make God's miracles on earth."

She was indeed the founder of the order, Moustapha concluded, but he cared only about getting Shafiqa back through the arch. So he squeezed his pink-robed form through a tiny window in the stairwell leading to the roof, tiptoed into the garden, and knelt right behind Shafiqa. She didn't notice him until he whispered in her ear.

"Shafiqa! You must come back through the arch, now!"

She didn't move, but her eyes opened. He reached for her hand, but she moved it away and shook her head. He waited, trying not to disturb the old lady's sermon. She was very influential in her time, and for several generations after her death, but her writings had been destroyed in the centuries that followed. Some volumes were burned during the Spanish Inquisition, but most were eaten by bookworms, like so many precious works by the great thinkers of those days. Somehow, her ideas lived on, passed down the generations by the women of her order. And with all these foreign women, who knew how far the seeds of her ideas had traveled?

Shafiqa looked at him, and, with her gaze, pulled his eyes to a thick book that sat at the old woman's side. He could read Shafiqa's mind and heart. This was an actual book of her teachings, a book that would not survive. Shafiqa wanted to read it, to know it, and to bring it back with her to the future. If Shafiqa stayed, she would have the chance to read that book, but she would be trapped in that time. She had to choose between to staying in the past and learning from her master, or returning to her own time and her family, having heard only a small fragment of the teachings of this woman.

"And most important of all," the old woman continued, "you must know that the fire of friendship, and its power, burns brightest and strongest when it crosses the greatest distances. The more unlikely it is, the farther it reaches, the more Godly it is, and the more it will bring us paradise on earth. Of all that I have learned, this, my sisters, is the greatest wisdom. Even if you were only to hear me once," she said, staring at Shafiqa with a knowing smile, "this is all you need. Trust that the friend is there, across the street, across the city, deserts, oceans, and sky. And know that the love that thrives in true friendship will heal the wounds of humanity. God gave us friendship to sow happiness and weave us together as one. Go now, all of you, and remember this. The key is friendship. Now, greet the sisters around you. Shake their hands and know their names. God is the Generous, the All-Knowing. Amen."

The women stood, then greeted and hugged each other, as they smiled through their tears. Even Moustapha was touched by the loving spirit on that rooftop. The old woman stood up and took a cedar cane in her left hand. She spoke to her audience, one at a time, hugging them, offering words of encouragement. But it was obvious to Moustapha that she was making her way toward Shafiqa, who stood still in excitement, knowing her beloved Master was approaching *her*.

"My dear," the old woman said as she reached Shafiqa at last, taking her hand. "I am honored that such a disciple as you has traveled so far to hear me today. But you must return to your home. Take what you heard here today. It is more than enough. Take it and share it with your sisters. Though many of my words might be lost, you have found the most important ones again. It is best that you take this simple lesson with you and bring it to life again."

"Thank you, Sister," Shafiqa said, bowing to kiss her hand.

"Now, stop that," she said, lifting Shafiqa up. "I should be thanking you for being so brave to come this far. Now, go with your companion, who is here to take you home."

"But I don't want to leave you!" Shafiqa said.

"Shafiqa, I am always near you. So be grateful you found me, and be happy you can share what you have learned with your own sisters."

"But our times are so hard, Sister."

"Yes, I know. Yet what you have seen and heard can carry you and a thousand others forward. It will ripple and echo on and on. Now, Shafiqa, go in God's peace. And you, my spirit friend," she said, turning to Moustapha with a smile. "Be gone!" And with that, Moustapha had Shafiqa by the hand, and they were flying over the city, back down the hill. They landed in front of the boarded-up arch, where Mike was keeping an eye on things.

Shafiqa savored one last moment in the past, breathing deeply. Then she nodded at Moustapha, smiled through her tears, and walked through the arch.

"She looks familiar, who's she?" Mike said quietly to Moustapha once she passed.

"Another stray one," he said. "Hopefully we're almost through with this business. All this human emotion and drama is exhausting."

Mike kept silent for a moment, not admitting that, while Moustapha was gone, and Ibrahim had stepped away from the arch, he had allowed Barbara to cross under the arch to the past. Of all the other students in the program, it was Barbara he could relate to best. And now he had a special bond with her. She told Mike how she and Shafiqa had spent the night, and how they had followed the men back to the zawia, and that she just wanted to look around for a little while, one last time.

Barbara had donned her white haik again and stepped through with a greater sense of wonder. She didn't go far, acutely aware that she couldn't risk being trapped in the past. But she knew it was the chance of a lifetime, to visit a *real* medieval souq once more, even if it was only for a few minutes. She intended to just circle one block, without getting lost.

"Rose perfume to sweeten the home!" a young lady called, carrying a wooden box of small bottles strapped around her neck. Barbara thought she looked like a medieval version of a cigarette girl from an old movie—a really, *really* old movie.

"I'll deliver the rest by next Saturday, God willing," a young man said, shaking hands with a shop owner selling brown leather satchels with long shoulder straps. "That is more than quick enough, cousin," he answered, slapping him on the back. "Keep up that pace, and you'll be way ahead of your competition." As Barbara strolled, she realized that in each conversation a new world opened up to her, a world that she had never known before.

She paused before a tiny shop selling dried flower blossoms: miniature roses, lavender, and baskets of other dried flowers she couldn't name. She noticed a basket brimming with delicate red tendrils of saffron. In modern times it was rare and precious. What she wouldn't give for just a little saffron from the past to taste, perhaps even a little to bring back home. But of course she had no money, so she just stood and took in the sight. An elderly lady sat on a wooden bench against its wall, eyeing her before saying, "My lady, can I help you?"

"I was just admiring your saffron."

"It is from our family's farm. My own granddaughters pick every strand themselves. Go ahead, try some." She used her bony arms to push herself to her feet and stepped slowly to the basket. "Here, please taste." She reached in and dropped some strands into Barbara's palm. She smelled them, then took some strands in her mouth. She had tasted saffron before, but this was different, more flavorful. She imagined making dishes with saffron from the 14th century.

"Why, it's wonderful!"

"Thank you, my lady."

A wooden door at the back of the shop opened, and through it, Barbara could see a tiled courtyard from which the sounds of drumming and *zaghareet* flowed out to the street. A woman who looked to be middle-aged came through the door into the shop. She wore a formal looking ensemble in a light rose brocade, pearl and gold earrings dancing as she nodded her head in welcome. "Welcome, my lady," she said to Barbara, a warm smile blooming on her face. "How may I help you?"

"Pardon, if you don't mind my asking, what are you celebrating today?" Barbara was getting bold, she knew it, but she had to grasp at every second she could.

"My daughter's engagement."

"Well, congratulations!" And without a second thought to the consequences, Barbara lifted her hand and let out a hearty zaghrootah. The ladies collapsed in laughter.

The middle-aged woman reached out and grabbed her hand, still laughing at this Frankish woman who could zaghareet like the best of them. "Welcome, please come inside." She pulled her toward the back of the stall and the courtyard beyond.

"But I have only a few moments."

"Of course, but you bring us blessings. Please come and give the bride-to-be your zaghrootah. By my husband's mustache, I have never heard a Frankish lady who could do that!"

Barbara was through the back of the shop in a moment, and she stepped into the courtyard. Trellises of rose and jasmine filled the air with scent. The mosaic tile work underfoot gleamed in blue, green, and yellow. Two dozen women had gathered there, dressed in brilliant hues—so many shades of orange, yellow, red, and pink. Silver and gold jewelry bedazzled her eyes. Some women were dancing to an all-women band, who were pounding out a complicated rhythm on frame drums. She was afraid she would faint from the beauty of the scene she had entered. "My name is Habiba," her hostess said. "Come, meet the bride."

The bride looked to be about 15 years old. She was a beauty, dressed in an exquisite brocade caftan of light-yellow linen embroidered with red and green geometric designs. Kohl rimmed her deep brown eyes. She wasn't at all shy, which surprised Barbara. Then again, there were only women present, her friends and relatives. When prompted by her hostess, Barbara let out her biggest, best, and longest zaghrootah. The women joined her in it and in laughter. Then, everyone who could got up to dance, and they beckoned Barbara to join in.

She was drawn in by a step the younger women were doing, and she tried to do it herself. It was not an easy step, for it was not an easy rhythm. And the step didn't start on the downbeat, Barbara realized, as she tried to copy the girls who danced the movement over and over. They lifted their ribcages as they stepped from side to side and shimmied their hips. All the while, they held out their arms in front and flicked their wrists. Then they began moving their heads from side to side, a move belly dancers call head slides. When the bride's mother got up to dance it, too, Barbara watched her and was able to understand it. *Oh my God, I'm doing it*, Barbara thought when she finally put the elements of the step together. She kept it up until the song ended. "I love this step!" she cried, and everyone laughed. They obliged her by playing another song and dancing the step some more. By the time they finished the second tune, she really had it. She knew it was the dance step of a lifetime. She would perform it in her shows, use it in her choreographies. And she could even *name* the step, for she had learned it from Habiba. This dance step would have a pure, perfect provenance, like an antique clock signed by its maker. Learning this one step had made the whole trip to Morocco worthwhile. She would call it "Habiba of Fez."

When the second song ended, Barbara made excuses to leave. Habiba made her promise to return another day. And as she left through the door to the spice store just outside, the old woman handed her a fist-sized cotton pouch filled with saffron. She ran down the streets and breathed a sigh of relief when she saw the arch still standing.

"How did you get through the arch again?" Moustapha said as she approached. "I told you, young lady, to stay inside and sleep. Do you know how much danger you were in?"

"I apologize, and I'm grateful for these few minutes." She raised her eyebrows at Mike and whispered, "I'll tell you later," as she passed through. She walked with a new confidence, as proud as a princess. It wasn't the fact that she had held up the arch during a battle of the spirits, keeping the time link open. And it wasn't the fact that she had become fluent in Arabic. No, it was because she had mastered an authentic dance step from medieval Fez.

As she walked to the front of the riad, she found Shafiqa there, and they hugged.

Shafiqa said, "I have to see the arch come down."

"Absolutely," Barbara said. So they waited there, around the corner from the alley, sipping spring water, checking on the arch every few minutes.

The door to the riad opened and Maureen emerged, carrying a small bowl in both hands. Maureen didn't recognize Barbara, who was still wrapped in her haik. Maureen walked slowly down the alley toward the gathering of men and djinn, and the arch.

"Who's that?" Shafiqa asked.

"My roommate, Maureen. She's a bit of a troublemaker. We have to watch this, come on." They kept their distance behind her as she approached the arch.

Ahead of Maureen, Ramses the cat had jumped down from the riad wall, walked up to Mike, and started rubbing against his legs. He purred loudly before sauntering through what was at that moment a single board opening in the arch, into the past.

"Here kitty kitty kitty!" Mike recognized Maureen's voice and turned toward her. As she walked toward the arch, she looked down to steady her hands as she held the bowl. "We've got milk for you, darlin' sweetie!" she called. Mike rolled his eyes. Why did women have such irritating cat voices?

She kept walking toward them, focused on the bowl. Mike said, "You can't go this way."

Only then did she stop walking and look up, her hands still holding the bowl. "Who died and made you sultan?" she said, walking forward again.

"But you mustn't, Ma'am," Moustapha said, reaching for her.

"Don't touch me! I'm going to give Ramses some milk. He is so malnourished. The people in this culture have absolutely no respect for animals." Moustapha tried to grab her, but she managed to jerk her arm free, spilling some of the milk. She stepped through the arch and walked down the alley. "Here kitty kitty kitty! Ramses, I've got milk for you!"

"I hope the cat doesn't get lost," Mike said, and they both laughed, turning when they heard Shafiqa and Barbara giggling behind them.

Maureen heard Mike, turned up her nose and marched on, calling Ramses until she reached the end of the alley.

"Don't worry about her," Moustapha said. "We'll get her back easily enough."

"How?" Mike said. "She's more than a bit stubborn."

"Trust me, this will not be a problem. I can fix this in an instant, but we'll let her wander a while. It just might do her some good. As for you two," Moustapha said to Shafiqa and Barbara, "Keep your distance for your own safety's sake."

"Let's go up on the roof," Barbara said. "I know a great spot to watch everything." In they went, and soon they emerged on the roof, refreshed with glasses of sweet mint tea. Barbara checked her watch. The students would be back from their classes within the hour.

Chapter 36

Hameed

"Where have you been the last two days? The truth now, boy." Hameed sat on the floor in a room off the madrasa kitchen that was used for grain storage. It had no windows and just one door. His boss had locked him in there after finding Hameed on the street, saying it would clear his head.

"I was helping some friends," Hameed said.

"Friends? What friends would keep you out overnight, away from your work, your duties? They are not true friends if they tempt you in this way." The madrasa supervisor ran his beefy hand over his bald head, then clasped his hands behind his back. Hameed was amazed that the man's fat arms and hands could reach that far.

Hameed's panic grew with the passing of each minute. He had to get back to the alley before they destroyed the arch. Otherwise he'd never see Ibrahim and the others again. He was sure he wanted to follow them, for he knew that his life at the madrasa would never change. He was an orphan, and his family had deserted him. His future was with his new friends. His eyes started to tear up.

"I see you are having at least some remorse," the supervisor said. "You have a lot of work to do, and though you're far behind in your regular duties, I'm not letting you out of my sight for the rest of the day. First, you're going to wash the courtyard. I've got my eyes on you. There'll be no more funny business."

Hameed's heart sank. Getting past the supervisor would be impossible. Hameed took a pail to the fountain where the men did their ablutions, but found it was dry.

"Sir, I have to go the hammam down the street to get water." Hameed said, hope dawning in his heart.

"Very well then, but hurry back."

Hameed was just leaving when the supervisor said, "In fact, I'll come with you. I'm not letting you out of my sight."

The hammam was only 100 paces from the madrasa. When they had taken just a few steps outside the madrasa, Hameed took his one chance. He dropped the pail and sprinted away.

"Come back, rascal!" The supervisor started after him, but Hameed slipped into the crowds and was gone.

Hameed's spirits soared as he flew down the hill, winding his way through the streets. He had to get through that arch. He was going so fast that he didn't see the horse crossing the street until it was right in front of him. He crashed into the heavy boots of its rider and fell to the ground.

"I'm sorry Sir, I didn't see you." It was one of the Sultan's guard.

"And just what are you up to, running so fast through the souq? You wouldn't be pinching some fruit from the market, would you now?" The guard got down from his horse and grabbed Hameed's tunic. "You seem to be in an awfully big hurry."

"Sir," Hameed's mind raced for an excuse. "My mother's giving birth, and I am going for the midwife. Please Sir, I must hurry." The guard let him go.

Ibrahim, stood near the arch, sizing it up. "We'll need the strongest rope we can find." He felt refreshed after a shower and a quick bite to eat.

Moustapha, who was no longer pretending to be an old woman, had rolled up his sleeves and taken off his head wrap, revealing hairy muscular arms and curly silver locks that fell to his shoulders.

"We have to break the link soon," the djinni said as he started to pace. "I sense something has gone wrong with Khalid. He should have been back by now. The Sultan's guards are no doubt rounding up the escaped prisoners. If they find this arch, there is no telling what kind of trouble we'll find ourselves in. So if he's not back in…."

"No. No matter what, we wait for Khalid. He's a fast runner; he can outsmart the guards."

"Humans, always taking risks, always making bad decisions," Moustapha said. "But it's true, you're in charge, at least in this world. And I suppose you want that woman, Maureen, back too?"

"Maureen's missing? I thought everyone but Khalid was back!" Ibrahim rubbed his temples as he contemplated what would happen if Maureen was lost. As much as she drove them all crazy, they couldn't just leave her behind in the 14th century. Especially her—there was no telling how *she* would change history! "I have to find her, we can't leave her."

"Are you *sure* you want her back?" Moustapha asked, enjoying the torture he was inflicting.

"Yes! I'll be in so much trouble if she…" Ibrahim said, starting down the street.

"Wait, there's no need to go searching for her. I'll take care of it. It will take just a minute or two."

Moustapha cupped his hands around his mouth like a megaphone and let out a piercing howl—part meow, part roar, part purr. Within seconds, half a dozen cats appeared, jumping down from ledges and walls, stretching in doorways. They started trotting toward Moustapha, their tails held high in happy anticipation. Unlike Ramses, most were scrawny cats who lived in the streets.

"We don't need *all* of you, do we!" Moustapha said, laughing. "No, my dears, we only need Ramses!" Moustapha raised his hands once more, letting out the strange call again. Within moments, Ramses turned the corner of the alley and joined his feline brethren as they gathered around Moustapha, all purring, rubbing their heads against his legs and standing on their hind feet, reaching their front paws up the front of his caftan.

"Yes, you are all good beings, but I'm afraid I've no food for you," Moustapha said, patting some on the head, pushing them down.

Maureen trailed along behind Ramses, still carrying the bowl of milk. "Look at all of you, so hungry! I would love to scoop you all up and take you home!"

Ibrahim picked Ramses up and took him back behind the arch. Ramses had enough sense to remain silent. Then Moustapha let out a wolf howl that scattered the cats in all directions in an instant, surprising Maureen so she dropped the bowl of milk.

"Why did you do that?" Maureen asked. "How *awful!*"

"We can't have all these stray cats around," Ibrahim said.

"I was just trying to give him fresh milk, you know how *starved...*"

"Yes, I know," Ibrahim said. "Why don't you take Ramses inside; there's leftover chicken."

Maureen stepped back through the arch and glared at Ibrahim as he passed Ramses into her arms and went toward the riad's front door. Ramses complied, purring.

Chapter 37

Heave, Ho!

Mike studied the arch. Most of its mortar had washed away over the years, so its strength seemed to come from the way its stones rested against each other. Ibrahim had borrowed a long coil of thick rope from a nearby construction site. He and Mike had slung the rope over the keystone at the top of the arch and tightened it, assuming that the group could pull on it together to break the arch. Mike remained on the present-day side of the arch, while Ibrahim stood on the other side with Moustapha.

"What do you think you're doing?" It was Abdul-Lateef, the owner of the riad. He was striding up the alley toward the arch. Oh no, thought Mike. What do I do now?

"Getting ready to pull down the arch. Ibrahim asked us to," was all he could think to say.

"Ibrahim? Where is he? What's going on here?"

"Wait here, I'll get him," Mike said, and he stepped through the arch and the boards. "Ibrahim, Abdul-Lateef's here, wondering what's going on."

Before they could respond, Abdul-Lateef pushed Mike aside and stepped through the opening into the past.

"What in heaven's name is going on here?" Abdul-Lateef asked. "You've gone missing for three days, and you turn up dressed in theater costumes. On top of that, one of the students is trying to pull down the arch, and he says *you* told him to. I think you owe me an explanation."

"Well," Ibrahim said. "You're going to find this hard to believe, but it's the truth. First, this is Moustapha, a djinni who is guarding the arch." Moustapha nodded, and Abdul-Lateef's eyebrows arched as he considered Moustapha and his disguise.

Ibrahim continued, "The arch is a time portal to the 14th century, to the year 1374 AD to be exact. It's been walled-in for centuries, until the rains opened it up. You can imagine how dangerous it would be if people from the past came to the present, and if people from the present went into the past. And now, the arch has to be destroyed, and fast."

Ibrahim took the stunned Abdul-Lateef by the arm and walked him further down the alley in the past and continued. "We would have been fine if your neighbors hadn't delayed the repair of the wall by going to court. But it cannot remain open any longer. We're about to destroy it. We're just waiting for Khalid. He's on his way and should be here any minute."

"How is he mixed up in this? The police have been looking for him and…"

"I know, I know. The main thing now is that we have to destroy the arch."

"How do you plan to do that?"

"We're hoping that if we pull the keystone out, the arch will cave in."

"You're going to need a lot more muscle to do that."

Abdul-Lateef shook his head and looked back through the arch. "Why should I believe this crazy story?"

"Look around. You can see it with your own eyes. Only, when you go back through, you'll forget everything I've just told you."

"Actually, from such a brief visit," Moustapha said, "for about a half an hour you will remember. But then these memories will fade. Fortunately, we will be finished in a short time."

"Supposing I believe you, destroying the arch might also cause the rest of the wall to collapse."

"Does that really make a difference to you, now that everything is held up in the Land Court? You don't even know if this wall will end up being yours," Ibrahim said, then added, "Trust me. We'll make it look like an accident, like the rainstorm took it down."

Abdul-Lateef was to about to say that the neighbor might sue if he learned they knocked down the arch. But his thoughts dissolved when he looked up at the neighbor's house. Instead of seeing the large satellite dish, he was astonished to see the tops of several tall cypress trees waving in the wind. At that moment, he believed, at least a little.

Abdul-Lateef strode back to the present and mustered some laborers working at a nearby construction site where he was consulting. Among them was a stonemason, who arrived with his hammer and chisel. Abdul-Lateef told them they were needed for a quick demolition job and promised them an extra fee for their help.

The mason stepped up to the arch and examined the stones for weak spots. He tapped each stone lightly with his hammer, and told Abdul-Lateef that a stone on the left side of the arch would be the ideal breaking point. Mike moved the rope to that stone and tied it tight.

The rest of the workers took their places in line behind Mike and took hold of the rope. They stared at the beautiful stones at the top of the arch, which glowed in the sunshine. Fortunately, the neighbors couldn't see them standing in the alley, or no doubt they would have come out to ask what was going on. Abdul-Lateef hoped it would be all over before the neighbors found out.

As they waited for Khalid, Abdul-Lateef had an overwhelming desire to look at the buildings of the past one more time. Ignoring Mike's protests, he stepped through the arch and took his time walking along the alley, looking at the buildings, feeling the walls, staring back at Dar Surour as it was in 1374. He made out traces of a rooftop garden, jasmine vines tumbling over the top. Sparrows chirped in trees that he couldn't see. Children laughed, and a goat bleated. He noted the lack of any mechanized or electric sounds, and he breathed deeply of the smells of the city of his forefathers.

"Khalid's coming!" Moustapha shouted from the corner. "Get ready!"

Abdul-Lateef stepped back into the present and took a hold of the rope behind Mike. The men were told to wait for his signal. They stood, muscles tensed, ready to spring into action. Ibrahim stood in the past next to the arch, watching Moustapha at the corner. A minute, then two minutes.

"Here he comes!" shouted Moustapha from the end of the alleyway. Khalid turned the corner and ran full speed toward the arch. When he was half-way down the alley, Hameed, who had been hiding behind a wall, jumped down and ran beside Khalid, hurling himself toward the arch.

"Hameeeed!" Mike shouted, "Come on!"

"That boy can't go through!" Moustapha said as he chased them toward the arch.

They reached the opening, and just Hameed was about to step through, Moustapha flew up to him and pulled him back. "He can't, it's too risky!"

Amazed that Hameed had made it, Ibrahim said, "It's for the best. If he stays in his time, he'd be considered a lunatic. We've talked it through with him. We can take good care of him, and he'll have a much better life."

"I'll be in so much trouble," Moustapha said. "Do you realize how serious this is? You can't do this!" Moustapha growled, working up a full froth of djinni anger.

"Watch me," Ibrahim said. "Hameed, are you sure this is what you want?"

"Yes, I'm sure."

"Okay then, come on," Ibrahim said. He wrapped an arm around Hameed's shoulders and, pushing Moustapha aside, they stepped from the past through the opening together. Once Hameed was through the arch, Mike pulled him back out of Moustapha's reach. Khalid stepped in behind.

Moustapha followed, his eyes slit in frustration, muttering, "This will be the end of me, I tell you. You have no idea what you've done here. Humans, always making crazy choices."

Ibrahim, Khalid, Hameed, and even Moustapha joined the others on the rope line. Ibrahim nodded to Abdul-Lateef, who instructed the mason to start hammering at the stone in earnest. He loosened it and stepped back. Abdul-Lateef shouted, "Now!" They all strained and pulled on the rope, and, as they kept at it, the stone began to loosen.

"Almost, one more time. Heave, ho!" Abdul-Lateef said, and they pulled hard. "*Bismillah,*" he said as the stone started to give way. For a brief moment, the keystone glowed green, as if lit from within. The workmen stared in disbelief, muttering, "I take refuge in God." Barbara and Shafiqa, standing behind the end of the line, repeated the phrase.

"Never mind that," Abdul-Lateef said. "Pull, now!" They strained once more and the stone gave way and fell to the ground, along with the other stones. The jewel-like arch stones lost their color, fading to grey and brown. Seeing this, the workmen called out to the Almighty for protection.

Khalid, Ibrahim, Mike, Abdul-Hameed, and Hameed hugged each other. Barbara and Shafiqa did the same.

Abdul-Lateef paid the mason and the laborers, warning them to keep quiet. They walked back to work, shaking their heads at what they had just witnessed.

"That was a close call!" Ibrahim said.

"Tell me about it," Khalid said. Then, noticing Shafiqa and Barbara for the first time, he said, "They know about this too?"

"Yes indeed," Barbara said. "We've been helping Moustapha for several days now." Mike gave Barbara a hug, and the others nodded to Shafiqa.

Khalid turned to Ibrahim as he backed away toward the street and said, "I'll be back first thing tomorrow." Ibrahim nodded in understanding.

Abdul-Lateef stepped up and said, "No, Khalid. First, we have some things to settle, you and I."

"Let him go, I'll explain everything," Ibrahim said, adding, "Khalid, go! Just go!" Khalid broke into a run and disappeared around the corner, on his way to see the one person he had feared he would never see again.

The remaining group looked down the alley beyond where the arch had been. It seemed ordinary, the same as any other. They stepped over the boards and stones and walked down the alley, listening to the sounds of the modern city.

Moustapha, who had been standing back, brooding over Hameed's breach of the time portal, sighed and approached the others. He was in shock that it had happened, after he had tried so hard to keep things in order, and after he'd trusted Ibrahim, of all the humans, to behave.

"Sorry about Hameed," Ibrahim said. "We owe you everything. We would hate for you to get in trouble over this. Can we put in a good word for you?"

"No, nothing can be done now," Moustapha said. He looked at the boy and tousled his hair. "You, young man, are going to have an interesting life. I can guarantee you that." Moustapha could only hope that the Powers that Be would overlook this one incident, because, after all, he'd gotten rid of Haqud for good.

Chapter 38

Reunion

Khalid ran toward home, overjoyed to be back in *his* Fez. He dodged the pack animals, the school kids on foot, the old folks out strolling, and the cart vendors selling sweets near the shrines. As he walked along the outer wall of Qarawiyyin, he ran his hand over its ancient bricks, astonished at its enduring grandeur, even after so many centuries. Once he reached his neighborhood, he broke into a full run.

He slipped his sandals off inside the front door, listening to the familiar echoes of his little brothers and sisters playing, and the cook's clatter in the kitchen, sounds he thought he would never hear again. After regaining his breath, he called out, "Mama, it's Khalid. I'm home."

"Khalid! Khalid!" His little brother Karim ran to him and jumped into his arms. "Mama's been so worried."

"Where is she now?" Khalid asked, carrying him further into the house, swinging him from side to side in an arc.

"Upstairs, having tea with the ladies," he said. "The aunties are here, too."

"Oh, I see," Khalid said. "Well, can you tell her I'm home? I don't think she can hear me up there." he said, setting his youngest brother down and watching him run up the stairs. Even though he was home, Khalid was still not sure he was finally safe, back in his own world.

"Khalid!" his mother cried as she hurried down the stairs, her caftan rustling. She wrapped her arms around him and hugged him tight. He breathed in her scent, rose perfume and lavender soap, and that's when he knew he was truly home.

"Where have you been, Son?"

"I'm sorry, Mama. I had to settle something, but that's past now."

She stepped back and looked at him, wondering what that meant.

"It's nothing. Just something I had to do. Everything's fine. Have the police been here?"

"They searched the house once, and they've stepped up neighborhood patrols. My son, why did you run away? You could have come to us for help," she said.

"It's too hard to explain. But it's nothing that you or Baba ever need to concern yourselves with. It's all in the past now."

"Look at your clothes! What in the world have you got on? And you're filthy!" she said, looking him over, turning him around.

"It's a long story, and we just had a big demolition job at the riad."

"I see," she said. "But you're home now? No more funny business?"

"Yes. Only, I need to take a bath, change, and call on…"

"Suhaila?" she said, smiling.

"But how did—" he said, but she cut him off.

"She's been here every day, asking if you'd turned up."

"I have to see her."

"I know, Son. She's at school today, go ahead now."

He plugged in his mobile to recharge it, took a shower, and changed. By the time he was dressed, two dozen voice mails clamored for his attention. He listened to them as he walked out to the taxi stand. Every one of them was from Suhaila.

He found her, standing on the edge of a group of students waiting for the bus, her hands in her jacket pockets. He came up from behind and stood beside her. She didn't notice him, and she stared into space as the rush-hour traffic sped by.

"Suhaila," he said, afraid to frighten her. But the traffic drowned out his voice.

"Suhaila," he said, louder, but she still didn't hear. What was wrong with her, he wondered.

"Suhaila, my darling," he said even louder. She turned at the sound of 'my darling', and her face lit up. Since they were in public, they couldn't hug, but he took her hands and squeezed them. Tears welled up in her eyes even as her smile bloomed.

One of the female students noticed the intensity of their reunion, and she got the other students to form a circle around them, to shield them from the eyes of strangers. They turned their backs and faced outside the circle to give the couple privacy. "Go ahead, hug him," one of them said. "Don't worry, it's okay." And so they hugged. One of the students glanced back and got the group to cheer.

That evening, Mike sat with his back to the sword-swallowing belly dancer and looked up at the ornate dome above him, in what was once the salon of a sumptuous merchant's riad. The students had been whisked off to a banquet and floorshow in an old riad, deep in the far end of the medina. There had been little time to discuss what had happened that day, for the Arabic teachers had given them a surprise quiz in the afternoon, and then they'd been told to meet up for an early dinner.

Mike looked across the round table at Ibrahim, who was obviously enjoying the dancer. The other students were transfixed, too. They lounged on low pillows, sipping wine. For the first time in weeks, Mike's mind was at peace. There were no more strange figures lurking in the corners, no laughing, no taunting voices. Apparently, Ibn Murad really had cleared things up in his head.

The drummer started to play a complex 14/8 rhythm, and the orchestra joined in. Mike sat up straight and turned to watch. He couldn't believe it. It was the spice merchant's song! He sang along with the oud player,

> *And she smiled as they turned to leave,*
> *Her guardian frowning at me."*

Ibrahim laughed at Mike and said, "Get up there and sing it with them." And he did. The musicians could scarcely believe it. Mike knew all the lyrics, the seductive melody, and the tricky syncopations. They hugged him and shook his hand at the end of the song, applauding him as he returned to his seat.

"Ibrahim," Mike said. "This song, it hasn't changed in 600 years. It's exactly the same as—"

"Where did *you* learn that song?" Maureen asked, disbelief in her voice.

"Oh, at university. We learned it in an ethnomusicology course. It's an old traditional tune," Mike said, winking at Ibrahim.

The master of ceremonies announced a special guest. Ibrahim signaled for Mike to turn around and look toward the stage. Mike nearly spit out his water. It was Moustapha, disguised as a magician with a long, curled moustache, with Hameed as his costumed assistant. Moustapha invited all the students to join him in the open area that served as the stage. Mike stood with them initially, but Ibrahim pulled him back to the table. Barbara, by chance, had stepped away from the dining room for a few moments. When she saw Moustapha speaking to the students quietly, Ibrahim called her back to the table. Moustapha hypnotized the students around him so they would forget anything they might have seen in the alley. Then he did a magic trick in which they were suddenly tied to each other with colorful silk scarves.

Chapter 39

Abdul-Lateef's Dream

Abdul-Lateef drifted out of sleep the next morning, but he didn't want to wake up. His dream had been so vivid. It wasn't unusual for him to dream about restoration projects, and about buildings in the old city. But this dream had been more intense than any he could remember. He'd dreamed that he was looking up at Dar Surour from the side alley, seeing it as it had been centuries ago. He remembered every detail, as well as the design of the buildings around it. And there had been something in the dream about the exposed arch, something urgent. But try as he might, he couldn't pull it from his memory.

He got up and put on his robe. Hearing him use the electric shaver, his maid brought his breakfast and left it on his drawing table.

Emerging from the bath, still in his robe, Abdul-Lateef stood over the breakfast tray and raised the glass of fresh-squeezed orange juice to his lips, savoring its fragrance. Setting the empty glass down, he noticed drawings he'd apparently done the day before. He didn't remember making those drawings, yet they were exactly what he had dreamed. He had filled three pages with detailed sketches. There were drawings of the corners of the riad's green-tiled roof, a sketch of flowers on the roof, grown in pots no doubt, peeking over the roof's wall. And there was a green-and-white striped awning—he'd drawn only the corner of it. "Some kind of natural gypsum finish" was written in his own meticulous hand. So was it a dream?

He sprinted two steps at a time up to the roof of his riad and looked toward Dar Surour, squinting and shading his eyes. There was no roof awning, no flowerpots. Nothing seemed different, until he noticed the pile of rubble in the side alley where the arch had stood yesterday. It must have collapsed in the storm, he concluded. And the old beggar woman was still sitting there.

A few minutes later, Abdul-Lateef appeared in the alley, dressed in his usual crisp blue cotton shirt, perfectly pleated slacks, and handmade leather shoes. He stepped over the pile of stones and scratched his head, not believing what he was seeing.

"You don't remember it falling down, young man?" Moustapha was staying on until things were resolved to his satisfaction—until he was sure the danger had passed, and that no loose ends remained.

"No, I don't," Abdul-Lateef said. "And how did it happen?"

"In the rainstorm last night, I guess," Moustapha said. *Djinn* were given permission to lie, when it was to safeguard humans from the tricks of their own minds.

"But wasn't there a group here trying to pull it down?" Abdul-Lateef asked. "That's what I'm trying to remember, Ma'am. And we were in a hurry for some reason."

"Perhaps," Moustapha said. "In any case, it is down now. I suppose the neighbors will be upset."

"In fact," Abdul-Lateef said, smiling, "I'm sure they will be. This might affect their claim. I'll have to look into that."

He wondered if he should rebuild the wall, or should they just leave the alleyway open.

"Sir," Moustapha said. "You don't remember yesterday?"

"No, Ma'am. It's as if my memories are full of holes. I imagine this is what it's like for the very old."

"Come here and sit with me," Moustapha said. "Just for a moment."

Normally, Abdul-Lateef would have waved off a woman like this. But this one was different, and he wasn't sure why. He crouched down next to her.

"Now I'm going to say this just once, and I hope you will remember it. You have just been through something that few people have experienced. Your dreams were real. You, and a group of others, including Ibrahim, Khalid, that American man, Mike, and even a group of your laborers—you destroyed the arch. Your memory of the incident will fade completely, and soon. But what you saw and what you learned will stay in your mind, though it will sink down very deep, to the bottom of your mind's ocean. You must trust this knowledge. Know that it is there, and don't be afraid if some of it surfaces from time to time."

Abdul-Lateef was about to ask something, but someone called his name from the side door of the riad. It was Ibrahim. "Good morning, Abdul-Lateef," he said. "See you at lunch. I'm going to run some errands."

"We need to talk about Khalid," Abdul-Lateef said, but Ibrahim was gone.

When he turned back to the beggar woman, he'd forgotten what they were talking about. Yet deep within, he had stored away her words in a secret protected place, and, in that place, he knew what the old woman had said was true. A sense of well-being filled his heart.

"I bid you good day and good health, Ma'am," Abdul-Lateef said as he stood up and brushed the dust from his slacks. He smiled and handed her a generous donation before walking back down the alley toward his office.

Chapter 40

The Pact

Mike couldn't sleep. He rolled onto his side and opened his eyes. It was still dark. He pulled the blanket over his head and shut his eyes, still hoping to get some rest.

He was stretched out on a cushion on the roof of the riad. The night before, there had been a rooftop music and dance jam that went on for several hours, but now only he, Barbara, Ibrahim, and Hameed remained. Each was wrapped in a blanket or two against the chill that came to Fez, even in deepest summer. They were, like him, sleeping on the cushioned loungers. Dawn had not begun to creep into the eastern sky, but the moon lit everything softly. Mike lay there listening to the night sounds. Ibrahim was snoring, but the others didn't seem to be disturbed by it.

After a while, Mike stood up, still wrapped in his blanket, and walked to the wall that overlooked the alley. Moustapha wasn't there. Mike leaned against the roof wall and gazed at the sky. The medina slept in peace. How different this was from the night when the djinn fought their battles.

He had so much to ponder. What would happen to them, those who had crossed through the arch into the past and had spent enough time there? Would their awareness and knowledge last, or would it fade in a few months? If he told anyone what had happened, no one would believe him. Ibrahim had said it wasn't just that—their lives would be in danger if anyone found out what had happened. And that's why Moustapha had called the meeting that would take place at sunrise, at five a.m., on the roof.

He'd gone back to sleep after that, for his head jerked up when he heard Khalid's voice, "Good morning, friends." He and Hameed had brought breakfast up to the roof and set it before them on a low table. "It's quarter to five. Rise and shine!"

Shafiqa entered the terrace. When she saw the others, her face bloomed into a smile, and she nodded. Khalid welcomed her to join them.

"Come on wake up, Ibrahim, Barbara. It's time." Barbara sat up and stretched, then remembered where she was and pulled on her hooded sweatshirt. She stood up slowly and joined Shafiqa on a cushion. Ibrahim was still asleep, and they giggled at his long, sweeping snores.

As Hameed poured the tea and coffee, the tinkling of the glasses, plates, and knives served as a pleasant alarm clock for Ibrahim, who rolled over and opened his eyes. "So I'm not dreaming this, am I? Is it already five?"

"Indeed, Sir," Hameed said.

No one spoke as they gathered around the breakfast, sipping their drinks and taking in the morning. Each had their own thoughts, reflecting on what had happened, wondering what was to come.

Ibrahim—finally awake, refreshed, and having sipped some coffee—would normally have resumed his natural role as group leader. But this time, he didn't know what to say. What could he say? He had no answers, only questions, just like the others.

They heard a *thump* on another part of the roof and turned toward the sound. Moments later, Moustapha appeared around the corner, walking, or rather waddling, toward them. No longer dressed like an old beggar woman, he wore jeans and a canvas shirt, just like a modern tour guide, although the clothes, even in a conjured-up custom fit, looked all wrong. He seemed uncomfortable walking in his new white sneakers, and he kept playing with the bill of his Yankees baseball cap.

At first, no one recognized him, but within a few moments, laughter filled the air when he said, "Good morning, my human friends. Yes, I know, it's not exactly my best look, but after all that time in a woman's caftan, I needed a change. A cup of tea and a croissant, yes, please, that would be very nice."

After sipping his tea and wolfing down two croissants with noisy gusto, Moustapha made a big show of brushing the crumbs off his jeans, ignoring his linen napkin.

"Well then, ladies and gentlemen. Let's begin. I'm sure you've been thinking a lot about what has happened these last weeks. And I know that some of you have been talking amongst yourselves about it. That is fine, of course. But you must know that what you saw, and what we did together in the old days, must remain our secret."

"What I'm telling you now comes from my higher-ups, the Powers that Be. First of all, know that whoever you tell about this incident will develop a fast-moving ailment that will claim their life swiftly, and no treatment will save them. Second, should word of your experience get out into the world, your own life, and the lives of all of you in this group, will be in grave danger."

"God protect us," said Shafiqa, Khalid, Ibrahim, and Hameed as one.

"Wait," Khalid said, "I already started to tell my friend."

"And what happened?" Moustapha asked.

"It was strange. It was as if she didn't hear me. She just said something like 'that's nice.' Is she in danger?"

Moustapha smiled. "No, not at all. Her hearing was veiled from it. Before you had the knowledge I just shared, no ill effect could happen. But from now on, don't tell her anymore about your experience, or she will die."

"If we told people, no one would believe us anyway," Khalid said. "Everyone would think we were lunatics."

Barbara said, "But if the story gets out somehow without us telling it, why would we be in danger?"

"For thousands of years, men have tried to find the key to time travel. You have actually experienced it, and you returned home safely. All of humanity would love to hear your story. But there are those with evil intent, who would like to alter history and take control of it. They would try to extract your knowledge first. You might pay the ultimate price for not complying. Most important of all, I've been authorized to tell you that Fez has other time portals, and they must remain a secret. Therefore, you must keep this whole incident quiet."

"There are more?" Khalid said.

"Yes, right here in the medina. I myself do not know their locations, nor do I know how many exist. It would be too dangerous for even me, a djinni, to know this. All the more reason to keep your knowledge to yourselves." The others said nothing, their minds reeling with this new information and its implications.

"So may I conclude," Moustapha continued, "that you will all comply with this, er, advice?" The others nodded. "Actually, it is more than mere advice. It is a direct order from, well, the boss of my boss and three layers above her.

And since you humans don't fall under our dominion, the order comes from your higher-ups, too."

Barbara smiled. "Did you just say there are female djinn in your senior management?"

"Oh yes, my dear. You have no idea," he said, rolling his eyes. He paused for a moment, then continued. "You must all understand the seriousness of your situation. Each of you has all the others in your hands. If just one of you discloses the secret, it could affect all the rest. So if not for your own sake, then for the sake of the others, please keep it quiet. Now, to make sure you are all in agreement, I have been asked to have you take an oath. But before we do that, I know you have many questions. So go ahead, ask away."

"I learned a dance step there," Barbara said. "Can I perform it, and teach it?"

"Yes you can," Moustapha said. "Anything you have personally learned can be shared, but you cannot say that you learned it in the past. You learned many things in Fez, but you do not need to say *when* in Fez you learned them. That goes for you, Mike, with your poetry and your music. And for you Shafiqa, for your group. And for you, Ibrahim, with your profession. Now, Hameed, you will have the biggest challenge, and this is why Khalid will keep you close, to make sure you manage to keep quiet."

Hameed's eyes begged for acceptance. "Please don't worry. I have been keeping many secrets all my life. In fact, for centuries!"

When the laughter subsided, Moustapha said, "No doubt, you will have more questions. We still have some days together before the students return home. So let us meet once more. God knows I may not have the answers, but I will do my best. We don't have much time before the others wake, so let us be done with the formality. Will you all please stand up and join me in a circle. Now, raise your right hands and repeat after me."

"In the name of God, the Merciful, the Compassionate. I swear before the Almighty that I will keep the secret of the archway, the time portal, the battle to save the city of Fez, and all my personal adventures connected to these things, a secret from all human beings who are not in this circle. So help me God." They lowered their right hands and moved in closer, holding hands. It was silent, except for a few sniffles.

Shafiqa said, "God the All Merciful, thank you for protecting us and our city, for the friends we have found, and especially thank you for the help of this brave spirit, Moustapha. Give us the courage to keep our peace, and to protect the secret knowledge you have given us. Ameen."

Chapter 41

The Sons of Fez

After the final exams were corrected, the students and faculty gathered for a formal dinner. During dessert, Dr. Charles passed out certificates of completion. Mike was beaming when he held his, knowing he would be able to skip at least one year of Arabic back home. He couldn't wait to drop in at his professor's office and start speaking in perfect classical Arabic.

"I would like to call Mike up to the front, please," Dr. Charles said. Mike made his way forward, wondering what was coming.

"At the end of each program, we give two special awards—one for most improved student, and one for all-around highest achievement. This year, the faculty and I—well, there was no question that, for the first time ever, one student has won both awards. Mike, even though we'll never know quite how it happened, you deserve both. You came to Morocco at the level of an advanced beginner. And now you have made exceptional strides in your proficiency such that you lead the program. That's quite an achievement. Congratulations."

Ibrahim, Khalid, and Barbara cheered the loudest. Hameed, who had been helping wait on tables, stood in the back and let out a loud whistle.

As their departure date neared, the students wandered the medina taking photographs with their newly-returned cell phones and cameras. They shopped with a final burst of energy, as they returned to their favorite shops, buying trinkets and small gifts for their friends and families. The well-to-do ones bought carpets and furniture, which they had shipped home. Ibrahim wanted little to do with all of this, so he called in a friend to take the students to the usual shops, giving up his commissions.

Instead of shopping with the students, Ibrahim roamed the medina alone. He walked among the craftsmen's workshops. He drank tea in the back alleys at the little stalls where the workers took short lunch breaks, playing chess on a piece of cardboard. He had a newfound respect for the artisans and their work. It used to be that he'd spend as little time as possible breathing the stench of the tanneries. Now, he found himself drawn there, spending hours watching the workers come and go, dying piles of leather skins in the very same vats where he had nearly drowned, and where the Sons of Fez had drowned Nimr and Samir.

Everywhere he went, the faces of the men from the brotherhood haunted him, for he saw traces of them all around. It was as if the guildsmen were still there, working at the same trades they had six centuries before.

Ibrahim had wondered about why passing through the arch didn't seem to change him. He already spoke English and Arabic. So perhaps there was nothing to be changed. But he found himself looking at the work of the craftsmen with a newly sharp discernment. He would stand in front of a shop, and he could immediately tell the quality of the work. He could tell if the materials and workmanship were substandard.

Now, he realized that a true master of a craft was a rarity. And he realized that he could tell who they were.

With this knowledge, he approached the craftsmen with new respect, and the effect was immediate. He completed orders for leather poofs, and he also made connections with the younger men who were used to dealing with overseas buyers online. For the first time, he trusted them, and they in turn welcomed him in a way he had never experienced there.

He spoke to Laila about his plan. She was shocked when he told her that he wouldn't be taking any more tours for a very long time. He said that he'd had enough of the road, and that he'd start importing from the Fez craftsmen online, and only the best.

"Laila? Are you still there?" he asked, thinking they'd lost their connection.

"Yes, my love," she said, sniffling.

"What's wrong, honey?" he said. "Are you all right?"

"Of course I am, I'm fine. I'm just so relieved," she said.

He had a debt to work off with her. He'd taken enough risks with their futures, especially the boys.

"Okay, love," she said, not fully convinced that he meant the part about not traveling. She knew how deep his restlessness ran.

The next morning, he set out to see what he could find that was of good quality. He found himself in an unfamiliar street, and he knew that he was meant to walk along it. Something drew him to the front of a small shop that looked as if it were carved out of an ancient wall. It had no sign, but he felt a strange attraction to the place. He had to bend over to get inside. It was lit with a single bulb.

"Hello?" he said. "Anyone here?" He was struck by the lack of an answer as well as by a strange feeling that had overcome him.

Knowing that sometimes shopkeepers went away for a moment or two, he sat down on a low wooden bench and waited for the owner to return. It was a kind of antique junk shop, with all manner of dusty trinkets, pieces of wood and metal, and a few old books. They were stuffed on makeshift shelves, in big baskets, and in wooden boxes. There were no prices on anything, and there was no sign or indication of who the owner might be.

His eyes were drawn to a shelf that was crammed with old pots and glasses. His eyes scanned the shelf and stopped at the sight of a small light-green glass. Somehow, he instantly knew it was centuries old. Yet how could he know this? He held the glass and found that it caused the nerves in his hand to tingle. What was happening? He touched the glass to his cheek, and his cheek responded with the same tingling sensation. He set the glass down at his side and began to scan the shop, shelf by shelf. What was this place?

His mobile rang. He was needed back at the riad to sort out payments for the bodyguards he'd hired. He left two 10-dirham notes and scribbled on a piece of paper that he'd bought the green glass, and that he would return.

Carrying the glass through the medina, he realized that the tingling sensation had stopped. He mulled over the adventures of this visit, and the mysteries he had experienced. For the first time in his life, he was sad to be leaving Fez.

Barbara and Shafiqa spent as much time together as they could. Shafiqa joined the students for dinner one night. Speaking in perfect English, she answered questions about her group's spiritual healing. In turn, Shafiqa invited Barbara to her aunt's home for a traditional meal. When they parted for the last time, they promised to stay in touch.

Maureen made use of her last days there by making daily treks into the medina, looking for the place where Mike said he had purchased his first gentleman's outfit. She had snuck into his room and borrowed one of his turbans with the unusual weave. She carried this fabric with her and asked every cloth merchant she found where it might have been made.

She could not understand how she had been suddenly able to understand, speak, and even read Arabic. She mentioned this mysterious new gift to no one, afraid they would think she was insane, which would have been the correct reaction.

In her quest to find the weaver of Mike's turban, she realized how valuable this ability was. For the first time, she felt an affinity for the place and its people, and she understood why someone might want to study Arabic.

As she searched, every person she spoke to seemed to recognize the fabric, and they confirmed that it was a traditional weave, but could not advise her about who made it. Most of them referred her to Atlas Weaving, a showroom and weaving concern on the far side of the medina. She resisted going there, assuming that there was some kind of commission scheme involved, but after days of no luck, and knowing the group would be leaving Fez soon, she relented.

Maureen had no trouble finding it, for as she made her way into that part of the medina, everyone she asked for information kept sending her closer and closer to the tanneries, then down smaller and smaller side streets until she reached an alleyway with a sign that read: "Atlas Weaving, Nizar Atlas, Proprietor."

She stepped inside the showroom, and her eyes were drawn to the bolts of linens and cottons in white and ivory stacked tight along the walls, so that they looked like pillars. She took a breath and took in the fresh scent of cotton and linen unadulterated by chemicals. She could tell right away that this shop had the finest fabrics she had seen in the medina, and she realized she had been foolish to waste time avoiding it.

She walked slowly along the wall of bolts, careful not to touch them, though she had to keep her hands clasped tightly behind her. These fabrics were too fine to be handled without first washing one's hands.

"Miss, may I help you?" a young woman's voice interrupted her reverie.

Maureen turned and smiled at a teenaged girl, who smiled and repeated herself, revealing a set of braces. The girl straightened the pleats of her dark-green skirt and clasped her hands at her waist, ready to help.

"Thank you, young lady, and good afternoon." The young woman bowed and smiled at Maureen's perfect manners. Maureen was surprised at herself. Something about this place and the fabrics made her speak formally. "I am looking for a traditional weave of fabric made of silk and cotton that I was told was woven in the medina, and likely by your shop."

The girl nodded and disappeared into a hallway at the back of the shop. Maureen followed her with her eyes and got a glimpse of a hall that led to what looked like a large production room for weaving. She could in fact hear the sound of wooden looms being operated by hand.

Maureen wondered why the girl had disappeared, and she was just about to leave, assuming that there was no one to help her at the shop, when a middle-aged man emerged from the back. He seemed to be out of breath, as if he had hurried to meet her. The teenager came behind and stood next to him, resting her fingers on the edge of the glass counter, blinking at Maureen in excitement.

"My daughter Jamila tells me that you are looking for a mystery fabric, a silk-cotton weave?"

"Yes, I am," Maureen said.

"Well, I'll have you know we've been waiting for you to visit us, as you've been referred here by many of my friends. Excuse me, where are my manners? I am Nizar Atlas." His smile lit up his round face, where two dimples appeared.

After exchanging the politest of pleasantries in perfect Arabic, a mix of dialect and more formal language, Maureen was invited to share her sample of fabric. She nodded and opened her cotton bag, then pulled out the turban, which she had wrapped in tissue.

She did this in a leisurely fashion, and one would scarcely believe she had spent days walking, asking, and finding only dead ends at hundreds of fabric shops and weaver's studios. She laid the package on the counter and opened the tissue in an almost nonchalant manner, as if this fabric were a mere curiosity, not an urgent obsession.

By then, Maureen had learned a great deal, with her newfound ability to speak and understand Arabic. She had learned to slow down, to be patient, and to respect the other party with polite and dignified manners, in what she had found to be an enjoyable old-world kind of way.

Yet there was something else. Maureen was surprised to find such a gentleman with a sincere interest in her quest, a kindred spirit who appreciated fabrics. He was in his mid-forties, maybe fifty, she thought. His white shirt was custom cut, and it was ironed to perfection. Discreet gold cufflinks adorned the sleeves.

She was delighted to see his eyes grow instantly large when she opened the tissue around the fabric and let him see it. When his hand reached out to touch the fabric in surprise, he held back, remembering his manners.

"Go ahead, please go ahead," she said. Moments later, she felt herself blushing, though Mr. Atlas did not notice, for he had stretched out the turban on the glass counter and was bent over it with a magnifying glass, feeling the weave with his powerful hands, which she noticed treated the fabric with delicacy.

He set down the magnifying glass and peered into her eyes, one brow raised. "Madam, I am sorry to say this is not one of our fabrics. I have seen similar weavings in old drawings, but never an actual piece. How did you come to have it, if you don't mind my asking? Truly, it is…magnificent, magnifique." For some reason, at that moment, Maureen wasn't disappointed by his news, and when he launched into French, she went right along with him.

As for Mike, he spent his last days apart from the other students. He slept on the roof of the riad and savored the night and dawn calls to prayer. He used his guidebook to find every mosque and every Sufi zawia on the map, trying to find the old muezzin with the raspy soulful voice.

By day, Mike wandered the medina, taking photos with his phone as he retraced the steps he'd taken with the guildsmen, seeking out each place: the madrasa, Nimr's villa, the site of the old prison, the carpenter's souq, and the tanneries. As he roamed, he fingered his remaining riyals from the past in his pocket like talismans. He sometimes whistled the guildsmen's call on his walks, hoping the men from the brotherhood would fall in next to him. He looked for them in the faces of the craftsmen, noting the turn of someone's nose, a distinctive pair of close-set eyes, or an unusual cut of beard that reminded him of his friends. He missed them, but he resisted returning to the location of the zawia. He wanted it to remain intact in his mind, afraid he would find it completely changed, or replaced by a row of shops.

On their last day in Fez, he gave in to his growing, almost frantic desire to find it. After getting thoroughly lost, he stopped in an open square. He turned in a circle to get his bearings, and his heart leapt. There it was, the brotherhood's wooden door. Though it had been painted glossy black, he knew the panels of that door—the distinctive carved wooden triangles and squares that formed star patterns and crescent moons. He approached it and ran his fingers over its surface.

"Excuse me, can I help you? No one's there until evening." Mike turned, and his heart leapt. It was the old man he had seen the first day he crossed under the arch. He was as elegant as ever in his tan colored cloak and white turban, his neatly cropped beard and mustache framing a wide smile that lit up his kind, dark eyes. His voice had a ring to it, somehow familiar to Mike.

Gathering his wits, Mike said, "Is it still the brotherhood?"

"Yes, indeed. The Sons of Fez. In fact, you're speaking to one of them. I am Younis." They shook hands.

"And do they welcome seekers?" Mike asked, still holding his hand.

Younis looked briefly in Mike's eyes and nodded. "Of course, my son, of course. You'll be welcome."

Mike blinked quickly as his eyes filled with tears, and said, smiling, "Thank you, Sir, until then."

"God willing, God willing," the man said, nodding slightly as he touched his right hand to his heart. "Until then."

Chapter 42

In God's Care

The alley is quiet now. The students are leaving tomorrow. All but Mike are in their beds. Those who are asleep are dreaming about what they have witnessed in the last few days. As for young Hameed, his nights will be filled with strange dreams for the rest of his mortal life. I've heard that human dreams are a gift from the Almighty. I know it is improper for me to say this, but why did God give humans, of all beings, the power to dream like that, and at the same time, deny it to us djinn? Oh, we seem so powerful and mysterious, but really, we are like those dreams themselves. We might appear real, but in the light of day and truth, we are the nearest thing to nothingness. As it is said, we are like smokeless fire.

Now the arch is gone, and I can only hope that, aside from Hameed, all the humans who walked through it are in their correct times. Still, one can never know, for Fez is a porous city of mysteries and secrets. Its ancient doorways and arches and alleys lead everywhere and nowhere.

No matter, it is not for me to judge why the Almighty arranged the world as He has. He alone is the All-Knowing.

As for me, my duty here is done. The breezes call me, from atop the mountain pines. I look forward to a nice long rest. And so I bid you farewell. In God's care.

List of Characters:

Abdul-Lateef – Architect and owner of Dar Surour.

Aisha Qandisha – Well-known troublemaking djinnia of Morocco.

Amin – Junior clerk at the Qarawiyyin Mosque.

Badr - Senior Clerk of the Qarawiyyin Mosque.

Barbara/Basma – American Arabic student and belly dancer whose Arabic class name is Basma.

Dr. Charles Khamis – Director of the Arabic Program.

Faruq al-Kandili – Second minister to the Sultan.

Habiba – Matron whose family sells saffron and dried flowers.

Hameed – Orphan working at the Madrasa Abu Inania.

Hammu Qaiu – Djinni husband of Aisha Qandisha.

Hamza – *Mu`allim,* or leader, of the Sons of Fez.

Haqud – Evil spirit from the 14th Century.

Ibn al-Khatib – Famous politician, author, poet, and thinker.

Ibn Murad – Imam of the Qarawiyyin Mosque.

Ibrahim – Moroccan-American tour manager, married to Laila.

Jenn and Carla – Arabic students from Texas.

Kamal – Head of the Carpenter's Guild.

Khalid – Manager of Dar Surour.

Laila – Wife of Ibrahim the tour leader.

Maha – Owner of a fabric shop.

Marcello and Dominic – Europeans visiting medieval Fez.

Maureen – Staff member and European medieval textile specialist.

Mike/Munir – American Arabic student. His Arabic class name is Munir.

Moustapha of the Mountain – Djinni in charge of the arch.

Naeem al-Tunisi – Tunisian carpet merchant.

Nimr al-Anmash – "The Spotted Leopard," a gangster.

Nizar Atlas – Proprietor of Atlas Weaving and Textiles.

Ramses – Orange ginger cat who lives at Dar Surour.

Samir – "Muscles Samir," a gangster.

Shafiqa – Member of a women's spiritual order.

Suhaila – Khalid's neighbor and ex-girlfriend.

Younis – Member of Sons of Fez.

Historical figures related to the story:

Ibn Abbad al-Rundi – 1332-1389. The character Ibn Murad is loosely inspired by this famous preacher and imam of the Qarawiyyin Mosque of Fez who was known as Ibn Abbad. He was imam of the mosque from 1375 until his death in 1389-90. He was born into a wealthy family in 1332 in the Spanish town of Ronda. After studying with his father who was a preacher, he traveled to the North African cities of Tlemcen, Fez, and Sale to continue his studies. He was a member of the *Shadhiliyya* order of Sufism that was popular with the common people as well as the ruling class. His most famous work is *al-Tanbih,* a commentary on the wise sayings of Egyptian *Shadhili* master Ibn `Ata Allah al-Iskandari. When he died, in 1389, it is said he willed his estate to the upkeep of the mosque, and that his bequest equaled the entire sum he had been paid over the years as imam. His other surviving works include a collection of letters he wrote to seekers answering spiritual questions, as well as some sermons he delivered at the mosque. The author recognizes that it is improper to imagine this spiritual person in this story, nevertheless his upright personal example inspired the fictional character Ibn Murad.

Ibn Khaldun – 1332-1406 – Legendary historian and author of the *Muqaddimah,* said to be the first book in Arabic on sociology and political theory. He held numerous political offices at the ministerial level in Fez, Granada, (Arab al-Andalus), Tlemcen, and Tunis. He interceded on behalf of his one-time rival, Ibn al-Khatib.

Ibn al-Khatib – 1313-1374 – A polymath and important thinker of the 14th Century, Ibn al-Khatib served as minister to Mohammed V, one of the Sultans of Granada in southern Spain. A rival to Ibn Khaldun, he was killed in Fez, reportedly for heresy, but it was due to political rivalries. He wrote about the spread of the plague. A prolific writer who was said to have struggled with insomnia, Ibn al-Khatib penned many famous *muwashshahhat,* or strophic poems, including "Jādak al-Ghaith" that is still sung in modern times.

Fatima al-Fihri – d. 880. Fatima, who earned the honorific title *Um al-Banin,* (Mother of the Children) was the daughter of a wealthy merchant, one of the founding fathers of Fez who came from the Tunisian city of Kairawan. In 859, she used her sizeable inheritance to found what would become the Qarawiyyin Mosque and University, said to be the oldest degree-granting university in the world, still operating today. Her sister Mariam used her inheritance to fund the construction of the al-Andalus Mosque in Fez.

Maimonides, also known as Mosheh Ben Maimun or Musa Ibn Maymun – 1135-1204 AD – A prolific polymath of the Middle Ages, Maimonides was a leading physician, philosopher, astronomer, and Torah scholar. He lived in Fez from 1166-1168 AD. His house is marked with a plaque in the Fez medina and is just down the alley from the Café Clock, near the Madrasa Bou Inania mentioned in this story.

Arabic Terms:

Adhan - Islamic call to prayer that is sung or broadcast five times a day from mosques worldwide.

Afreet - Devil or ghoul.

Al-Andalus - Andalusia, or the Iberian Peninsula under Arab rule.

Allahu Akbar – "God is Great."

Amazigh - A person of Berber ethnicity, plural *Imazighen*.

Babush - Moroccan leather slippers.

Banat Hilal - Daughters of the Crescent Moon.

Bismillah al-Rahman al-Raheem - In the name of God the Merciful the Beneficent. *Bismillah* is a short version, used when beginning something, or sometimes, entering a room.

Chouara - Tannery district of Fez.

Couscous - Traditional North African dish made from semolina grains.

Darija – Moroccan dialect of Arabic.

Djellaba - Men's caftan from North Africa.

Djinni/a - Male/female spirit, can be either good or evil. *Djinn* can marry and have children.

Fez al-Bali – The Arabic term for the Medina, the old quarter of Fez.

Fezzi - A man from Fez; a woman from Fez is a *Fezzia*.

Fatiha - Opening verse of the Qur'an.

Fi Aman Illah – Go in God's care.

Gandoura - Loose caftan-like garment worn by men of the Sahara Desert.

Gnawa – Spiritual brotherhoods who perform healing and trance rituals using music and dance to call up saints and spirits from Islamic and African traditions.

Guenbri – Gnawa string instrument that sounds like a gut-stringed bass guitar.

Habibi - My love (to a man); *Habibati,* my love (to a woman).

Haik - Traditional white cloak or wrap worn by Moroccan women.

Hajhuj – Fez term for the *guenbri,* a gut-stringed guitar played by the gnawa.

Hammam – Traditional bathhouse; plural, *hammamaat.*

Hamsa - Traditional hand design, the "Hand of Fatima," said to give protection from evil.

Hijri – Related to the date of the *Hijrah,* 622 CE, when Islam was founded. The Islamic calendar is called the *Hijri* calendar.

Imam - worship leader of a mosque.

Imazighen – plural of *Amazigh,* indigenous people of North Africa.

Insha'allah – God willing.

Qarawiyyin - The central mosque of Fez. The term means "people from Kairawan," a city in Tunis, hometown of many early Fez residents.

Kuttab - Traditional children's school for memorizing and learning the Qur'an.

Lalla - Moroccan term for "lady."

Lila - Moroccan for "night" (*laila* in classical Arabic). Also refers to an evening ceremony of gnawa musicians.

Maghrib – North Africa, from Libya to Morocco (Egypt is not included in this). Literally means the place in the west where the sun sets.

Maghribi - Male person or thing from North Africa.

Maghribia - Female person or thing from North Africa.

Maqam - Middle Eastern musical mode or scale (plural *maqamaat*).

Mashallah – "What God has willed."

Mihrab - Prayer niche in a mosque indicating the direction of Mecca.

Minaret - Mosque tower where a muezzin announces prayer time.

Moulay Idriss – d. 791 AD, founder of first Muslim dynasty in Morocco; also helped found the city of Fez.

Mu`allim - Learned one; in a *Sufi* brotherhood, the man in charge. Also the man in charge of a group of gnawa musicians.

Muezzin - Person who calls the faithful to prayer from a mosque.

Muqaddim/Muqaddima – Leader of a gnawa ceremony who makes sure the ceremony goes smoothly. In Fez, they are usually women.

Mushtari - The planet Jupiter.

Muwashshah - Strophic poem, often set to music, usually with a love theme.

Nuun – The Arabic letter "N."

Nusnus - Coffee that is "half – half," espresso and cream.

Qaf – The Arabic letter similar to "Q."

Qaraqib - Metal hand clackers used in gnawa music (like large metal castanets).

Riad – Moroccan term for a city mansion. (Riyadh means gardens in Arabic.)

Shesh – Traditional Tuareg men's headdress.

Sidi - Moroccan term for "Sir"; *Ya Sidi* means, "O Sir."

Sirwal - Pants, pantaloons.

Souq – Marketplace.

Sufi - Muslim mystic; follower of one of many Sufi paths to enlightenment. See *Sufism.*

Sufism – In Islam, the inner or esoteric path to spiritual development. There are many differing Sufi traditions or schools.

Sunduq - Chest or box, also treasurer's office, institution where funds are deposited and disbursed for a special purpose.

Thuya - Moroccan hardwood tree, known for its beautiful striations; rare in modern times.

Tuareg - Saharan tribes; not Arab, but Amazigh (Berber).

Um Kulthum - Famous Egyptian singer of the 20th century.

Wadi - River or valley.

Zaghrootah - Trilling cry of excitement usually made by women; plural, *zaghareet*.

Zawia - Sufi brotherhood gathering place, literally "corner."

Zuhra - The planet Venus.

Suggested Reading

Becker, Cynthia J., 2020. *Blackness in Morocco: Gnawa Identity through Music and Visual Culture.* Minneapolis: University of Minnesota Press.

Burckhardt, Titus and Stoddart, William. 1992. *Fez: City of Islam.* Cambridge: The Islamic Texts Society.

Clarke, Suzanne. 2008. *A House in Fez: Building a Life in the Ancient Heart of Morocco.* New York: Pocket Books.

Lebling, Robert. 2010. *Legends of the Fire Spirit: Jinn and Genies from Arabia to Zanzibar.* Berkeley: Counterpoint.

Renard. John, S.J. (translator). 1986. *Ibn ʿAbbad of Ronda: Letters on the Sufi Path.* New York: Paulist Press.

Shah, Tahir. 2009. *In Arabian Nights: A Caravan of Moroccan Dreams.* New York: Bantam Dell.

Tafsout, Amel, (2013, October 20). *Entering the Sufi Spiritual World of North Africa: Sufi Brotherhoods and Trance Ceremonies in the Maghreb.* Gilded Serpent.

Witulski, Christopher. 2018. *The Gnawa Lion: Authenticity and Opportunity in Moroccan Ritual Music.* Bloomington: Indiana University Press.

ACKNOWLEDGEMENTS

Thanks to all those who helped bring this work to life. Editor Marcia Lynx Qualey made the text clearer and crisper. Proofreaders Sally Butler and Gary Campbell searched every sentence for imperfections. Several readers, including Frances Elliott, Jo Grossmann, Patricia and Eric Hanson, Gwen Sayian, and Amel Tafsout gave important feedback and suggestions. (Any cultural gaffes or errors in the text are mine alone.) Jennifer Bunting offered wise publishing advice and encouragement. Don Campbell was always encouraging. Miss Dickens faithfully attended revision sessions at her favorite spot beside my computer.

I am grateful to Jean Courter, Cassandra Shore, and Addi Ouadderrou of Moroccan Caravan Tours for their roles in introducing me to Fez. It should be noted that the only things Addi has in common with the character Ibrahim are his winning smile and handsome good looks. Addi is a fabulous tour guide, and I am grateful that he led my first visit to the Medina of Fez.

ABOUT THE AUTHOR

Kay Hardy Campbell is the author of A Caravan of Brides: A Novel of Saudi Arabia. Kirkus Reviews called it a "masterful debut" and "a mesmerizing Middle Eastern tale to be savored from beginning to end." - Kirkus Reviews – (starred review)

A life-long student of Arabic language, culture, history, and music, Kay majored in Arabic at University and lived in Saudi Arabia for several years. She writes about Arab culture for *AramcoWorld* Magazine, and is a director of the Arabic Music Retreat. On her first visit to Morocco, she felt instantly drawn to the city of Fez, particularly its medina, sensing that history was very near. She and her husband live in Maine.

www.kayhardycampbell.com